PAPER CLIPS
EASTERN SCOTLAND

Short stories by writers
from Eastern Scotland

Edited by

SUZI BLAIR

NEW FICTION

First published in 1993 by
NEW FICTION
4 Hythegate, Werrington
Peterborough,
PE4 7ZP

Printed in Great Britain by Forward Press.

Copyright Contributors 1993

Foreword

New Fiction is an imprint born through demand.

Such is the popularity of writing as a pastime of today, the opportunity to get 'into print' is increasingly difficult. Competition is tough and plentiful - rising at about the same level as opportunity shrinks. In the midst of a market that proves financially rewarding and worthwhile to only the blockbusters and bestsellers, new and less well known or unestablished writers bear most of the burden of lack of platform.

New Fiction is achieving its twin aims of building such a platform for fresh talent and publishing stories accessible to a broad range of readership.

The Paper Clips collections gather together a diversity of stories by contemporary writers who succeed with the essential magic, that has made storytelling a part of life through the ages. It is intended that individually the stories allow a quick and easy injection of entertainment. Collectively, they should present a buffet of subject and style with much 'dipping into' potential. Ultimately, Paper Clips represents a 'thumping good read' from writers living in Eastern Scotland.

Suzi Blair
Editor

Contents

The Flight Of Time

by

Jill Bennett

It was an idyllic day. Bees buzzed about seeking nectar while a dog lay prone in the shade. The heat haze shimmering on the horizon sanctioned a laziness normally foreign to the area. There was however, an air of expectancy, tension even. Three men, with shaded eyes, stared up at the sky. Cirrus clouds sped, tendril-like across their focus but refused to reveal what they sought.

'It won't be long now,' commented the oldest of the men, ceasing his vigil to light his pipe.

'How can you be sure Jock?' replied the one known as Steery Duncan.

'I can feel it in m' bones.'

Steery gave him a sidelong look, his ferret face mirroring his impatience with the old. 'Your bones are crumbling old man and so is your brain.'

A cat slunk by in the undergrowth, unnoticed.

'You mark my words,' returned Jock taking a long draw on his pipe. The other man, a youth really, remained silent.

Five minutes stretched into ten, then fifteen. Steery Duncan was getting restless. He surveyed the cracked earth with a jaundiced eye and spat out his frustration. The spittle narrowly missed a scurrying spider. It was the youth, Davey, who broke the silence.

'There it is! There it is!'

He jumped up and down like an agitated ant. Steery took his hands out of his pockets. 'Where?'

Davey pointed to the east. 'There! Do you see it?'

Steery saw it and his eyes lit up. 'It's a good time.' He allowed himself a smile. 'Open the door to the loft Davey.'

Jock took the pipe out of his mouth. 'Aye, it's a winner Steery.'

His companion put a friendly hand on the old man's shoulder. 'If it is Jock, I'll buy you a dram.'

They all stood back and watched the pigeon circle over the loft. Steery willed it down.

'Home you come my beauty. That's it.'

The pigeon homed in on the loft. Very deliberately, Davey picked up the cane, ready to prod it into the loft. He knew what he must do. Get the ring off the pigeon's leg and run down to the pit office to get the time verified.

Three pair of eyes watched the pigeon flutter down to the roof of the loft. It commanded as much attention as Noah's dove returning with the olive branch. Suddenly, for no apparent reason it swerved and flew up again into the heavens.

'Damn,' cursed the earthbound owner, 'bloody pigeon.'

'Something must have frightened it,' observed old Jock.

'I'll give it something to be frightened of; I'll wring it's bloody neck.'

The pigeon circled again as if surveying the home base. Below, the long yellowing grass rustled. The pigeon decided to land and the onlookers held their breath. It was the bringer of peace.

The homer fluttered down a few yards from the loft and started to peck at the ground. Steery stood by the loft and started his ritual intonation.

'Peas, pud pud pud. Peas, pud pud pud.'

Like some canny sheepdog, Davey steered the pigeon to the loft. Steery's eyes fastened themselves like safety pins to the bird's tortuously slow advance.

'Peas, pud pud pud,' he chanted, his voice registering a falsetto on the word peas. 'Peas pud pud pud.'

The bird's button eyes blinked. Food. The pigeon stretched its weary wings in readiness to span the few short yards to food - and its mate. It never made it. A ginger, furry streak met it head on. For a split second, shock robbed Steery Duncan of articulate speech. When it did come, it poured out like some overdue eruption.

'Christ!'

The expletive was an assault on the day. The word rose in the still air and hung there - a silent discordant echo. It galvanised Davey into action. He picked up a stone and threw it at the retreating cat. His aim was true. The cat let go off the pigeon and it took off skywards.

At about the same time that the pigeon made its escape bid to freedom, a door opened and out hurled a wizened virago with broom in hand.

'What did you say Steery Duncan?'

'That damned cat got my homer woman. What do you expect me to say?' shouted Steery trying to take the offensive.

The old woman's face, cobwebbed by lines, creased into crumpled paper. 'Take the Lord's name in vain will you!' she screeched, quite beside herself. Steery backed away. His mother came after him, hitting him, whenever possible with her broom. 'Wickedness! Blaspheming idler that you are!'

'Leave off woman,' cried Steery, using his arms to protect himself, 'I didn't mean it like that.'

'Just like your father, God rest his soul, a liar and a blasphemer. I think I've spawned one of Satan's own imps to be talking like that!'

2

She renewed her thrashing with a vigour which belied her years. Steery could only take evasive action and appeal to his friends.

'Get this woman to stop before she does herself an injury!'

His appeal fell on deaf ears.

'You, more like,' pointed out Davey unable to conceal a huge grin. He turned to Jock. 'This is better than the pictures.'

Jock chuckled into his beard. 'That's right Bella, give it to him. Teach the young pup some manners.'

The pigeon entered into the loft unnoticed.

It's An Ill Wind . . .

by

Jay French

Noiselessly in the dark the knife in Willie's gloved hand eased along the sash of a back window at 'The Laurels'. It was an old-fashioned type snib and slid back at once and with cat-like economy of movement Willie hoisted himself over the sill.

As he had known in advance he was now in the larder. Unerringly he shone his torch on the door into the hall and padded over. The next door on his right led into the dining room in which he had a shrewd idea of what he would find in Miss Alice Gladthorn's antique Victorian side-board. Even these days wealthy old ladies' treasured possessions ran to pattern; family silver black with disuse but the real thing; priceless figurines with luck unchipped; maybe a complete yellowed set of ivory chessmen.

The dining-room door knob turned glibly in his grasp. The hour was two am but the ornate mantel clock stood silent at seven. Not a sound outside either. 'The Laurels' was detached and at the far end of a cul-de-sac. Willie knelt. Started expertly examining, selecting, discarding items. Swiftly into the sack at his feet went the good stuff as he thought fleetingly of the old dear asleep upstairs, a bit sorry for her really, for unsuspectingly when he'd called a fortnight ago on the pretext of seeking gardening jobs she'd asked him to prune a privet hedge, then invited him through the house for a cuppa when that was done. That had suited him fine.

She'd been taller than he was but then he wasn't a big man, only five foot four. Her hair had been frost-white cut mannishly short, her eyes a kindly blue and her out-of-date idea of security had been to hang a man's hat in the hall and have a stout walking stick in an oriental jar there. It would have been cleverer of her, Willie thought, if occasionally she'd brushed the dust off the hat. Her trusting sort was becoming rare.

He could tell by the weight the spoons were silver all right. He was in luck tonight, making a good haul. He always worked by himself for himself. Who else was there to work for? He'd never had a family, only an orphanage upbringing and the only girl he'd ever wanted to be someone for had died twenty years ago, the victim of a hit and run motorist. Since then he'd never wanted to be anything at all really. Turning to petty crime had somehow just happened. His loot as a loner might be limited but so was the risk and he always chose to pinch from only those to whom the loss would be no real hardship. He was a kind of modern Robin Hood, he thought.

Lifting out a tall silver coffee pot his ears caught a whisper of sound. He stiffened. The wind? Wind didn't cause floorboards to creak though. He remained squatting like a toad, eyes unblinking. One night his luck might not hold and he didn't intend to be caught ever. He was gingerly tipping the matching cream jug and sugar bowl into the sack when there was a sharp click behind him and the room was flooded by blinding light.

That moment was to live vividly in his mind for the rest of his life for it was when he slewed round that pain slammed through his lower back and nailed him to the floor. A scream rose in this throat, came out through gritted teeth as only a strangled wheeze. The torture sliced again. He couldn't move, could scarcely breathe.

In the same moment in the doorway Alice Gladthorn's hand fell like a stone from the light-switch. She stood gaping at the man crouched on her carpet. Unbelievably he was making no move to spring towards her. Conserving his energies, she thought wildly. Recognition of him hit her - the man who'd clipped her hedge. Fool that she'd been! He was stockily built and that meant strength. She ought to be doing something, but what? Useless to scream in this detached house and the telephone was far off in the kitchen. His eyes were screwed up, his lips curled back showing good teeth but in a gargoyle-like snarl. Brazen he was. No stocking mask for him.

Her hand flew convulsively to the empty gold locket round her neck which she was never without, even in bed. Long ago she'd discarded the faded image of the man she'd loved and lost but the locket was pure gold. This intruder would murder for a thing like that. They did. You heard every day about such things. He was struggling awkwardly to get up now. Blood pounded like a trip hammer at the back of her neck. With my blood pressure I'll die before he gets across to me. I won't feel anything and only be a headline in tomorrow's paper, she thought.

He was on his feet now, but crookedly steadying himself with one sinister looking black gloved hand clutching the edge of the sideboard, the other still round at the small of his back. What was he holding in it? One of her heavy silver candlesticks to bring it down swiftly on her skull?

Fascinated she watched him swallowing whilst sweat trickled down his forehead. The hand behind his back suddenly jerked forward and to her amazement there was nothing in it after all. If I didn't know better I'd swear he was ill, she thought but when a low pro-longed animal cry tore from his throat Alice knew she'd been right and from way back in her nursing days she diagnosed lumbago. Once she herself had suffered a never to be forgotten acute attack when lifting a patient. Fervently she wished she'd taken her usual sleeping tablet tonight and never become part of this dangerous, impossible situation. She didn't listen to his agonising muttering too closely. Such a man wouldn't be praying exactly, although he ought to be, considering the predicament he was in - a burglar caught in the act, not by any human agency but by pain. It was really a kind of judgement, for once cobra-like lumbago struck, it could again and anyone in his profession prone to it would be as effective as a policeman with no feet.

Greatly daring - for if this was an act she was for it, she stretched out a hand. 'Here, hold on to me. You're in pain,' she offered.

Willie gaped. Was she mentally defective? Couldn't she see the bulging canvas bag on the floor, his discarded torch? Next thing he knew he was in a big lug chair looking into a cut crystal goblet with a meagre teaspoonful of brandy in the bottom. He didn't drink. Never had. The fumes of the stuff were making him cough and pain snarled in response. A gas fire started to pop at his side. Warmth was stealing up his legs. He shook disbelief and brandy fumes from his head. She was all right, this lady. She had nerves of steel and no intention of calling the police either! Returning his gaze Alice studied him. Was he like herself, completely alone in the world with no one to care what he did, why he did it or where he finally finished up? Glancing at his haul in the sack she thought how she'd long ago lost all interest in having silver teaspoons.

'I'll put those things back now out of the way,' she said with decision. 'I reckon we could both do with a cup of tea.'

Every week that summer when she asked Willie came to do a bit in the garden for her, or to chop sticks or carry coal for she insisted on an open fire. He'd done his last burglary; somehow lost his taste for it. Anyway after a bit he rightfully owned all the silver and never gave it a second thought and Alice Scott, nee Gladthom has long since reached the conclusion that she did after all have a purpose in life, even if it had taken some time to reveal itself.

For a start local folk often asked her how in the first place she'd come to know Willie and in reply Alice just vaguely spoke of her sleeping pills and Willie having lumbago. Satisfied, everybody now concludes they met in the doctor's waiting room and so the pair of them both sit at nights in the firelight smiling over at each other, remembering amusedly how in order to go straight he had to be bent double and reflecting that it's an ill wind . . .

Interview Technique

by

Diane Gooderham

Miss Edwina McKay looked up with some distaste as the next applicant entered the room. her pale blue eyes appraised and judged mercilessly. She was well known amongst her colleagues for her snap decisions and it was said, though only behind closed doors and away from those piercing eyes, that she decided if an applicant deserved the position within the first thirty seconds of the interview.

With one glance she took in the unshaven face (not so much designer stubble as five o'clock shadow), the kipper tie (dreadful she thought) and the wide amiable smile that was almost a leer.

Her glance dropped to the form which now headed the pile on her desk. Inside the first printed box which requested *name* was written Charles Platt in a large uncultured hand.

'Please take a seat Mr Platt,' Miss McKay said in a tone which although polite could never have been deemed cordial. It was certainly not a tone to put one at ease.

'So Mr Platt,' she began once he was seated, 'I see from your application form that you were made redundant two years ago and that you haven't worked since.'

'Not for the want of trying,' Platt said candidly.

Unimpressed she continued, 'And you were employed by the Factory in what capacity?'

'I was a sheet metal worker.'

'I see. So what appeals to you about working for us here at Flemmings?'

Platt took a deep breath and stared off into the middle distance thoughtfully for a few seconds then said, 'Well I reckon it would be real cosy working in a big store like this. Nice and warm in the winter not like I was used to at the Factory. Outside in all weather and me with a bad chest as well.' He stopped and gave a little cough as though to verify this.

Then, having collected his thoughts, he went on: 'Also my wife's sister Cathy works in the canteen so I know the food's good and we could travel in together taking turns to drive and save a bit on fares.' He flashed the smile at her again.

Miss McKay did not actually sigh, not audibly anyway. She had been Personnel Manager too many years for that but the muscles of her face tightened to keep the mask in place.

'I see you've given some thought to this position.'

'Oh yes. It would be awful handy for me here.'

'But you have no previous experience of shop work?'

'No but Miss Tyler at the Job Centre thought it might suit me.'

'Did she?'

'Yes, she's always be very helpful to me. She's been advising me on interview technique. In fact she's even lent me a book on it but I haven't read it yet.'

'What a shame,' replied Miss McKay without a trace of sarcasm.

Unabashed he continued, 'You know I've been going into that Job Centre for the past two years and every week she's found me something to try for. That woman is what I call unswerving. Unswerving I say. Never known anyone put herself out as much I really haven't. She's the most dedicated Public Servant I've ever met and she hasn't had it easy herself these past eighteen months. Her father's been in the hospital with his kidneys you know.'

He paused for a moment and sighed. 'I'm going to miss her.'

'Why is she leaving?' asked Miss McKay allowing a tinge of undisguised malice to creep into her usually tepid voice. She had heard quite enough about this paragon of virtue.

Platt smiled a little coyly at her as if he and she shared some wonderful secret that neither were permitted to speak of and said, 'Well you never know what's behind the next corner do you?'

Enough is enough Miss McKay decided and intending to redirect the interview to its close began to extol the merits of her employers. 'I think I should tell you that Flemmings are an excellent firm to work for. Not only do employees enjoy a delightful working environment but they also benefit from four weeks paid holiday per annum, in-store training, the Company pension scheme, staff social club and canteen (which you have already mentioned) and 10% discount on all staff purchases.' She stopped triumphantly, her eyes gleaming behind her glasses.

Feeling that something was expected from him Mr Platt lent forward and said, 'Well that'll be very useful with Christmas coming.'

The spell broken Miss McKay again perused the form and asked, 'So bearing in mind that we have received three hundred applications for this post and that you have no previous experience, what do you feel are the qualities that you possess which could make us choose you?'

Stunned, Platt looked about him for a minute or two then, with a little laugh said, 'I suppose I could say that I get on well with folk and I've got a good head for heights.'

'Yes, seeing as this is for the position of Lift Operator I imagine that should put you in the front running. And we mustn't forget that sense of humour must we,' she added with very little of her own noticeable.

Now into her stride and with the end in sight she began her dismissal speech, 'Anyway, as I was saying Mr Platt there has been a fair amount of interest in the vacancy and I do have quite a few other people to see before I can give you an answer so you can expect to hear from us in a week or two,' spoken in a voice so lacking in enthusiasm that few would have been waiting for the Postman to call.

'Oh well,' said Platt, 'that'll be after my holiday I expect.'

Thrown slightly by the applicant's lack of urgency Miss McKay asked, 'Going away are you. Somewhere nice?'

Platt positively beamed at her, 'The Bahamas,' he said. 'We've never been before.'

It was Miss McKay's turn to be stunned. 'The Bahamas! You're going to the Bahamas?'

'Yes, the wife's always fancied it so we booked it yesterday.'

'Well I must say I'm surprised. I wouldn't have thought that anyone who could afford a trip to the Bahamas would be interested in a job as a Lift Attendant.'

Mr Platt took a slow deep breath and said, 'Actually I'm not now love. It's just that when Miss Tyler phoned up and told me about the job I didn't have the heart to tell her. She wasn't to know and she does try so hard to help.'

'I'm sorry, I'm not quite with you,' Miss McKay said. 'What didn't you want to tell her?'

'Aye, I was just coming to that,' Platt continued in his calm steady way. 'It was last Saturday you see, an exceptionally bad day for score draws you know.' Then as a little aside he added, 'except for me of course. Do you watch much football.'

Miss McKay shook her head to indicate that she did not.

'That's a pity 'cos it's a grand game. Anyway it was that match between Dundee and Partick that clinched it for me, 1 - 1 and that last goal was a corker, did you see it. . . oh no you wouldn't have. Well I let out such a whoop when that went in I can tell you.'

He looked at her slightly blank expression reflecting utter disbelief and rather unnecessarily added, 'That was it then, I'd come up on the Pools. I shan't have to worry about working again now.'

'So why did you come here?' Miss McKay enquired.

'I told you, Miss Tyler has tried so hard. I think she could do with a bit of help herself.' He winked at her knowingly.

'The wife suggested she might like to come on the trip with us. It would do her the world of good.'

With that Mr Charles Platt smiled once more his larger than life smile of a truly happy man and left.

For some minutes afterwards Miss McKay stared at the door in contemplation and then she sighed. She had always fancied a holiday in the Bahamas herself.

Reflections

by

Gillian O'Donnell

Laura tossed the newspaper aside and finished her drink. Nothing but Seasonal spectaculars - did the programme planners think that the whole world was celebrating tonight!
Did they not realise that for some people there was nothing left to celebrate. Did they
never watch their own documentaries and heed their own statistics - how could they not
know that more people commit suicide over the Christmas holiday period than at any
other time of the year?

Not that she was contemplating such drastic action, simply that she wasn't feeling entirely festive this New Year's Eve. A sudden wave of self-pity washed over her - and why
should she feel festive after the year she'd had! She poured herself another drink and
sank deeper into the comfort of her chair. All the pain and loneliness which she had tried
so hard to disguise over the Christmas came rushing back, somehow more acute after
its temporary absence. With it came a pang of guilt, everyone had been so nice to her
that somehow it seemed ungrateful to now be feeling sorry for herself. It was not even
as if she needed to be alone this evening. She had been invited over to friends for a
meal, and she'd refused - refused because she honestly didn't think she could bear any
more of the well-intentioned, cloying niceness which had been her sole diet during the
Christmas period. Rather than face another round of syrupy sentiment she had chosen
to be alone.

But with only the tartan clad TV spectaculars for company she began to question the
wisdom of that choice. Perhaps it would simply be better to ignore the whole issue by
opting for an early night - but a voice inside cried out that then she would merely be delaying the inevitable, delaying matters for another year. But why shouldn't she - who
could blame her! And anyway, it wasn't even as if she was Scottish - why should she
feel obliged to celebrate New Year? Except . . . except, that she had always done so -
after all, it had been their special time. She closed her eyes and suddenly found that she
could recall their very first meeting, their first New Year's Eve. It had hardly been the
most romantic of situations, a watch night service in a draughty church. Her father had
been reading the lesson and had dragged her along for moral support, that and to stop
her going to Becky Kennedy's threatened all night party! Mike had been visiting relations
with his parents and had not been given any option about attendance. They were barely
sixteen and when the service was over they had merely exchanged coy pecks on the

cheek and then fate, in the form of Mike's father, had taken a hand. Despite the initial lack of enthusiasm from both his wife and their friends he had suggested that they set off on a round of first footing. The Scottish custom of visiting friends', and strangers, houses into the early hours was quite unheard of in this area of rural Norfolk and yet somehow he had won them round. Then somewhere along the line she and Mike had connived their escape and ended up at the Kennedy Farm together - only to find that the party had never materialised and that Becky and the rest of the household were fast asleep. It was on the long tramp back to civilisation that she and Mike had exchanged their first real kiss. The frost had sparkled underfoot and the stars had sparkled above them and he had made corny jokes about it being the perfect setting for a wild romantic novel and she had laughed at this lunatic Scot and thrown herself into his arms swearing undying devotion - and then suddenly they weren't laughing any more. The effect had been startling and they had walked the rest of the way home in embarrassed silence, ill at ease with the night and each other.

But eight long years later that same draughty church had heard them make their solemn declarations of love, and two years after that they had returned to christen their baby girl. Laura smiled remembering Melanie's birth, that was another New Year she wouldn't easily forget! The baby had not been due until mid - February and had surprised them all by making an unscheduled and rather hurried appearance halfway through Mike's first Sergeant's Mess Function. They were on a posting at RAF Rheindalen at the time and Mike had only been promoted in the October. He'd been away on a course at the time of the camp Christmas Ball and so the New Year's Eve party had been their first taste of Mess life! It had all seemed rather unreal: the men all immaculate in mess-kit and the women whirling around the floor in rustling evening gowns with the promise of champagne at midnight and more at four o'clock for those hardy souls who managed to dance through the night and survive until then, when a full English breakfast would be served. Laura had loved it all, enjoying every minute of this ridiculously elaborate evening when suddenly painful reality intruded on the dream and she had found herself collapsing in a screaming heap on the dance-floor. Melanie had arrived within minutes of the bells and long before the ambulance, creating a minor sensation which guaranteed mass coverage in the station magazine and even managed to make the cover of the RAF News, much to Mike's horror!

There had been many other Mess Balls and parties since then, at bases all over Britain and abroad, but no more children. Melanie's premature arrival had been the first warning. The next two never even made it beyond the earliest stages of pregnancy and then a son, born and buried within two days in an unmarked grave in a private cemetery while on tour in Northern Ireland. Laura drank deeply, she'd only seen the grave once - regulations prevented Mike returning to Ireland once his tour of duty in the province had

11

ended and so their tiny boy lay unnoticed in a shroud of weeds. She'd thought then that she'd faced the worst that life could deliver - fought the biggest battle and come through it intact. A fighter, Mike had called her a survivor. She had been too! But life has a way of dealing out the unexpected and just as she felt she was holding her own once again the unthinkable had happened. One minute Melanie had been laughing and talking, excitedly telling her all about the school play, the next she had been lying like a broken toy. The car had come from nowhere, taking the corner at tremendous speed and mounting the pavement before coming to a halt with its bumper mangled in the playground railings.

They'd gone away together that New Year, not wanting to face the parties any more and needing time to be alone - to re-adjust. They'd never envisaged themselves as a childless couple, both of them came from large families and they'd naturally assumed that there would always be children around them. Now the pressure of the tribes of nieces and nephews jarred while their own parents' interminable talk of 'the grand-children' set their nerves jangling discordantly. So they had spent New Year alone, exiling themselves from the crowds of revellers by hiring a holiday cottage. On New Year's Day they had walked in silence along a deserted Northumbrian beach and each blamed the biting wind for the tears in their eyes. They never spoke about it afterwards, but loved one another enough to know that they had resolved to make a new beginning.

A new posting that summer meant the chance to start afresh, to re-invent the past once more and build a new future amongst strangers. Oddly, the end of the year had seen their first real row. Mike had been on duty and reluctant to spend New Year's Eve alone Laura had accepted a friend's spur of the moment suggestion to go up to London and join in the celebrations in Trafalgar Square! It had been a memorable night. All around them people had been laughing and joking and while officially all alcohol had been confiscated in actuality everyone was indulging in high party spirits. Somewhere someone had started up playing a jig on the fiddle and Laura had found herself being swept up by a large and jovial Irishman and whirled around in time to the crazy music. When it finished she was near the fountains and as Big Ben's chimes rang out she found herself being caught up in the surging crowd and propelled towards the outer edges of the square. It was then she saw the policeman, struggling valiantly to maintain some sort of order and looking increasingly harassed. Something about his air of bemused desperation had reminded her of Mike and impulsively she had flung her arms around him and planted a huge kiss on his cheek. Unfortunately she had not been aware of the lurking television cameras and the kiss and policeman's startled reaction were instantly beamed live into thousands of homes around the country! *Not* to mention the gatehouse where Mike was on guard duty! The subsequent frost lingered well into the spring.

Laura stretched and smiled at the memory - despite everything she had enjoyed that dance and would have willingly relived it, row and all, rather than face the New Year's Eve which concluded that year. Even now, after all this time, it still felt impossible. For this was the nineteen nineties and yet it seemed that the accumulated wisdom of the years counted for nothing as once again a familiar scenario was re-enacted and men marched away to war. Or rather they didn't march, but clambered into hired coaches to be driven to airports and flown out to a desert land which didn't even permit a wee dram of whiskey to celebrate the passing of the year, or to steel the nerves against the unima-ginable horrors of chemical warfare. Not that it ever came to that, but it was close - too close! Alone in married quarters which seemed achingly empty that night Laura had drunk more than ever before and yet still wakened perfectly sober in time to hear the news bulletin at six the next morning. That had become the pattern of those following war dominated weeks - a drink before bed to stop the dreams and then waking early to watch the nightmare news. A desperate fight to remain sane in a world which had appar-ently gone crazy. The daffodils had been blooming when Mike returned, and he'd laughed and taken her in his arms and said that she was silly for worrying and kissed her tears away. But in his sleep he twitched and moaned and waking would not speak of the things he'd seen but said that she was a fighter, a survivor to have coped so long with so many fears without cracking up.

And now, now she was on her own again. Only this time he would not be coming back and somehow she didn't think she could go fighting. She was sick of surviving - now was the time to surrender. She rose silently and went up into the bathroom, taking the bottle of drink with her. While the bath was running she undressed and carried through the box of tablets from her bedside table. The bathroom was warm and steamy when she en-tered, its muggy vapour enfolding her in a gentle embrace. A scent of roses hung in the air and she lifted out a large white towel from the airing cupboard. For a moment she hesitated, surely a towel was no longer necessary. The combined effect of the drink and tablets would be sufficient to lull her to sleep and then she would merely sink under the warm scented water and...

She stretched up to replace the towel and in doing so caught sight of her reflection in the mirror. She paused, suddenly realising that this would be what they would see when they eventually discovered her. Carefully she wiped away the condensation and for the first time in months looked seriously at her reflection. The image in the mirror appalled her. Did she really look so awful? Had she really let herself go so badly? Shaken, she peered more closely and then stepped back in the hope that a different perspective might alter the view. She breathed in, but even with this minor alteration there were still lumps where once there had been curves. She had never been exactly slim, but she had always been able to cover the fact by her stylish dress sense. The fact that she would

13

now be found naked alarmed her - suddenly it seemed alarming that she would be so exposed. Her hair too was disappointing. She could not remember allowing it to become so lank. What had happened to her that she should look so much like a stranger?

Slowly she sank into the bath and lay quietly amid the foam, thinking. Then she washed her hair and wrapped it in the white towel. Returning to the bedroom she set about removing the hairs from her legs and from under her arms. Next she applied a face mask and began a thorough manicure and pedicure. A search in the wardrobe unearthed her hairdryer and styling tongs, further rummaging produced the only remaining set of silk underwear - a legacy from Mike's unaccompanied detachment in the Far East.

It took over an hour before she dared to face her reflection once more. This time the image was less alarming. She smiled at the transformation and the highly glossed lips smiled back at her. The effect was startling and she sank down onto the bed overcome by the sudden recognition of a glimpse of her former self. Was she really still there - the hopeful young girl who had dwelt so long inside the disappointed and frightened woman she had become? Did she still exist? The girl who had kissed a boy on a frosty night? The woman who had danced until dawn and drunk champagne for breakfast? The mother who had wept and mourned her children and then rebuilt her life on a windswept beach? Was she there, the fighter - the survivor? The impetuous kisser of policemen, the dancer of wild jigs with strangers - had she come through the terrors of night and emerged victorious? Could she now be recalled? Was this who tonight was for?

Inside her head Laura could hear Mike telling her to go for it! Fight, survive!! But as she pulled on her brightest coloured clothing Laura knew that what she was doing now was not being done for Mike but for herself. Tonight was hers and hers only, for now she had no-one but herself. She would fight, she would survive and in doing so she would start to live again. Now fully dressed she returned to the bathroom and disposed of both the tablets and the drink. In the living room she turned on the television and opened the window. Outside a thick frost had formed and the heavens were jewelled with stars. She breathed in deeply, allowing the chill air to fill her lungs and clear her head - drinking in the sense of hope and expectation that clung to the fringes of the year. Then the hooters on the boats along the river began to sound and in the distance a clock chimed the hour.

Rough Justice

by

Wendy Craig

Elaine had been sitting in the waiting room for four hours, every so often someone with a clipboard would come in shout the next number and name and lead the witness into the court-room next door. It was like taking cows to the slaughterhouse she thought, when she looked around the court-room however she regretted this thought as many of them looked like they had already been to a slaughterhouse. She still couldn't get over how lucky she had been. The man opposite her had a 'Glasgae smile', a large slash from the side of the mouth to the ear. The next guy had stitches down the side of his head where he had been struck by an iron rod. Then there was Lynn whom she had befriended sitting next to her, she had been in hospital for a week with a broken rib cage and head injuries where she had been pounded with boulders. They had been together for several hours now and the room of twenty witnesses had formed into several groups to chat and ultimately disclose their horrors.

'What aboot you then Elaine, what wis it the bastards did ti you?'

Elaine cast her mind to the night of the event and felt embarrassed to relate her feeble story. It wasn't feeble at the time, but now next to all the nightmare scenarios she had just heard it seemed that way. For the first time ever she had this overwhelming sense of valuing her own life, all she could think of was what could have been, she valued the experience of sitting talking to these people.

'Well mine isny that bad compared ti everybody elses, am just really lucky you know. A wis walking hame fi work aboot eleven o'clock and as a walked along Ingram Street a felt sort o uncomfortable, a felt like someone wis following mi, know wot a mean? So a sped up a wee bit and turned the corner ti go intae ma flat and these two girls ran up behind mi and backed mi up against the wall. Everything happened that quick you know a kin hardly remember it noo. The older lassie wis telling the younger wan ti grab ma bag. A really think it wis their first time as they were quite wary. A think a realised this so a started ti fight back and struggle fir ma bag. They both tried ti get ma bag and there wis a few kicks and punches. A had a compulsion ti scream and this seemed ti scare thim. A think they saw someone coming up the street so they took off, but a still had a tight grip o ma bag.'

'Brilliant, they never got nothing off yi then,' beamed Lynn, 'they're called the City Street Gang you know. It's been going on fir weeks, there's a load o thim mugging fir money fir drugs. So did yi go ti an ID parade then?'

'Ye, a wis summoned a few months later. Ma pal had persuaded mi ti call the police that night and after statements and what-not they told mi a wid hear fi thim. A wis beginning to think that wis the end o it but no, a wis asked ti attend the ID parade.'

'So, who did yi pick oot then,' asked Lynn curiously.

'A tall, dark-haired girl, number seven she was.' She thought about the ID parade and remembered how terrified she had been. She wasn't convinced that the accused couldn't see through the one-way mirror. It was silent and dark on her side and she looked into a brightly illuminated space where ten figures stood in a row each holding a numerical placard. She let her eyes wander slowly along the line and they rested on number seven, she had looked familiar. She did each one again very slowly eliminating the suspects one by one. She came to number seven again, moved then returned to seven, it was the eyes she recognised, they were evil eyes, dark and solemn verging on black. She was sure this was her, the hair was longer but it would be after all these months.

'I think it's number seven,' she had whispered to the CID inspector. She rushed out the room as she was sure everyone could hear her great pulsating heart bound off the glass wall. Lynn broke her thoughts, 'right folks it's dinner time, anyone coming ti the cafe?' A few filed downstairs and into the cafe queue. Elaine glanced over to the window and couldn't believe what she saw.

'Lynn a might go back upstairs, a don't really want to sit in here, look over there, that's the girl a picked oot the ID parade, come on.'

'No bloody way, we've more right in here than them you know, we're the victims Elaine. This is a right farce this so-called court system, the prosecution and accused in the same room, the one a picked oot is there as well.'

Elaine felt their eyes pierce into her back, she had a sick feeling in the pit of her stomach. She didn't feel hungry at all she was too full of fear. 'This is outrageous,' she thought, 'why should a be persecuted like this, I feel like am in the wrong, what if a picked the wrong person though?'

After lunch Elaine is told she is the last witness number fifty, she will have to come back tomorrow. She can't believe she has to go through another night of anguish and knotted insides. On the way home she furtively looks over her shoulders, she doesn't want any repercussions from this court business.

'Witness number fifty, Elaine McShaw.' She's led into the witness stand and wishes there was a seat. Her whole body is numb and she concentrates on not fainting through nerves. She glances to the accused box, four boys and a girl sitting giggling and nudging each other.

'So Miss McShaw,' boomed a lawyer who stood up and walked round a table in the middle of the room. 'Will you please describe the events of the night in question the 24th March 1992.'

Elaine reiterates her story in a blur of sentences.

'So, Miss McShaw, you believe this girl here, pointing to number seven, is one of the girls who attacked you on this same night.'

'Yes.'

'I can't hear you Miss McShaw.'

Elaine forced out a louder 'Yes.'

'Are you positive this is the very same girl?'

'I think it was her.'

'Oh, so you think it was her, that will be all Miss McShaw.'

A huge wave of relief pushed her out the box, she didn't care what happened now she just wanted to get out of this suffocating room.

Two weeks later she receives a phone call from Lynn. 'Well, they were found not guilty, can you believe it? Am so mad Elaine a swear am gonna get thim, fifty bloody wit-nesses and a verdict of not guilty, a ask ye. Am organising a gang to get thim, a know who they are, we're gonna find thim. Are yi in?'

'No Lynn, count me out, a jist want ti forget the whole escapade.'

The extreme bitterness and anger she felt subsided after a while. It was so unfair she couldn't work it out at all. She thought she had done the right thing but the outcome was so perverted, so ironical.

She was always met from work now, her friends would take it in turns to walk her home, always two or three of them. It was Saturday night and the Glasgow rain was pelting from the smog-filled sky. She waited for ages but no-one came so she started to walk, she tried to catch a cab but there were none in sight. She was struggling against the wind and rain when they grabbed her and bundled her into a dark alleyway. A blade was shoved under her chin and two pairs of drug-filled eyes met hers, she recognised those eyes just before number seven pulled back the knife and lunged it deep into her chest.

'You won't identify me again ya bitch,' she hissed.

They left her in a pool of rainwater and blood, her coat over her head, the pockets ripped and bereft of money. No-one will notice her for a while, they'll only think she's a down-and-out sleeping up an alley.

Is this what they call justice? The innocent suffer and the guilty live on. Rough justice has come full circle and will continue on and on, round and round, drawing the circle of crime which can never be broken.

17

Incurable?

by

James Anstruther

'Ha, ha, do you remember Les, what old Sir Colin said to us the day we joined?' asked Joe. As the joke had already gone the rounds three times that week, Les answered right on cue:

'Be loyal to the company and the company'll look after you.'

'And here we are . . . wondering . . .' Joe continued, waving his redundancy cheque and looking around for the Gents, ' . . . if these have any more value than the paper I'm just off to use.' They were still laughing when he bellowed from halfway across the pub: 'We should ask Steve - our Company Accountant.'

Stephen joined in the bitter-sweet laughter. Lacking Joe's paranoia he was sure their money would come through OK but being a mere clerk he was, as everyone knew, hardly the one to ask. It was only a week since volunteers had been requested. Not only were none forthcoming, but yesterday everyone in the company took the proverbial one step backwards, everyone that is, except those attending tonight's hastily arranged fare-well party who'd been told, 'Don't even pick up your pencils. Your desks will be cleared for you and the contents forwarded. Thank you.' Stephen like the others, felt bitter; but for him this was tinged with a strange optimism. He was not altogether unprepared.

His bitterness had only developed in recent years but had, he knew, its roots in his early days with the company when his fiancée Elisabeth had wanted him to move to a more scenic part of the country, away from those bleak industrial estates. Coming from a farming community she'd insisted: 'This is no place to bring up children . . . ' and was he thought, quite right. He didn't have the excuse that work was scarce, and had actually changed jobs several times during his then, twenty-seven years; but though he'd no great ambitions, he'd seen this new post as an opening to a stable career and as reasonably financially rewarding. That in his opinion, was an important factor to be considered when raising a family.

'I can't promise that you'll be on this side of my desk in ten years,' said Sir Colin overstating his point on the young accounts clerk's first day thirty years ago, but we do reward hard work Stephen.' Lies. All lies - not that Sir Colin was directly responsible for yesterday's decision, having sold out to new management, headed by Timothy Warwick-Jones three years ago. Many more people than Stephen were to realise however, that doing a good job in this company was not enough. It was who you knew, not what you

18

knew. By the time Stephen realised his loyalty to the company was totally one-sided, Elisabeth had called off the wedding and eventually their relationship foundered. He couldn't blame her. His evening studies consumed more time than they spent together and she was evidently, regarding his career, longer-sighted than he.

'Another fiver for the kitty! Everyone agreed?' shouted Joe approaching the table.

'Yes but nothing more for me Joe,' said Stephen dropping a note into the ashtray. 'I'll have to go.'

'Oh I forgot you're on doctor's orders - sorry Steve,' said Joe handing him back his note. 'You know I can't get over how rotten they've been to you mate. They get you to put all your knowledge of the company's system on a database and then decide to replace you with a glorified computer operator.'

'Oh I've learned a few things though . . . ' said Stephen putting on his scarf.

'Yeah, haven't we all? When do you plan to go?' said Joe.

'Oh, so far it's just a thought and I've a few things to take care of before I go.'

'Where's that? . . . ' asked Les ' . . . Thailand?'

'The Philippines I think, but I'm not sure yet.'

'I believe Warwick-Jones is heading out that way in a week or so mate . . .' said Joe, ' . . . though he's not looking for the same thing as you, ha ha. He probably just wants some cheap labour.'

'Enjoy yourself then Steve.'

'Send us a postcard.'

'Keep in touch.'

'Watch your wallet . . . ' came the various farewells from fond workmates knowing they might never see him again.

Stephen's trip was initially planned as a holiday until his doctor's disturbing diagnosis. Walking home from the pub he recalled the conversation.

'You did ask me to be direct with you Mr Watson.' Dr Meredith apologised.

'I know . . . ' said Stephen, resigned.

'With treatment you can still have a few good years.'

'Tell me one more thing . . . ' said Stephen, carefully wording his question, though Jack Meredith was broad-minded enough as to need no polite subtleties in conversation with patients of long standing. 'Is it communicable . . . I mean . . . in any way?'

'No. It's non-communicable so you can go on your usual summer holiday without at least that on your conscience.'

That was a couple of months ago. He had started a course of treatment to which he was responding well and neither his employers nor workmates had any idea of the severity of his illness.

Successful computerisation of the company accounting system relied heavily on Stephen's typical assiduity and dedication which he maintained despite health worries and his increasing suspicions regarding the company's future plans. Even yet his sense of loyalty was undiminished, though he'd never really forgiven them for Sid's death . . . years previously. Sid had been Stock Controller for longer than anyone could remember. He was older than Stephen and whilst they weren't exactly close friends, together they shared an interest in electronics, keeping abreast of innovations and were both radio 'hams'. His wife had recently died and he lived only for his job and his hobby. Stephen fondly remembered him on one occasion confiding, 'I know why you take all these foreign holidays lad. No one can ever replace someone you've really loved can they?'

When Warwick-Jones took over relishing his role as 'new broom'; he'd computerised, within a year, the stock control system; automated the stock retrieval and made Sid redundant. Although he was given a reasonable farewell package, everyone knew it meant little to Sid and his suicide, whilst a terrible shock, was with hindsight, predictable.

In the two weeks following the clearance of his redundancy cheque Stephen was keeping himself busy spending a great deal of time in his workshop. He read a lot - mostly technical manuals, and wrote - mostly airmail letters. He arranged bank transfers and plane tickets; sold or gave away all his furniture, crockery and objéts; slept on an old mattress and dined out every night. After a final examination with Dr Meredith he arranged his cessation of tenancy with the local housing department. He wished he had more time but it was now or never.

'Smoking or non-smoking Mr Watson?' the check-in clerkess enquired.

'Smoking please and an aisle seat if possible.'

'Would you like me to put that through as well sir?' she nodded at his holdall.

'N . . . No it's hand luggage . . . ' he said clutching it firmly.

'No problem, check in by 7.30 at the latest please.'

Checking his boarding pass over a coffee, his thoughts were racing. 'With a bit of luck it'll all be over in a few minutes. Gone without a trace.' He glanced at his watch and re-crossed to the check-in desk.

'Excuse me please. Has a Mr Warwick-Jones checked in for this flight?' he asked nervously.

'No I'm afraid not sir,' said the clerkess gazing at him quizzically.

'Oh I just wondered. It's just - he's a colleague of mine,' he reassured her.

'I'm not sure if I can go through with this,' he thought crossing to the phone booths. 'God give me strength.' He was glad that there were no youngsters about; dismayed that the booths were all occupied.

'Damn it. I hadn't planned for this . . . ' he said out loud, now sweating profusely. Wiping his brow with a handkerchief he looked up at the clock. 'God please, I need a line.' As if in divine response a businessman hung up at that instant and dashing forward Stephen opened up his holdall, grabbed the receiver and dialled the number; smiling as his call was answered. Burying the handset in the clumsy accoustic modem he'd home-wired to a lap-top, he flipped open the computer lid and within a few well rehearsed keystrokes, saw the magic words appear on the screen:

> directory *Company Accounts*

> enter password *XXXXXXX*

> subdirectory *Sid* > subdirectory *Virus* > file *Destroy*

Choice: type

         R = Recoverable
or
        I = Incurable

    followed by *Return*

'Last call for Flight Number 157 for Manila via Bangkok,' the tannoy announced as Stephen placed his lap-top back in the holdall.

The Proper Job

by

E Walker

There he goes - him from No. 6, all set for his day at his proper job, complete with neat little briefcase. The little smirk he gives me as he passes is maybe him thinking about the daft story I told him the other day.

Well, he was sounding off yet again about how he couldn't understand why I liked my work as a window-cleaner and was it really true about the stories he had heard.

'Stories?' I said.

'Yes, you know, you're bound to see a bit of life in the raw, if you know what I mean?'

All he left out was the nudge, nudge, wink, wink!

So, just to keep him happy I said, 'Oh, aye, I was lucky the other day. Mind, it's only once in a blue moon you get the chance.' This really had him sitting up and taking notice so to put him out of his misery I told him about the young woman I had seen, just as she finished her bath.

'You should have seen her - a wee beauty, blonde, blue eyes with curves and dimples all in the right places. Man, she was something, I can tell you, better than any calendar picture in that braw office of yours.'

The poor chap almost choked on his drink as he mentally reviewed the glamour girl I'd described to him. Patting him on the back I left and had a wee grin to myself as I hurried home to the lovely blonde - 'My toddler, all rosy from her bath and ready for a cuddle from her Daddy'.

In my last 'Proper Job' I worked shifts and never saw my family. Redundancy put paid to that. I'm a lucky man - with a proper job and time for the blondes in my life! My wife and child!

The Long Memory

by

Roland Portchmouth

It was mid-January.

The Firth was frozen over from shore to shore. It was the first time it had happened in living memory. Well, almost. Gulls stood on the unfamiliar ice-rink, as did the few resident swans. Nearer the beach, herons gazed forlornly from their usual stand with dull-eyed disbelief at the changed scene.

Experts who said the tidal waters would not freeze wondered where their theories had gone wrong. Overnight, air temperatures had plummeted; but for the Firth to ice up like this was unknown. Certainly to locals. Not to old Dougal, however. His memory was longer than theirs. Longer, in fact, than it should have been by rights. No one else could recall the time he claimed to have walked out on to the ice and made holes to fish through. Nor other things he hinted at - like using ice as a deep-freeze for the fish he caught.

Nobody knew Dougal's age or much else about him. But then he was not a mixer - from natural reserve, some said; others, because he was a bit 'peculiar'. Maybe because he had nothing to say, he said nothing. Except to the birds and animals: with these, he conversed as though with life-long friends. What passed between them was their own secret.

Today was so cold and slippery, few people were about. Some had business to attend to, but they did not loiter, except to exchange shivering views on the freak weather. From time to time, a Council gritter passed. What traffic there was, moved slowly, for roads were like polished glass. In the village, only sheltered or well-heated homes had water. People with none, phoned neighbours to see if they had any. Lucky ones went round with buckets, and made arrangements back home to ration the supply. House-holders were locating exposed pipes in attics and elsewhere to pack extra lagging round them and stave off possible bursts.

But no one was unduly worried. Inconvenienced, yes, but hopefully not for long. By evening on the second day, nothing had changed, and a few were getting anxious. Water supplies from neighbours had been replenished several times, and by now everyone knew the telephone numbers of plumbers advertising emergency service.

A third day came and went. And a fourth. By the end of the week, more and more people were becoming uneasy. Still no explanation for the unprecedented cold snap was

23

forthcoming, although possible reasons were aired. These ranged from a deflection of the Gulf Stream round the coast, to a tilt of the earth's axis, with a corresponding shift of the North Pole and the Arctic Circle.

Willie McNab, who studied such matters from avid reading of the tabloids and from science programmes on TV, was in triumphant mood.

'That proves it!' he pronounced to George Carstairs, who had been so careless as to get caught up with him. 'It's all a load of rubbish and scaremongering - this talk of holes in the ozone layer and global warming. Everyone's on about ice-caps melting and sea levels rising!' His arms swept round the frozen Firth and shore lines. 'What price their theories now! Does *that* look as if the world is warming up?!'

'It can warm up as soon as it likes, as far as I'm concerned,' responded George, retreating quickly into the corner Supermarket. It was not easy to get away from Willie, whose object in life was to blast the media.

Inside the Supermarket, George caught sight of a note pinned up. A meeting of village folk had been called for 7 o'clock that evening in the Pavilion to discuss the crisis.

Despite the short notice, the meeting was well attended. Villagers, muffled to the eyes, sat around among clouds of condensing breath, waiting for someone to take a lead. Andy Murray stood up from near the front.

'Ladies and gents,' he said, with a doubt in his voice that this was the correct way to open. 'Thanks for turning out. As you know, it's a week now since this freeze-up started. Robbie here and me, we thought we ought to do something about it - like call a meeting.' Robbie sat in solemn acquiescence at his side. 'There's not much water in the village, and supplies of other things - food and fuel and so on - are running low. Deliveries aren't reg'lar, and could get worse, I reckon. Unless the weather lets up, it won't be long before things get serious.'

'Got any ideas, Andy?' called a voice from the back.

'*I* have!' called out another. Wilma Duffy.

Everyone looked her way, hopes rising.

'What's that, then, Mrs Duffy?' asked Andy.

'Speak to old Dougal,' she said.

Disappointed groans went round the hall. A few clicks of annoyance and derision.

'Dougal?' echoed Andy. 'What help is Dougal?'

Wilma Duffy got up from the bench. 'Old Dougal says he was around when it froze like this before. Not that I believe him, any more than anyone else does. But if he *is* older than the rest of us - and if he's right. . . '

'If he's right - what then?' interrupted Andy.

'Well, he's still here, isn't he - so he must have lived through it. How did he do it?'

She sat down with hands on her lap and the air of one who has made an unassailable point. The idea, at first dismissed as daft, somehow caught on. No other suggestions were offered, and it was decided to have a word with Dougal. Andy and Wilma were delegated to call on him at the disused tackle store where he had made a home for himself.

He was in when they knocked, and met them with an impassive stare. It was no good wasting words with Dougal, and Andy came straight to the point, reminding him of his claim to have witnessed an earlier similar freeze-up in the past.

'What we'd like to know, Dougal,' he said 'is - how did you manage?'

Dougal looked at them blankly. 'Manage?' he said.

'How did you get things? Water, for instance?'

Dougal brightened. 'Water?' he repeated. 'I melted the ice, of course - made a fire of sticks and melted the ice.'

Andy and Wilma exchanged glances.

'What did you do for food? It must have run short, didn't it?'

'Food?' echoed Dougal. 'I caught it.'

'Hunting, you mean? What did you catch?'

A far-away look came to Dougal's eyes. 'Mammoths,' he said. 'Me and the lads got 'em. Mammoths take some getting, mind you. But they last a while. Specially in the deep-freeze.'

The report of Dougal's Ice Age reminiscence circulated rapidly with the return of Andy and Wilma to the village. He *was* older than the rest of them, then! Old enough to be admitted to a particular Home near Inverness for his own sake. It was warmer there, anyway. And three meals a day. So he did not share the general relief in the village when the cold snap ended as suddenly as it began - still unexplained. Nor was he around during the thaw to take part in the mopping-up operations, or to see how soon everyone got back to normal and forgot the crisis.

Dougal did not forget. But then he had a good memory. Went back a few million years.

A Letter Hame

by

Maggie Stephen

3rd January 1993.
Mum,

Ken this? A'm sittin in this cafe, an the sun's beatin doon on me. A've got a braw cup o coffee in front o me. Thur's only wan thing a coud wish fur on a day like this. A wish this effin cafe wis in Kirkcaldy instead o New bleedin Delhi!

Ye mind hoo abody sayed it wis braw A wis comin tae India. They sayed whit hot it wid be, an whit braw things A wid see. They aw sayed whit nice it wid be tae see the Taj Mahal an awthing like that. Well, it's hot, an things are aw braw, an A seen the 'Taj' as we tourists are meant tae say. But it wisnae as braw as some o the things A coud see if A went back tae Scotland. Dinnae git me wrang. A'm no exactly complainin aboot it here. But if A wis back in Scotland A coud see aw thing an no be a tourist. That's whit's causin aw ma problems the noo. Aw the Indian blokes at the Taj were wantin tae tak ma photie. Wan wid come up an say, can A tak yer picture, an A sayed aye. Thin thur's aboot ten pals appears fae naeplace an they're aw wantin a photie! Yer aye saying that A'm no exactly guid lookin, so A dinnae ken how they're so interestit in me! That's jist wan o the many irritatin things whit happen here every day. Ye cannae jist blend in, like ye coud if ye were walkin doon the High Street. Yer somethin special here. Some folks wid be away wi thirselves here. A'm no ower fond o it.

A can sit an eat ma breakfast in this wee roadside cafe, everyday. A coud hae ma denner an ma tea here anaw, an the lot widnae cost me mair than a bag o chips fae Overton Road. An ye even git porridge fur breakfast! Only thur no shair o the spellin, so it's porag or porradge or even porrage banan. Usually A hiv pain porrage, that's whit it says on the menu. Tae you an me, that means porridge on its ain.

A can sit here an feel the sun on me, an a wee scruffy dug will come sniffin aboot ma ankles. It comes each mornin, lookin fur some scraps, or a wee pat on the heid. Some folks clap it, but thur aye warnin ye aboot rabies, so A dinnae bother, jist in case. A jist sit here in the mornin an wait fur the wee auld Indian mannie tae come aroond wi the papers on his bike. He comes wheezin along the street, amid the dust an the traffic an aw thing. He looks aboot sixty, but it's hard tae tell, cos yer skin gans aw withered an dry really early if ye live in a hot country. Roond he comes, an he sells me the Times o India or the Indian Express. A've bin tryin tae read aboot whit's gaun on in Bosnia, but the

Indians irnae really shair aboot it. They hivnae got naebody like Kate Adie tae gan in thair an tell ye aboot it! In the paper it'll say somethin like some people got shot in Sarajevo, but we're no shair cos we wisnae thair. An A think the only way they ken even that is cos they've phoned up Kate Adie an asked her! Sometimes A see the news on the telly, but it's no much better. Ye widnae like it, Mum. Imagine that - nae Reporting Scotland!

A'll be sittin here eatin ma breakfast or whitever, an A'll hae tae pit up wi some awfy things. It disnae hauf turn ma stomach some days, it's that stinkin. There's some smells A'm no gaun tae tell ye aboot, cos ye wid be ill thinkin aboot it. Some are nice, like the spices they hiv piled up in the mercats an the incense whit burns aw place. An there's some cookin smells that are braw tae, although A coudnae say exactly whit they wur. But there's a smell o animal dirt, an human dirt tae. A think ye ken whit A mean. A seen an elephant wanderin through the city the ither day, so ye can imagine whit kind o state the streets will be in if that's a regular occurence. A can see things like the Indians blowin thur nose as they gan along the street. Nae hankies, mind. They pit thur finger against one nostril tae block it, and they blow doon the ither ane. Aw the snot o the day comes oot, an it gans boing-a-boing-a-boing, until it finally breaks free an plops on tae the road. Abody's belchin an fartin at ye as ye walk along. Naebody cares aboot that sort o thing here. A think it coud even be polite - try tellin that tae Auntie Effie! They aw stare at me cos A'm a lassie by masel. So A walk along the street an A belch back at them. A dinnae see why A shudnae. A quite enjoy it! An, course, ye shud aye mind that 'Whin yer in Rome . . . '

Thur's aw kinds o things tae look at, jist whin yer wanderin aboot the street. But the Indians only want tae look at you! A feel like the main attraction at the circus some days. Aw the wee bairns come runnin up, an they can aw say at least a wee bit in English. If thur no askin fur money they say, hello, an which country please, an even A love you! Ye widnae believe it unless ye seen it fur yersel. But then there's loads o folk wantin baksheesh tae. They come up an they say baksheesh madam, baksheesh, or they shout whin ye gan past. Baksheesh means gie's some money, an it can be a bit hard tae git roond. A'm rich here, believe it or no. Some o the people think ye shud spare them a few rupees cos ye hiv mair than them. An why no? It's jist like you wantin mair pension aff the government, Mum. The trouble wi baksheesh is, if ye gie money tae one person, ye hae tae gie it tae them aw. So A try tae say no.

Abody's tryin tae sell ye somethin tae. They wander efter ye tryin tae sell things like postcards an wood carvins. This wan yisterday come up tae me wi this sack in his haund. He sayed Snake Madam, Snake Madam, an he wis hingin on ma airm, but A wisnae interestit. If ye are, they tak this poor dopey snake oot the sack, and they play the flute an charm it. Then they tell ye that thur wantin money fur daein it. Thair wis wan

27

A seen, an he wis sittin at the side o the road playin tae this snake. A took a picture o it, but thin he sayed he wis wantin ten rupees fur me takin the photie! A sayed no, an A walked aff. But whin A looked back, the snake hid turnt aroond in the basket, an it wis lookin at me really mean. So A ran awa roond the corner, cos A thocht he wis sendin the snake efter me! Ye hae tae be careful here, cos thair isnae much comes free.

A've only been frightened the once. That wis whin A wis waitin in this railway station fur ma train. A heard aw this commotion ootside, like chantin an shoutin. A didnae ken whit wis happenin. These guards burst in tae the waitin room where A wis. They were aw massive an they aw hud guns. A thocht something dreadful wis aboot tae happen. But it turns oot they were guardin this man whit wis the leader o wan o the political parties here. Aw the Indians were stondin aroond him an bowin, an kissin his haunds. A jist sat tight in the corner, an the guards offered roond a bag o oranges fur abody tae tak wan. That must be the equivalent o kissin bairns! Things calmed doon efter that, but A wisnae hauf worried whin it first happened.

A dinnae ken whit A'll dae at the end o this month. A might gan up tae Kathmandu, cos A've been tellt that the Nepalese are right friendly, an ye can git a drink thair. A'm no hauf needin ane! It's an experience here, but it's big, and it's miles fae hame. It's weird walkin aboot a place an no meetin anybody that ye ken. But A've paid aw this money tae git here, so A cannae gie up. But if ma fairy godmother turnt up an sayed that A coud hae A wish, A wid ask that A coud be back hame eatin ma pain porrage wi you, right this minute!

Tak care o yersel, ye hear, an dinnae fret.

Lots of love,

M.

Black Widow

by

John Johnstone

Normally Simon Hughes enjoyed the two mile walk from the small town of Inverdrummond to his isolated cottage in the heart of the Scottish countryside. His job as an assistant librarian involved him spending so much time among dusty old books that he welcomed the chance to stretch his legs and stroll quietly home, breathing in the clean fresh air which, after a day spent in the stuffy confines of the District Library, tasted more intoxicating to him than a pint of ice-cold lager. Tonight however was different.

It had been a pleasant enough evening when his diminutive, slightly balding figure had emerged from the library, blinking owlishly in the light cast by the rays of the sun as it set slowly behind the hills in the west. Now, however, there was a sharp, autumnal chill in the air and a thick fog was starting to roll in from the moors. Simon imagined that Sir Arthur Conan Doyle had had just such a night in mind when he wrote about the demon hound which was supposed to prowl the countryside around Baskerville Hall in search of fresh victims. As he walked, Simon could almost hear its menacing, baying howl and feel its panting, fetid breath upon his neck as its slavering jaws opened wide in readiness to tear his throat open with savage ferocity.

Simon gazed anxiously around him and of course there was nothing there. He was completely alone.

'Damn it, Hughes,' he cursed vehemently to himself. 'You've been reading far too much Stephen King recently. Perhaps you should stick to something less racy in future. Like Enid Blyton, for instance!'

But, as he pulled his heavy overcoat more tightly around him, it was more than just the cold that made him shiver. He could not shake off the ominous feeling that someone - or something - was watching him.

On such a night as this, he was more than usually glad to see his small, white-walled cottage with the thatched roof and the neat, trim garden in which the roses were still in full bloom. As he put his key in the lock and let himself into the house, the fog had closed in completely, covering everything like a shroud, and it was beginning to rain.

Once inside, Simon turned on the gas fire and welcomed its warmth as it drove the chill from his body. He switched on the television set and the image of the young female newscaster, whom he had always found so attractive, flickered into view. She was just completing an item of news that Simon immediately wished he had heard in full.

'And so everyone in Inverdrummond and the surrounding areas,' she was saying, 'are being warned to make sure that all their doors and windows are securely locked until this dangerous maniac has been recaptured. Those in remote areas are advised to stay indoors if possible. And now the weather . . .'

Simon's heart was thudding apprehensively in his chest as he gazed through the curtains into the night. The rain was hammering heavily against the window-pane and the air seemed filled with brooding menace. On the other side of the desolate moors stood the asylum and Simon knew full well that it contained inmates who were so evil and so sadistic that they made Hannibal Lecter look like the Jolly Green Giant. Carefully, he went round the house checking that all the doors and windows were securely bolted and wished, not for the first time, that he had had the foresight to invest in a shotgun.

Under the circumstances, Simon Hughes spent a restless evening. He had originally planned to at last begin work on that epic novel which he had been promising himself for years he would write but never somehow seemed to find the time to begin. But each time he sat down at the typewriter some noise, real or imagined, would immediately send him racing round the house to check that all means of entry into his home were still secure. Each time they were, and he cursed himself with increasing impatience for his timidity. Eventually, around 11 pm, he was just about to go to bed when there was a loud, frantic hammering at the front door. His heart seemed to skip several beats as he nervously walked down the hall, his hand tightly clutching the heavy paper-weight he had instinctively reached for when the knocking started.

'Who's there?' he shouted fearfully, his voice trembling.

'Help me,' a woman's voice screamed out. 'For God's sake, you must help me.'

At once Simon unbolted the door and threw it open. Standing there was a young woman no older than about twenty-five, with long auburn hair cascading over her shoulders and wearing a white cotton dress that was soaked through by the now torrential rain. Simon noticed that one sleeve of her dress was torn and that blood was seeping slowly from a cut on her left hand in which she held a small travel bag.

'Let me in,' she implored Simon. 'He's probably still out there.'

Simon immediately stood aside to allow her to enter the house and ushered her through to the warmth of the living-room.

'I was hitch-hiking to Inverdrummond,' she explained, trembling as she sat down in the armchair by the fire. 'A guy picked me up but, as soon as we were out in the country, he stopped the car and tried to rape me.'

She buried her head in her hands and began to cry loudly, her body racked by uncontrollable sobs.

'I'll phone the police,' Simon decided, picking up the telephone that stood on the small mahogany table that rested against the far wall. As he did so, there was no comforting buzz from a dialling tone, only silence.

'The phone's dead,' he gasped, sudden anxiety flooding through him. 'Look you better stay the night. We'll go to the police together first thing in the morning. You'll find a dressing gown through there in the bedroom. You can wear it while your clothes dry out. I can bunk down on the sofa for the night.'

The young girl ran over to Simon and flung her arms around him.

'Don't leave me alone,' she begged him. 'I'm frightened.'

As she pressed her firm young body seductively against him, Simon felt a strong desire stirring within him.

Simon Hughes slipped quietly out of bed, taking care not to disturb the sleeping figure of the girl who lay beside him. Wearily, he donned his dressing-gown and wandered through to the living-room. Still fresh in his mind was the memory of the yielding softness of her smooth, energetic young body, the intense, almost violent passion of her erotic love-making as, their bodies joined as one, they had almost forgotten the bleakness and danger that lay outside.

Simon slumped into an armchair and gazed at the clock on the mantelpiece which told him it was nearly 5 am. Almost automatically, he turned on the radio where a news bulletin had just begun.

'A murder enquiry is under way in the Inverdrummond area,' the news reader was saying, 'following the discovery late last night of the body of a taxi driver. He had been brutally stabbed to death. His death is thought to be connected with the escape from a nearby asylum yesterday of Angela Penman. The public are again warned that this woman is extremely dangerous and should not be approached under any circumstances.'

Simon sat bolt upright in his chair. Angela Penman? Yes, he remembered reading about the case at the time. She had been a prostitute who had murdered around a dozen of her clients. They had all been stabbed to death and their bodies horribly mutilated. He recalled that the tabloid press, with its unfailing lack of good taste, had dubbed them the 'Jill The Ripper Murders'.

At that moment, a slender female hand reached out from behind the armchair and grabbed hold of Simon's hair. Her other hand, holding a large carving knife, appeared and expertly slit his throat with such savagery that he was almost decapitated. As the blood flowed freely from his severed jugular, Simon slumped lifelessly to the floor, a red warm bubbling pool growing large around him.

The auburn-haired figure of Angela Penman walked round from behind the armchair, a mad sadistic grin on her face, her eyes gleaming with evil pleasure. Again and again she plunged the knife into Simon's corpse, her maniacal laughter reverberating round the room.

Jill

by

G M Gall

It was going to be a lovely day. Even before she had got out of bed Jill had realized that it was a beautiful morning, birds were singing and rays from the young sun lay aslant the grass outside her window. Dewdrops were glistening in the sun, soon they would dry and a warm day would follow.

Now breakfasted, Jill awaited her boss, he always came to take her to work. For three years they had been working together and Jill felt that she had really fathomed his thought processes. Sometimes the work would take them to other places, then there would be strangers to meet, different ways of doing things, but always they came home in the evening, then they would part.

Jill wished that she could stay with her boss, but his wife thought otherwise. Always she seemed indifferent to Jill, cold even, and would not tolerate Jill entering the house. So she had to stay in this old place which had seen better days, with no company to cheer her. Work was always a joy; whether working alone with her boss, or with others, there was usually a feeling of companionship, a cheery word, something which she missed of an evening and on the interminable Sundays.

But today was not Sunday, the boss would be along any minute, she wondered what vehicle he would have today. The vehicle was the first clue as to where they might be working. She liked the occasional changes of venue, was still young enough to savour the different places, somewhat to the amusement of her adored boss.

An engine - the boss was coming. With a light step and a shake of her skirts she made for the door. Footsteps outside, she could hear them above the sound of the idling engine, a rattling of the latch, door swinging open, a shaft of light on the floor, 'Good morning Jill, how are you today?'

Jill wagged her tail.

Dinner

by

Bob Brown

Even though it was fuelled by an extra glass of wine, Stewart had a good idea. He was just finishing his dessert when he noticed the old lady struggling with her umbrella while she held the door open behind her with her foot. Wouldn't it be fun, he proposed to his friend Bart, to secretly pay for her dinner.

'We'll be long gone by the time she asks for the check. Give the old bird a thrill,' he said.

It would be fun agreed Bart. All they had to do was wait until she ordered, let her waitress know what they were doing and leave enough to cover her bill.

They chuckled together when she ordered, saying to each other that they hoped it wasn't something expensive, fully aware that they could afford anything that this local's place had to offer. Stewart motioned to the waitress to come over. Her smile grew as she understood what they wanted her to do. How sweet she thought, nodding that she understood. She showed them what she had written on the order pad, fish and chips, with water to drink. Stewart gave her enough to cover the bill and plenty for a dessert and tip. They made the waitress swear to secrecy. On the drive home, Bart laughed at how confused the old lady would be as he reached over to turn up the football scores on the radio.

Mrs Martin Andrews did not often go out for dinner often. Besides being expensive, it was not enjoyable to go alone. She was at the age when most of her friends didn't drive at night any more so just about all of her activities were during the day-time. Winter meant especially long lonely nights at home. She decided two weeks ago that since today would have been Martin's birthday, she would take the bus the short distance to his favourite restaurant. Going out to dinner was not something usual, and it wasn't something enjoyable either, so much as it was the right thing to do. Martin was always doing things for her when he was alive, his widow could always make the effort to be nice in a way he would have liked.

Her thoughts wandered as she fussed with her fork at the fish and chips. For the first time in years her daughter didn't call on her father's birthday. Perhaps it has been long enough for her to forget. Her son, she laughed, he would never think to call. Yet, tomorrow he might send a dozen roses. Martin's birthday was always hard. The memories of

34

years and years flooded back in torrents. Too many. Upsetting her that she couldn't grasp one and hold on to it.

She escaped her thoughts by looking around the cafe. It was a clean simple place as befitted the small town where she came to be married. An assortment of tables and chairs crowded the room like the hodge podge of colours and sizes of her neighbours at the bus stop. Customers she didn't know hunched over their meals and turned their backs to make their own little worlds. The table where the young gentlemen sat was being cleared, two tables were crammed with squirming young families. A young couple oblivious to everyone else occupied the table in the corner and a middle age couple sat at the one in the middle. Two of the tables were empty but fully set, waiting for people to arrive. She smiled at the stages of the lives around her. So much happiness and so much sadness from the same thing. The cafe would be complete, she thought, if one of the empty tables had contained an elderly couple and the other an older man. She was sure Martin wouldn't object to her ogling a nice gentleman for he knew she loved only him.

She asked the waitress to bring her the menu again. Cake would be nice, for Martin's birthday. They didn't have any which was probably for the better. It would have been silly to order cake pretending that it was his birthday cake . Maybe she was losing her mind a little to think such a thing anyway. She reached into her purse so she could pay for her meal and catch the 8.30 bus home.

What was the waitress saying? Mrs Andrews didn't understand. How could someone have paid for her meal? No, this was crazy.

'No one pays for me,' she said, digging in her purse and bringing out the coins. I have the money right here. Why won't you take it?

The waitress was insistent. She thought that the idea was cute. It was so very thoughtful to help out an old lady. Why wouldn't she understand?

Mrs Andrews listened as well as she could. She began to realize that someone she didn't know had paid for her dinner. That didn't make sense but that is what happened. So she didn't have to pay for her dinner. The waitress said that the bill had been paid. There was no bill. She could simply get up after her dinner and go home.

This was not right. A person can't go out for dinner and not pay for it. She looked around to see who might have paid for her dinner. All the other people were eating as if nothing was happening. The waitress said it was someone who had already left. Mrs Andrews was becoming more and more upset.

'This is not right. Please allow me to pay for my own dinner,' she said.

The waitress told her that since her meal had already been paid for, to take more money for it again would be illegal. That made sense to Mrs Andrews and she certainly did not want them to do something illegal. The waitress was called over by one of the families.

So Mrs Andrews sat at her table and tried to understand what this was all about. A stranger bought her dinner. Was that bad? It felt bad. Maybe it was the strangeness. This was not the sort of thing that occurred every day. She could understand if this happened to a young girl, and the young man had stayed around to accept her thanks. But she was an old lady and whoever it was had left. It had been a very long time since a nice young man had bought her dinner. It had been a long time since she and Martin had dinner together.

Did someone feel sorry for her? Maybe that was it. Whoever it was thought she was poor or wanted to brighten up her day. That made some sense. She would rather have had some company than to eat alone. But, she probably would have declined going to someone else's table or accepting a strange man at her's.

It was probably a joke. A cheap way for someone to have a laugh at her expense. Confuse the old lady. Give her something to worry about. That was it. A cruel thing to do, but that's how people are nowadays.

Listen to me, she thought, am I going daft or what? Someone bought an old lady her dinner, it was as simple as that. Is why he did it so important? She decided it was a question of dignity. Why he did it was important. But he had gone. There was nothing she could do about it. It wasn't like he was a beau and she could say no. He would never see her again, maybe never even think back on buying the old woman her modest dinner. That left it up to her. She had to figure it out herself.

It was, she had to admit, an extravagance to eat out. She had enough money and had it in her purse. It was her choice and she was willing to make the sacrifice. Coming to dinner here was something she could do to touch a little of Martin. He was so far away. This brought him nearer. Dinner wasn't the important part, it was the thinking about it, the thinking about him.

She motioned for the waitress to come over.

'Were you left a nice tip?'

'Yes, a very nice one.'

'Good.' Mrs Andrews reached down for her umbrella that she placed under the table then got up so she wouldn't miss her bus. 'Martin was always a very generous tipper,' she said to the waitress. 'Goodnight dear.'

Eye Of The Storm

by

Ruth Walker

'I will not be beaten by the wind and the sleet.'

Bethany repeated this phrase to herself as she surveyed her handiwork. She had painted the rusting iron poles for the clothes line a defiant shade of green. She had had to work quickly, before the next snow shower, and the phrase she repeated was to become a constant accompaniment to her work over the next few weeks.

She had bought Pine Tree Cottage a few months ago. Then, in the full glory of summer, she had been mesmerized by the bee hives on the hillside opposite, and the steamy sunshine by the river. A profusion of vegetation, and the flash of a bird's wing had made her heart soar. Then, the vine in the greenhouse drooped with a glowing array of wine red fruit, now it stooped at a drunken angle with a mouldering mish mash of rotting berries. Bethany had been eager to buy the cottage, and also a little afraid. It would be a new interest, an outlet for her creative talents, but it was also a turning away from her more social interests and the friends of the past. Indeed, so engrossed had she become in the hanging of curtains and the arranging of rooms that she had forgotten more than one social occasion.

Later on, she would admit to herself that she was not too sorry to have missed out on things, and it led her to marvel at the energy she had expended in the past on getting to places on time - functions, parties, charity does - and all for what reason. Latterly, she had attended functions partly not to hurt other people's feelings, or because she was too weary to say no, but, in the distant past she conceded that the real reason was to find a man. All that careful dressing up, that lingering in smoky foyers intensely preoccupied with programme notes, the missed heartbeats when he did notice her, the deep gloom when he walked past her without a turn of the head - it was far healthier and less wearing to cultivate ones vines.

It was a key decision moving to the Cottage, Bethany felt. In a few years she could see herself gathering wood in an old pram just like her neighbours, or cultivating leeks, or birds of prey. People around Pine Tree Cottage indulged in such pursuits, with all the energy that Bethany, in earlier years had devoted to finding a man.

When she first moved in, it was all fun. It was magic to see the fire spring to life in the grate, to admire the birds feeding at the bird table, but it was to be a long winter. People

37

were to remember it as the Year of the Storm, or the Year of the Floods, of The Year of the Snow, for all these natural disasters happened in her first winter there.

To combat the cold, Bethany put on layers of assorted clothes, so that she looked like a clown, pink faced, in tights and woolly socks. The fire made her clothes grimy, so she buried her romantic environmental sentiments and invested in a washing machine.

It arrived astonishingly early one winter morning. Bethany clutched her shawl around her like an old woman as she opened the door to the icy cold. Outside, it looked like the interior of a deep freeze waiting to be defrosted. The trees wore a livery of feathery white.

'Minus twelve out there, darling,' the men remarked cheerfully as they unloaded the great white ice cube of a machine. They rattled it indoors on a trolley, and wheeled it into the kitchen. A very tiny fire remained alight in the grate. Bethany was almost hysterical when she saw that the men had left the front door wide open, allowing her precious heat to escape.

'For heaven's sake - it's cold out there - let's get the door shut.'

They shuffled papers in front of a white and dazed Bethany.

'It's too cold to test the machine - the tubes are frozen. You'd better try it a few hours later, when it has had time to thaw. It's been on the lorry all night, frozen solid it is.'

When they had gone, Bethany sat and stared at the alien white lump in her kitchen. Outside, a hoar frost threw every blade of grass into relief.

After she had steamed up the windows with several kettles of boiling water, and had covered her clothes with smuts of coal dust, she decided it would be safe to try the machine. It seemed to take most of the day for the machine to complete its many programmes, but then it was made in sunny Italy, where time did not matter. After many hours she was left with a cylinder of dubious coloured water, and some half washed clothes.

'Reckon it's the pump,' the engineer advised her on the phone. 'I'll be with you next week.'

Bethany hung the semi-washed clothes on the line, and brought them in not long after, totally frozen into flat, sculptural shapes. When the cold lasted for another few weeks, Bethany thought about getting in some storage heaters to supplement the unsteady heat of the fire with its back boiler that heated the water and a few radiators in fits and starts.

But all such considerations palled into insignificance on The Night of the Storm. Bethany had gone to bed at the usual time. She was dressed in her now usual ridiculous assortment of clothes. She left the bathroom light on and the door ajar, as she had not quite got used to the blackness of the nights without street lights in the country. The next she knew, she was awake, and it was not yet five in the morning.

At first the wind outside was mildly disturbing, like a tossing or crashing of waves at the times of the Equinox. She could hear things banging and crashing outside, and then pieces of wood, and pots and cans being hurled around. The sound intensified, till the wind became a vicious, moaning thing that licked at the windows and snarled at the doors. It seemed to be right over her head, then a little further away, and then it was back, more vicious than ever. The bathroom light that had shone so bravely, flickered in time to the wind, spluttered, then went out completely. The blackness around her was impenetrable.

Frantically, Bethany groped around the floor beside the bed to where she thought she had laid her torch. She remembered it was on the dresser, and she staggered out of bed to get it, then tried to keep the sound of the wind out by pulling her quilt over her head. Gradually, like a thunderstorm, the wind sounded further and further away.

Shivering and clutching her torch Bethany got out of bed, and went through to the kitchen. The fire in the grate looked dead. She thought about putting on a kettle, and remembered there was no electricity, so she put a pan of water on the Calor Gas stove instead. The pan soon hissed and bubbled, and she sat listening to the retreating wind, with a candle stuck on the table in front of her. Breakfast by candlelight, she mused. How unutterably romantic. She got up and tried to see out of the window if there was much damage. The landscape was sepia coloured, and eerily still. She added a few layers of clothing, and tried to revive the fire. Little use now for washing machines and electric heaters, she thought as she snapped some twigs and set a match to make them roar.

When daylight returned, people appeared in the landscape, white faced and drawn, to view the damage. Bethany could see the roof of her shed was ripped off. The glass house that held the indolent vine had remained intact. Bits and pieces of information slowly made their way up the valley. The road was blocked by fallen trees. They had brought the electricity line down, and the phones were out of order. The river had burst its banks further up, but Bethany's land was safe with its lade burn.

Later in the day, when the sun came to warm the landscape, she went for a walk to see things for herself. Coming back, with her hands full of firewood, she met someone coming over the bridge into her garden. She could see it was Nathan, who farmed the few acres at the top of the ridge.

'I came to see if the vine had weathered the storm. I thought you'd have a few panes of glass missing at least.'

Bethany only knew Nathan slightly, she had been far too busy with her cottage to get involved in local affairs.

'I seem to have been remarkably lucky,' she said simply.

Together, they stood on the wooden bridge over the lade and surveyed the scene. Bethany's carefully cultivated plants were bashed and broken. The iron clothes poles were askew, ripped out of the earth. The branches of trees had snapped and toppled. Whole roots of trees on the hillside above them had been prised from the ground.

'Come in and have some coffee, at least I have some Calor Gas.'

As the two of them sat quietly sipping their coffee in the kitchen, Bethany couldn't help reflecting how pleasant it was to be sitting there, with the sun streaming in as though the Storm had never happened. Once upon a time, she might even have found the scene just a little romantic. Instead, she offered Nathan another biscuit, and it was gratefully accepted. I must learn to cultivate my neighbours as well as my vines, she told herself, smiling at Nathan.

Icy Looks

by

M Mitchell

They were an unlikely pair, the Duvaliers. She, Lucille, tall, blonde, athletic and beautiful. He, George, short, balding, overweight and short-sighted. She, still young, with a
mind like a steel trap, he, an ageing alcoholic, prone to make mistakes. His last had
been to invest the money for which she had married him, in a crackpot speculation, losing it all. ·

She detested him for that, even more than she detested him before; only the cushion
of his money had allowed her to suffer his slobbering over her body. Now she treated
him with contempt, almost as a servant, but, totally besotted by her, he put up with the
icy looks and the disdain with which she berated him for his mistakes.

It was her idea that they turn to crime and he was her willing accomplice, but only in a
minor way, obtaining and organising the equipment she needed for each job. It was Lucille, with the inside knowledge gained as a once-favoured guest of the ultra-rich Swiss
society, that burgled the luxurious homes. The lithe body that he craved was adept at
scaling walls, reaching balconies and escaping with jewellery and negotiable bonds. The
planning and execution was all hers, and any attempt on his part to make a few suggestions would be met with that blue-eyed icy look.

This latest job would be her last. It would be the hardest ever, the alarm system one
she couldn't by-pass. Her only chance of escape would be to cross the border at the
nearest point, unguarded, because the route to it was down a glacier of sheer ice. She
was sure she could do it, and *would* do it. Her young, handsome lover would be waiting
for her and they'd start a new life together.

The only obstacle was George. He knew too much. Could not be left to spill all to the
police.

Calmly, she slept through the evening, and then made ready. She went through the
check-list of equipment with George, who was drunk. He always turned to the bottle prior
to her doing a robbery, but he blearily assured her that her pack, in the car, contained all
she had ordered.

She was breathing hard when she got to the car. She would normally have checked
her gear, but George had taken so long to die!

She had leaned over his chair from behind, bringing the knife across his throat. To her
horror and dismay, instead of slumping down, he had surged to his feet and turned to

her; his eyes like those of a wounded animal. He'd tried to speak, perhaps her name, perhaps a curse, but all that came was a spray of blood. As he tried to grasp her she struck again and again, her face an icy mask, until finally he lay still. She'd had to change and put her blood-soaked clothing into the incinerator.

She left the car some distance from the remotely-sited villa, ski-ing deftly across deserted countryside to her target. The act of robbery itself was easy, the villa deserted, the safe combination known to her.

She left, again on skis, going hard now, taking chances where necessary; the police would be on their way, alerted by the alarm. She had discarded the rubber-covered grapnel, and the dart gun with which the guard dogs were neutralised. Most of the weight in her back-pack was loot, beautiful loot, even she had not expected the gold bars as a bonus.

When she reached the start of the glacier, she glissaded to a halt, unsnapping her skis, casting them and sticks aside. She rummaged in the pack ready to attach her equipment to her adapted boots. Her movements became more hurried, what the hell had George done? She felt a box and pulled it out. In the bright moonlight, the picture of a laughing girl in a bathing costume seemed to mock her. She tore at the box, spilling the contents, scattering the tubes of absorbent material around her. Then, she began to laugh, hysterically.

'Oh, George, you really did it this time. I said, 'pack my *crampons!*.' Weeping now, she fell to her knees, and was aghast to find herself sliding, ever faster, down the glacier. Her arms flailed, her nails tearing at the ice, but her ice-axe was strapped to her discarded bag, and her boots slid helplessly without the toothed attachments George had omitted to pack. With a wailing scream she plunged into a crevasse.

When she regained consciousness, hours later, wedged where the crevasse narrowed, she knew that she was near death. Her lower body was mangled, her arms pinned. Water was dripping down onto her head and shoulders, from where the sun, far above, melted the lip of the fissure. It soon froze again, where she was. It was a freezing weight in her hair, creeping inexorably down, matting her eyelashes, sealing her nostrils, despite the warmth of her breath. There was not much of *that* left, however.

Her last thought was that bungling George would have liked to see *this* particular icy look!

Calling Me Back

by

Mary Gordon Dawson

Last night, in a dream, I seemed to visit my old home. The house in which I was born and lived with my parents and my brothers and sister. We had lived there until I was about twelve years old and then we moved to another house and another town. But I never thought of the new house as home, not like the old one. Why I should dream about it now after so long I really don't know, unless it was the sense of security and comfort I had known then and needed to find again, my husband having recently made an unfortunate gamble on the stock exchange, as a result of which we had lost everything and things were getting desperate. It's strange the way the mind works on, when one is asleep.

My grandfather had lived in part of the old house. He was a retired sea-captain and when it rained and we couldn't get outside, he would often ask us in to his study for tea and biscuits while he told us wonderful stories of his life at sea. My brothers and I would sit silent and wide-eyed taking it all in. Although I rather think that he invented some of the more colourful ones just for us.

In my dream I walked down the path to the great sycamore tree at the foot of the garden. It had been one of our favourite places for playing in and we would spend hours climbing and swinging from it on a long rope with a tyre for a seat. The tree could be anything we wanted it to be, our imaginations conjured up all sorts of adventures. When it was windy it could be a tall sailing ship bound for the Azores to join Sir Richard Grenville and help save 'The Revenge', or being blown by the trade winds to exciting places with wonderful exotic names. We could almost smell the spices and sweet perfumes as we passed the shores of Zanzibar and Calabar. Other times it might be a space-ship travelling along the milky-way on our way to the planets. On hot sunny days we would climb to the higher branches where it was cool and read a favourite book or just sit and watch the patterns the sunlight made on the shimmering leaves.

I could see the little river at the bottom of the garden where we fished for tadpoles and minnows, and where I once fell in when the rope I was swinging on broke. My brothers had loved that.

At one end of the garden was the big brown shed where we put on little plays that I had made up, all about princes and princesses or pirates and treasure. We made our costumes from the old-fashioned clothes that were kept in an old trunk in the cellar and

43

we charged the audience, which consisted of our friends from school plus any unwary relatives with time to spare, one penny. Then we put the proceeds - which might amount to the grand total of one or two shillings - in an envelope and took it to the Red Cross lady up at the local hospital for the wounded soldiers. They must have been staggered to receive such a huge donation.

I could see the garden seat where we sat and watched a total eclipse of the sun one day. Everything went quite dark and quiet, and I remembered that we had to buy special dark glasses so that we wouldn't be blinded. I don't think it lasted very long, perhaps only a few minutes, but I believe it was quite an unusual thing to see in this country.

In my dream I wandered through my grandfather's vegetable garden and his orchard where he kept his bees. We would find him there nearly every day with his large floppy hat on, covered with a net to protect his face and neck. He had often warned us that we must always tell the bees about anything important that happened in the family, like a new baby, a wedding or a death, otherwise they would fly away and we wouldn't have any honey - and we did.

I didn't go into the house in my dream, probably because I don't remember much about it as we were encouraged to be outside as much as possible unless it was cold or wet. But I could see the steps that led down to the cellar under the house which we used as an air-raid shelter during the war. At night, during those dark years, we wore our siren suits ready to move into the cellar when the siren went. I could still feel the terror of the night raid on Clydebank when a few bombs fell quite close to us. We could hear them come whistling down and held our breaths waiting for the explosion. But we were lucky and they landed in the golf course where they did no harm at all except make a few more bunkers. (Afterwards, of course, we all had to go and see the huge craters they had made). My baby sister slept undisturbed through it all in an old-fashioned basket-work pram that had been in the cellar for a good many years.

To us the cellar was a place of great mystery as most of the things in it were very old. There were piles of books, some of them in French, German and Greek, that had belonged to my mother's old uncle, but some of the things were of much more interest to us, like the two old chests with brass locks and corners. One of them held the clothes we used for dressing-up in and in the other, among many things that belonged to grandfather, was an old ship's compass, a telescope and a brass sextant. Sometimes, on rainy days, we were allowed to play with these treasures. But the cellar was also very dark and had a musty smell about it, and there were corners in it that we kept well away from. In my dream I kept returning to it as if I were looking for something and I felt that this was important, and when I awoke I remembered that there had been something else in one of those trunks that I had forgotten all about, until now.

With a sense of rising excitement I remembered it clearly now, and I knew exactly what the thing was that had been in the trunk for so long. At the time, no-one in the family, not even grandfather, had given it a second thought. He told us that he had won it in a game of cards from another sailor on one of his many trips abroad, and he believed that it had come from the Easter Islands. We children had played with it and thought of it as our lucky charm. Of course, I had no idea where the trunks would be now but I remembered that we would often hide our treasures away in a secret place in the garden where no grown-ups would think of looking for them and I wondered if they might still be there.

I felt that my dream was calling me back to my old home so that I could recover this, which I now knew to be, a valuable and much sought-after relic of an ancient civilization. If it was still there it could solve all our financial problems and maybe leave us a little left over. We could certainly do with some luck just now.

As soon as possible I set off next day on the journey to my old home only to find when I arrived, that the inevitable changes that were bound to have happened after so long had changed the place completely, and as I drove down the road that I had walked so many times in the past, I had great difficulty in finding the landmarks that I had once known so well. The two railway bridges had completely disappeared and the road had been widened. The fields and footpaths were now covered by hundreds of new houses. But worst of all, when I arrived at the spot where our house ought to have been, I couldn't find it.

The five tall Lombardy poplars that had been opposite my bedroom window were still there, so I could work out from them where the house ought to have been. On the site now was a huge modern filling station. The garden had completely disappeared under tarmac and the river was no more than a little burn, overgrown with weeds and brambles. But the sycamore tree was still there, larger than ever, and when I went over to have a closer look found it much the same as it had been those many years ago. Could I possibly find our hiding place after such a long time and would there still be anything in it? The trunk was thick with age and I had to walk round it looking for our secret hidey-hole. Perhaps it had closed up over the years and crushed whatever might have been inside. My heart sank until I realized that if it was still there it would now be much further up the trunk than it was before. I stood back and looked up and sure enough, almost out of my reach, I found it. My hand of course was bigger than it had been and the opening was quite tight, but there was still room for my hand to move about, and yes, there was something there. I pulled it out and my hands shook as I unwrapped the old cloth which covered it and I almost cried out with disappointment when I discovered that it wasn't what I expected. It was a diary, my old diary with my name engraved on the front and in surprisingly good condition after all those years in the tree. I put it in my pocket. I would read through it later.

Had I made a mistake? Perhaps the talisman hadn't been hidden there at that particular time after all. I reached up again and put my hand once more into the hole. I couldn't feel anything but my hand wasn't quite reaching the bottom of it. I looked around for something to stand on and found a large stone which I rolled over to the foot of the tree. I stepped up and this time I managed to get my hand right down into the hole and I found something hard and round at the very bottom. I tightened my fingers round it, pulled it carefully out of the hole and stepped down from the stone. This was also wrapped in an old cloth but this time I wasn't disappointed for when I unwrapped it, there lying in the palm of my hand was the thing I had hoped for. It was an extremely ugly and primitive carving of a man, measuring about eight inches in height, but fashioned out of a beautiful shiny and smooth wood, very dark brown to almost black in colour. It was certainly, to my eyes, an ugly thing but its colour and workmanship was superb and I knew it was worth a fortune. It had turned out to be a very lucky charm after all.

I wrapped the carving up in its cloth and put it safely in my bag. Then I turned once more to have a last look at the old sycamore and ran my fingers over the rough bark wondering if any memory could possibly remain of the children that had once played happily there so long ago.

Me, Vinny And Jane

by

Hugh Clark Small

Me, Vinny and Jane. We're sitting in my parent's back garden, it's the middle of Summer and we're sharing a lunch of cheese, bread and salad. They've got the old deckchairs out from the shed. The faded cotton contours of green and red stripes nestling against their warm skin. It's their third visit this month. They're old friends from way back before the accident; always threatening to marry me off before I hit thirty and teasing me about old girlfriends I've lost touch with. They're the kind of couple who deserve the 'made for each other' tag. I'm not jealous or envious or any of that shit, just glad they've held onto the principles they used to talk about. Kindness, love and all the corny, benevolent rhetoric you hear so much about and see so little of.

Jane gets mayonnaise on her chin and she tries to lick it off. Me and Vinny are laughing at her futile attempts. The tongue darts in and out of her mouth, then swings and stretches down towards the white blob. She misses every time. She bends down, defeated, to get a paper napkin and her loose vest tumbles in front of her. I catch a quick glimpse of her left breast. The pink nipple excites me. I still get aroused down there like anyone else. I avert my gaze swiftly at Vinny. He's cramming his face with the cheddar and the bread. I realise that no one has seen me and, in doing so, the stolen moment becomes sacred. I wrap it up and store it away in my memory.

Vinny finishes chewing and says he's going inside to get some of the beers he put in the fridge. It's just me and Jane for a couple of minutes and I'm imagining what it's like to be going out with her. She keeps me and Vinny in order when our language starts turning vulgar. Not in a reprimanding way, but with a smile and a gentle shake of the head which makes us melt inside and turn immediately to something more wholesome. I often imagine her as the sister I never had. Even now, while she's rummaging through the salad bowl looking for the last slice of tomato, I see us a children growing up through some make-believe series of events; birthdays, holidays, Christmas mornings, squabbles and secrets. Holding each other's hand through adolescence until we reach the stage we're at now. I love her.

Vinny comes back out with three beers and a wooden box precariously balanced on a chess board. I love him too. He asks me if I fancy a game and I say I do. We both look at Jane for approval. She doesn't mind at all and flips her sun-glasses down from her forehead onto the bridge of her nose.

47

Jane lies back and pushes her face up at the sun. For a moment we're transfixed by her simple beauty. Vinny smiles to himself then he gets up and places the old bird-table between our chairs. He rests the chess board on it and we begin to set out the pieces. Every game is played for keeps. We joke about past grudges but, as soon as we start, an air of tension takes over from the garden's calm.

Half an hour of silence later we've taken three pawns each. Our brows are wrinkled with master plans of conceivable strikes and improbable surprises. We've drunk all our beer and started to share out Jane's. She's still dead to the world. The sun has grown hotter and it's shining white on her mirrored lenses. The humidity has sapped up all our strength. I look at Vinny and see, like me, that he can't be bothered racking his brain any further when he could be relaxing. We call it a stalemate and toss the pieces back into the box. There's a ladybird crawling over the black and white squares. It flies away when Vinny lifts the board off the bird-table. He replaces the table in the corner of the garden then he peels off his shirt before settling back down on the deckchair.

The disturbance wakes Jane. She's lost for an instant until her mind collates the events of the day. She asks who won before she asks how long she'd been sleeping for. I'm touched by her unselfish nature as Vinny gives her the answers. Then he kisses her on the cheek and tells her how beautiful she looks. Not in the sarcastic way I used to do with girlfriends, but with an easy flair which makes me wonder how on earth I ever shirked from telling the truth. When she notices her empty bottle, she raises her sunglasses, then her eyebrows. Vinny looks at me only because we both look so guilty. I ask him to bring out three more. He returns with two. One for me and one for Jane. He's driving, and, although I know he'd really like one, he's still sensitive to my feelings.

Jane picks up her acoustic guitar and strums out two or three chords to check the tuning. There's a full-bodied sound as all the notes scatter up into the blue sky. She's got a classy voice. Someone once told her she sounded like Patsy Cline, but Jane didn't know who Patsy Cline was so she missed the compliment. She puts the plectrum between her teeth and starts doing some complicated finger-picking. I've nothing but admiration for her. She tried to teach me how to play after the accident, but I was all fingers and thumbs and left handed to boot. Even she had to admit defeat on that one.

I was staring up at the cloudless sky and listening to the sweet improvised music she was making. Inside, I was trying hard to push back all the bitterness, but it was hard when you placed it face to face with the boundless sensation of the moment. Knowing, moreover, that the music would end and the sky would soon cloud over. They would go and the night would replace them.

As if she herself had witnessed the conflict in my face, she started strumming and began singing 'Heartbreak Hotel' in her best mock-Presley voice. It was the panacea I needed. A minute later, me and Vinny were blowing out long hollow notes on the empty beer bottles. She did 'Hound Dog' after that, by which time we were clanking the bottles together and barking and howling until the sweat was dripping from our brows and our cheeks were sore from laughter. Then she replaced the guitar on the grass and I knew the awkward moment was about to come.

She looked over at Vinny who was dousing his face with a lettuce leaf. The tears of joy and the beads of sweat were rolling down his face. Despite their intrinsic difference, they intermingled and ran together as one, stemming from the same well of emotion. We all knew the hours had slipped from our grasp and that it was time to part. Jane said she thought I'd better go inside in case I got sunburnt. They started clearing up the mess and put the deckchairs back in the shed.

The metal frame of my chair was hot to touch. Too hot, indeed, to rest my bare arms on. I wheeled myself up to the door and waited for them to come up the path. Jane, carrying her guitar and looking like some bohemian goddess amongst the kaleidoscope of flowers, bent down and gave me a huge kiss on my dumb-struck lips. My mother came out and shook hands with Vinny the way she always did, formal and distant. It gave me the uneasy impression that she had been watching all the while for their departure. I felt like a child again. A spasm ran down my leg and my hand stuttered with the nervous twitch.

They said they'd try and make it again next weekend; they'd phone to confirm. My mother needlessly complicated things by mentioning a couple of appointments I had at the hospital. Then we all said goodbye and they set off up the road to their car. They always parked the car out of my view now. Because of the memories they said. Theirs and mine.

My mother helped me indoors, all the while prattling on about the excruciating noise and the neighbours. But I wasn't listening. I was looking intently at the ladybird crawling up my arm and recollecting what a precious day it had been.

Laying To Rest

by

Lorn Macintyre

Doctor Aonghas Macdonald came home on the last ferry, in a coffin. His feet were point-ing to the ramp, and for the hour long crossing his remains lay beside a refrigerated lorry. The seamen talked in Gaelic about the doctor, who was known throughout the is-lands. He had been a good piper, and on his instructions his ivory and silver pipes were in the coffin with him. When the ramp went down they carried him off on their shoulders to the hearse that had backed down the pier.

Morrison the undertaker had received his instructions by fax from the doctor's lawyers in Edinburgh because there were no known relatives. The doctor, who was 49, had never married. He had been a quiet studious man who had written an important paper on an infectious disease. He had also been a keen lepidopterist, going about the island with a butterfly net and a torch as a youth. He had discovered a new type of moth which had actually been given his name.

No flowers had come with the coffin, which was driven twenty miles along the coastal road to the small town. The driver had to stop often to let sheep cross. The coffin was carried into the parish church above the bay in which the doctor had been christened and in which his parents had been married. He was the son of the local schoolmaster and any island woman who had been a great Gaelic singer. His own Gaelic had been impec-cable. A black bordered card among assorted tools in the ironmonger's window on main street intimated that there would be a short service before interment.

Two women came off the ferry that evening. They were travelling separately, and the driver put each of their cases in the boot of the bus waiting on the pier. They paid their fares - return tickets - and sat in different parts of the bus.

'Where do you want dropped off, ladies'? the driver asked.

'The Hebridean Hotel,' both said.

It was the best hotel in the small town. Though it wasn't on his route he took the bus up the steep hill to the hotel above the bay. The two women had rooms with private bathrooms, with views of the bay. They sat at separate tables in the dining-room, each with a candle burning, eating seafood from the a la carte menu. One had prawns, and broke them up in her fingers; the other forked the meat from lobster claws. One had a glass of Spanish wine; the other sipped mineral water with ice and lemon.

They went into the lounge for coffee, sitting with their individual silver pots and little dishes of petit fours on doilies. They were both beautiful and dressed at the height of fashion, with rings on their fingers, lacquer on their nails. One had a Celtic cross at her throat. At the desk they both ordered a call for eight o'clock the next morning. Both slept soundly, their windows open on the bay.

The church wasn't full for the service because Doctor Macdonald had been away for so long that a generation didn't know him. The two women walked up the brae. One was dressed in a black costume, with a pillbox hat from which a veil hung. The other was wearing a dress patterned with flowers, and a wide brimmed straw hat. Their heels were high.

They entered the cool vestry of the church, each taking a hymn book from the beadle in her gloved hand, and sat in different pews near the front, where the doctor's coffin rested on trestles. The minister called for *abide with me*. One woman was a mezzo-soprano, the other a contralto, and their voices went out through the vestry and across the bay where a man cutting bracken heard them and sat down to listen. When the minister asked the mourners to join him in prayer the two women put their gloved hands together and closed their eyes.

'We remember Doctor Aonghas,' the minister said.. 'We remember his love of learning, his devotion to his profession, the purity of his Gaelic.'

The coffin was carried out of the church to the heavy tread of the organ. The two women joined the other mourners, walking behind the slow hearse up the hill, past the ruined smiddy where the dead man's people had plunged the hissing iron into the trough of water while hooves from all over the island waited to be shod.

A local man closed the gate of the cemetery behind him and turned to the two women. 'You can't come in here, ladies'.

The woman in the floral dress arched an eyebrow. The other one lifted her veil with spread fingers.

'Women don't go to funerals in these parts,' he explained.

But the one in black pushed open the gate, and the other woman followed her up the gravel path to the doctor's family lair which had been opened by one of his school friends. Macdonald had had no close friends in the community, but the undertaker had phoned around to find eight names to put on the cards for the allocation of cords. He had the cards in his hand, calling out the head cord first. A notable piper came forward to take it, but the woman in black was already by the undertaker's side. Her glove plucked the card from his hand. The undertaker looked uneasy, but called out the next six cords. The eighth was for the feet. He was about to read the name but the other woman stepped forward and took the card.

The minister went up to the two women and put an arm round each. He spoke to them, and they whispered to him, their lips close to his ears. He nodded, then opened his bible to read a prayer.

The woman in black took the strain of the head cord, the other woman the feet cord. The heels of their elegant shoes were buried in the earth. The three men on either side took the strain as Doctor Aonghas Macdonald was lowered into his grave. When the coffin was on the bottom both women threw in a handful of soil.

The deceased's lawyers had authorised the expenditure of £100 in one of the hotels for whisky and sandwiches for the mourners. Both women drank whisky neat. When locals tried to make conversation they turned away to the windows, to gaze out over the bay as if they were expecting a boat to come in.

'I've never seen a woman at a graveside in my life before,' an old timer complained to the minister. 'And I've certainly never seen one, far less two, getting a cord. Why did you give them the cords?'

'They have come a long way' was all the minister would say.

The two women went back on the afternoon bus with their boat tickets in their gloves. But this time they sat together, talking, pointing out seals on a rock, a yacht tacking up the sound. On the ferry they ate a meal together, and afterwards went into the bar where there was much laughter.

It was said on the island that one of the women was Dr Aonghas's common-law-wife, and that the other was her sister. Other stories went round in Gaelic. The doctor had collected more than moths.

Darg's Castle

by

C Gibbons

It was late at night and so quiet. So quiet that Danny started to feel weary, as time crept passed midnight. He was so determined to finish the final level of Darg's Castle, even though his mother had told him to be in bed by ten thirty. Danny had been playing his favourite computer game for hours that day. A particular game that he could not reach the end of. The screen of the monitor seemed to swallow Danny's small frame, as his face drew closer to the screen in a attempt to concentrate harder on the final level of the game. So late he thought, but Mother was out and the baby-sitter sat watching television downstairs, unaware Danny still played his computer. Slowly, Danny's eyelids began to feel heavy, the screen started to blur, colours and shapes merged into one dark haze, as the light faded swiftly. He seemed to be falling towards it. . . through the screen. Danny could only watch, his mouth agape in awe, as a large sudden blur of colours surged through and around him. Danny fell down, down to the bottom of what seemed to be, the one place which was in his computer game, He floated down in the dim light towards the floor, now almost sure in his mind that he had fallen into a dungeon. He landed with a hard thud to the bottom of his feet which numbed his legs, sending him sprawling onto a patch of old damp and dirty straw. Danny sat where he was and glanced around, knowing something was wrong. He wondered how he came to be in this place, a place which he had seen so many times before, the place being the final stage on his computer game. This stage had been the one he could never finish, always being defeated by the black dwarf. Fear began to take hold of him. He tried to think how he arrived at such a strange place, such a cold, lonely and scary place. It seemed just a few minutes earlier that he played happily on his computer, in the warmth and safety of his small bedroom. Danny slowly stood up, brushing straw from his pyjamas thinking what a strange dream he was having. Danny looked carefully at the objects in the room. After pinching himself on his arm a few times to try and wake himself up, it dawned on him a frightening reality, even as weird as it seemed, that he actually stood in the dungeon of his favourite computer game, Darg's Castle.

The cold damp musty air of the dungeon, pushed its way through Danny's pyjamas. A strong smell of mildew and mould began to drift up his nose which made him cringe and shiver. Apart from his body and feet becoming cold, a warm sensation spread suddenly on his face. Danny realised that he must be blushing, probably due to the odd surroundings he found himself in. That idea vanished when he felt the warmth really turning into hotness. He searched for an answer, as to how he could be stuck in a game which he had played on so many times before, but no answer came to mind, only, he must be dreaming in some way. Danny had an unusual feeling that someone, or even something was watching him. Unsure of what to do or which way to turn his head to look, Danny discovered what watched him. The need to be at home safe and warm away from this terrible place, suddenly increased as he stared at the thing watching him intently. There were two large wooden tables pushed up against the left side wall, standing end to end. Danny stared in disbelief at the huddled shape under the nearest table. From the scruffy form, a single dark red eye was casting its steely glare at Danny's face. The heat came from the one red eye. As Danny stood terrified, the silent form slowly, cautiously, edged its way out from under the table. Only a heavy shuffling sound of the stone floor came from the dark shape, as it stealthily crept its way towards Danny. The pounding of Danny's heart increased with each awkward shuffle of the black shape, as it emerged from under the table. The heat on his face from the thing's one large red eye, grew more intense with each shuffling step the figure made towards him. Danny tried to run and run, but his legs were paralysed. Danny saw no place to run or hide in the room, even if he could move. He tried to think of a way out from the computer game, but losing a life had been the only result in the game. At this point however, he only held one life which could not be lost.

'We meet once again,' squeaked the dwarf as it lowered its burning glare.

'Please let me go home now. My computer did it not me,' Danny replied in a frightened voice.

'There is but one path home for you,' remarked the midget sarcastically.

Danny could see a possible way home now as he asked, 'What do I have to do?'

'Kill the beast in the room, but quickly before he awakes,' sneered the dwarf.

A long needle was produced from the dwarf's cloak and held out to Danny. Danny felt he had been given a chance to escape , as he carefully lifted the needle from the dwarf's filthy palm. With feeling back in Danny's legs, he jumped forward and rolled under the farthest table.

Danny got to his feet slowly looking around the gloomy room for a beast of some description. In the middle of the room he could see a large comfy armchair, with its back facing him. A soft carpet of straw totally covered the stone floor. At the far end of the room, reached a stone stairway into the ceiling. There was nothing else in the room at all, only the armchair. Danny looked at the needle in his hand, looked to take the easier way, up the steps fast. He ran to the steps only pausing on the first step, as a gentle wheezing from the armchair behind froze his actions. He turned to see a small wolflike creature pounce at him form the seat of the armchair. Danny closed his eyes screaming and lunged at the mad dog with the needle. The wolf howled and screeched out as it slammed into Danny's chest, bowling him over onto the straw at the foot of the steps. Danny jumped up and slipped on the bottom step in his slippers and clambered swiftly up the stairway.

Danny awoke early the following morning, rubbing a painfully sore chest. Birds were whistling happily outside his bedroom window, which ruined his idea of drifting back to sleep. He could vaguely remember a strange kind of dream, but he did not know why he had such a sore chest. His stomach told him it was breakfast time, as he swung his legs out of bed and looked around for slippers. He reached under the bed where the slippers were usually found and screamed out loudly as his hand brushed over some loose straw. Danny shot his face towards the computer, which had suddenly flashed words onto the screen despite power being off. Danny started to cry as he read the words of the monitor, 'Congratulations for completing Darg's Castle, standby for the special bonus dungeon level.'

The Spare Room

by

Athalie Bushnell

Anne Lucy folded up the letter and put it back in its envelope, a perplexed frown on her face. She had lost touch with her great-aunt Emily who, according to the solicitor's letter, had left her a legacy. For that was what it was, she imagined, even though the letter only referred to the contents of the spare bedroom - 'to my great-niece, Anne Lucy.'

Aunt Emily always had a soft spot for me, thought Anne - and I for her, come to think of it. She remembered the visits she had paid to 'The Beeches', Coppice Drive, Inverness, frequent during her early childhood but fewer and fewer as the days and years had gone by. With a pang of conscience she wondered if the old lady had been lonely and longing for a visit from her favourite great-niece. Ah, well! Anne should have made more effort to spend some of her hard-earned leisure with her grandfather's youngest sister, but it was too late now. At least she could treasure what she had been left of the contents of the old family house.

She took the solicitor's letter out again and made a note of the telephone number. She would phone on Monday morning and arrange to go up to Inverness and see what 'the contents of the spare bedroom' were. Over the phone on Monday, Mr Miller, the solicitor, sounded very pleasant and arranged to meet her himself at Inverness station and drive her to the house in ' Coppice Drive' before taking her back to his office to complete the formalities.

The following day as the train drew into Inverness station she wondered how she would recognise Mr Miller. However, she need not have worried, as there was only one man on the platform who could possibly be a solicitor. It was the middle of the morning and the only others on the platform were two elderly women and a couple of youths in jeans and T-shirts.

When, seated in his Ford Escort, she confessed to what had been worrying her, he laughed and said 'Snap!' Apparently the same thought had crossed his mind again but, Miss Lucy, as he insisted on calling her, had been the only passenger alighting from the train of a suitable age, so that he had recognised her at sight.

As they turned into Coppice Drive and stopped outside The Beeches it all looked very familiar; she half-imagined her great-aunt would come bustling out to greet her. She was brought back to reality, however, when Mr Miller took a bunch of keys from his pocket, opened the front door and stood aside for her to enter.

At once it was evident that the house was uninhabited: what is it? she wondered, that gives empty houses such a feeling of gloom - even when the sunshine is flooding in. No, she thought, gloom was the wrong word: 'lifelessness' would be better, for houses were inanimate objects and it was only people that turned them into homes.

Automatically she ascended the stairs following the solicitor, who threw open the door of the spare room where Anne herself had always slept on the few but delightful over-night visits to her great-aunt. The room looked just as she remembered it; the big double-bed with the brass knobs - the solicitor was saying something about them being very fashionable nowadays and telling her of a good firm of auctioneers if she should want to sell it locally.

'It is quite in order, if you wish to take any of the smaller items with you' - she only half-heard the words Mr Miller was speaking.

'Why, oh why,' she said to herself, 'must solicitors use such inhuman language: items, indeed - souvenirs, using the REAL meaning of the word, would be more appropriate.' And she crossed over to the dressing-table and picked up her great-aunt's green glass scent-bottle which had always fascinated her as a child.

'I'd like to take this with me' she said - 'and the silver pin-tray. I'll have to think about the rest. Oh, the little clock as well, they will all go into my bag,' and she picked up the carved wooden miniature grandfather clock off the mantelpiece. No one had seemed to know whether it had been made as an apprentice-piece, a child's toy or a sample of a woodworker's craftsmanship but the family had always treasured it and it would be her cherished possession.

She wandered round the room, picking up various articles, fingering the curtains - the same ones which she had used to hide behind when she was a child. Perched on the window seat, hidden behind the curtains, she had created a world of her own - until the grown-ups had discovered her.

'There is also a small suitcase under the bed,' - and Mr Miller was already pulling it out - 'I wondered if you would like to take this with you and sort out the contents at your lei-sure - it's not at all heavy.'

'A good idea,' said Anne. She didn't remember the case, but quite probably it con-tained some mementoes of those childhood visits which her great-aunt wanted her to keep, and she had no wish to unpack it in front of a stranger.

'Yes, I'm finished,' she said in answer to the solicitor's unspoken query, and together - with the suitcase - they went downstairs, locked up and were soon sitting in the solici-tor's office, drinking coffee.

'Your cousin who now owns the house is in no hurry to sell,' he told her, 'he wants to give you - and the other legatees - time to decide whether you wish to remove your prop-erty or have it sold locally. Let me know what you wish to do as soon as you make up your mind, though, as unoccupied property is always a temptation to burglars, squatters or vandals.'

Thanking him, she assured him that he would certainly know her wishes within the next few days. She was not one for lengthy deliberations.

Back in Edinburgh, she lifted the small suitcase off the rack and made for the Dunbar train which would take her home. Two hours later, having cooked and eaten a meal, she opened the suitcase with the key Mr Miller had handed over.

Wrapped carefully in tissue paper was 'Teddy.' She had almost forgotten Teddy. Each time she had visited The Beeches he had been fetched out for her to play with. Originally he had belonged to great-aunt Emily when she was a child: indeed it was only a year younger that its owner had been. Anne reckoned that would make Teddy nearer 80 than 70: she wondered if he was one of the ones fetching thousands of pounds in the salesroom now, but she expected not. No one in her family had that sort of luck. Anyway she would rather keep him out of sentiment and because great-aunt Emily had wanted her to have him.

There was the traycloth she had embroidered at the age of ten as a Christmas gift to her great-aunt, a copy of 'Alice in Wonderland' with the original Tenniel illustrations; she could remember being read to at bedtime from that copy of 'Alice'; a photograph album covering several of her visits to 'The Beeches,' a Mickey Mouse overall kept there for her use - and something red at the bottom of the case.

Mystified, Anne held up a red track-suit - about big enough for a twelve-year-old. She was quite sure she had never seen it before - and equally sure that her great-aunt belonged to a generation which would never have worn a track-suit.

All that was left in the case was a folded piece of paper:

'Dearest Anne,' she read 'I knew you would claim the little grandfather clock, and a few ornaments, and I had no need to pack them up for you, but I thought you might have forgotten Teddy, I'm sure he would want to be with you. I am also enclosing the little red track-suit (never worn) which I bought for your twelfth birthday which was to have been spent here. But you decided you would rather go to stay with a friend of your own age. Well, dear, an elderly aunt understood - but gives it to you now as a token of her love.

All the best,

Great -Aunt Emily.'

The tears were streaming down Anne's face as she folded it up again and put it back in the case, ashamed of the selfishness of her twelve-year-old self.

Endless Thoughts

by

Dawn Barclay

I sat alone inside my car. It was lovely and peaceful here, just what I needed until . . .

The White Morris Minor drew up in front of me. Inside it were an old couple who affectionately acknowledged one another. The engine stopped and the pair of them sat there looking out onto the rippling waters and beautiful green scenery.

I loved it here, always had. Whenever something was not going well I would come down here to think it over and reminisce. This was a place of strength and security. Many a time I had come to the conclusion of a dilemma here and hopefully today I might find one.

As I gazed out the water on the lake streamed softly down then carefully splashed against the huge embankments. The large solid trees at the other side waved their branches calmly in the slight breeze showing off their new foliage.

I started thinking again when another car pulled up beside me. It was a bulky family car which sounded like a chimps tea party was being held in it. The mother smiled at me apologetically as though she was sorry for interrupting my thoughts, which her children had. The children, a boy aged about nine and two girls aged seven and five, kept shouting for food and drink from their personal parental slaves. The father, unsurprisingly, was becoming very annoyed.

He got out, slammed the door shut and marched to the boot of the car. There he produced a picnic basket to shouts of delight from the children. The mother looked once more at me and shrugged her shoulders. They were the type of children I would hate to have myself but if I did have children they would not be anything like that anyway.

Children - one day, maybe never. I had always insisted on never having any but as time wore on my maternal instincts began to play on my natural emotions. They bring such joy, happiness, upset and pain. I could remember the feelings of pain I had felt as a child and never wanting any of my own going through it.

The old couple in the Morris scrutinised the young couple and the behaviour of the children. In their days a clip round the ear was in order and usually did the trick. They seemed irritated that their tranquil visit was being disturbed by three young nippers, who, despite their feed, persisted to behave like spoilt little brats - which they were!

Suddenly, a red car came zooming into the park and screeched to a halt at the last minute. The guy in the car immediately picked up his carphone and frantically started dialling. The call was short and to the point with the emphasis on loud talking and the use of abusive words. I watched him with a little amusement in my inside mirror. I had not realised how many facial expressions a person could have or how quickly they could change. After the first phone call he appeared more relaxed, skimmed over some papers and called more people on his phone.

I held considerable suspicion with carphones. I believed that although many people had them for their businesses some of them did not have them wired up. They just had them to pose with, make themselves look good and executive-like. The young guy behind me was certainly putting his to good use, either that or he was making his debut for an Academy Award! It was one of them.

Things had started to settle down again and once more I reached into my thoughts. The breeze was becoming stronger and the waves were being pushed towards the banks with some force causing the water to crash on the earthy slopes. My dilemma was becoming more like this, the more interruptions I had the harder it was for me to concentrate.

My thoughts were beginning to come together when yet another car arrived. It was an older type car, body had been abused a bit. The kind where the driver has music blaring out of it so no-one would notice the noise the actual car made or hear the bits falling off. It reminded me of my first set of wheels!

The boy driving it looked like he had recently passed his test. He was trying to appear really confident but was rather flustered as he reversed into a space a couple along from me. If he had turned his radio down he might've been able to concentrate on his driving. His girlfriend sat there happily enjoying the outing. When the car was parked a few jokes were obviously made and they both laughed. Their laughter soon turned to more serious talk. The girl shook her head most of the time during the conversation. He was suggesting something improper or she had a serious problem with her head!

When was the last time an improper suggestion was made to me? Probably last night and that is why I was here. Well, it was not improper more of a shock. It was something I had not thought about but something somebody else had. Plain to them but a thought that had never entered my head.

I watched carefully each person in the car park. There was the old couple who were very contented, sharing their lives and experiences with one another. They had probably been through a lot together and were there for the other.

The young couple were going to go through some very bad times regarding their children. The parents seemed happy together but the children were tearing them apart.

The businessman was single and free, a bit like myself at the moment. He was decisive, assured not at all like me especially right now. He had everything to go for and lived life to the full. He had no responsibilities or ties such as a wife and family.

Then there were the teenagers in the car dying to become grown up but scared at the same time. Nothing could happen fast enough for them as they wanted it all now. They would give everything to be the person of their dreams.

Here I was stuck in the middle. I wanted what everyone here had. I wanted someone that would care for me and make me laugh. Someone who would be a faithful husband and a good father to our children. I wanted my own status, my own identity, my freedom. most of all I wanted someone to be there at the end. Someone I could talk to and they would understand, realise what I was saying.

I wanted it all and now I had to try and think of a solution. I did not know how long it was going to take but I was determined to get there even if it took me forever - but I hoped it would not!

Never Count Sheep If You Want To Sleep

by

Howard Murphy

Feeling rather tired and weary I headed off for bed but, spent so much time, tossing and turning, shaking the pillows, and in the counting of endless numbers of sheep. The elusive slippery arms of sleep kept letting me go.

Perhaps the counting of sheep was not such a good idea; for the memories of those skipping, jumping, impish bundles of wool, brought back too many memories. Of course these could not be the usual ones of the idyllic pastoral scene. Oh No! My remembrances of these creatures are so far from that peaceful scene.

Days spent in the Welsh Hills tupping and topping the male sheep, or gathering the flock in for dipping and then later the rounding up, from every nook and cranny on the high mountains tops, those willful, stupid, creatures to be driven down along the narrow, dangerous, steep sided paths to the floor of the main valley. They were then penned in stonewalled enclosures, for the shearing an act that took place under the strong summer sun, scorching unprotected flesh. The heat increasing the smell of dog and sheep droppings, together with the odorous stinking sweating smells of working men. My mind now is full of the noise of bleating sheep, barking dogs and the various shouts and whistles of the men, and the splashing of water, as the shorn sheep passed through the cleansing, medicated water troughs.

Men had been gathered together from all over the district, high mountain isolated farms, hill farms of the lofty valleys, and the larger roadside farms with the lush green meadows. One thing that they had in common, was the desire to see all the sheep quickly shorn of their valuable coats-money, hard earned, to be placed in the bank. Cash to pay off debts! Cash to invest in more woolly backs, cash for the future!

Eyes, would often be raised on watch for bad weather signs. The shearing needed to be finished before the rains of summer fell. Each man had drawn lots hoping in his heart to be first, free from the worry or to have the most suitable weather conditions according to his drawn place.

Lots you may say! Lots? Surely that's gambling now man!?

Let the visiting Pastor, more used to the ways of towns and city's, raise that subject from the pulpit! I can tell you now, without fear of contradiction that those God fearing men, would turn him, at once into that biblical statue of salt. But this time it may be proper to

62

say, a block of ice as he was dammed by those hard, piercing, cold steel eyes his perdition to be marked in the very books of the Chapel forever.

Yes, Chapel (Free-Church) men they were, and proud of it too! For they in the daily happenings of their life experienced every aspect of God's teachings. Their voices in songs to sing, in heavenly joy, of praise and thanksgiving would rise to their lips to harmonise with the work, or task they were doing - the majority of the singers, members of the local 'Male Voice Choir.'

Men they were too. Small in stature, but strong in limb of body. One leg always appeared to be shorter than the other. Perhaps it was the way they stood. Although to a young fellow, with an over active imagination, the shortness of the leg came about from walking the steep sides of the craggy mountain valleys.

You might say, that sheep and shepherds go together. Visiting 'English Gentry,' were sorely puzzled when no answer came to their grating plumstone tones, 'I say shepherd , do tell my good lady wife, how far you have walked to-day. I sa . . . y sheppp . . . herd!' For these men of the hill farms, who had to turn their hand to any type and method of farming the term, 'Shepherd' would be considered to be far too limiting and too high -and-mighty a tag to be attached to them.

At least those hours bereft of sleep have gone steadily by whilst thinking of sheep. It's just as well there is no tally man to record those passing, empty hours! For if there was, I think his eyes would have been long closed tight, no marks on his tally-stick to make!

I wonder if he might dream of sheep?

Three o' clock, the church clock tolls. It's a sad sound drifting over the stillness of the night air. This time of the night when the body feels so cold, so tired, always is a depressing time. When sadness, and the feelings of loneliness seem to strike deeper, and harder, too. In the Welsh the word *hiraeth* defines it so well; *longing, nostalgia, grief, homesickness.*

Awakened from those dream incurred nostalgic memories of the Welsh Hill-farms, over the hill from Kilrenny Mill the noise of the cock crowing is loud and clear. I'm pleased not to be living any closer to that discordant sound - a sound that must split the morning air, each and every day. Although, as Shakespeare wrote in Hamlet:: ' The morning cock crew loud, and at the sound, it (the ghost) shrunk in haste away, and vanished from our sight.' So , perhaps now, I can be certain that any ghostly apparitions will not appear the light can be switch off.

It's four-forty three, on this Sunday morning. Standing at the window breathing in the fresh clean air, looking out I see the moon dipping down below the horizon. On the harbour wall, the tall, slim silhouette of the heron can be seen. There it stands against the rays of the rising sun. When the whisper and sigh from the waves of the incoming tide laps against the rocks below, here in the bedroom the sense of silence is felt even deeper.

In the shadow of a split and weathered rock the sentry-like figure of a white gull stands. It's shrill, keening call cuts the air like a razor edged sword echoing over the gentle peaceful sound of the incoming tide. The piercing cry falls to rebound, from the movement of waves and dawning sky. It brings to mind a thought melancholy, but apt. A thought of the entreaty of a tired lonely being, seeking peaceful sleep!

Time, however, moves on. So too, does the natural forces of nature, taking the waters from the harbour, as the tide flows back from the Firth of Forth to the sea. The piquant smell of seaweed rises to fill the room, comforting. Yes! Strangely comforting is the acrid smell, thought provoking too. My gloomy, tired mood changes, as thoughts of moonlit nights and windswept days fill my mind. Pictures clear, of blue alluring eyes smiling.

Sleep gently starts to make its presence felt, eyes close to open; heavy-lidded eyes, with joyful pictures filled, filled with dreams of the dancing figure running free in the wind with her arms outstretched to fly like a bird; voice singing happy, joyful songs.

Sleep, in tendrils of comforting winding, binding threads, draw me down; draw me down to sleep.

To sleep.

The restless night is done.

Take heed of this, never count sheep, if you want to sleep!

Friendship

by

Lyn Pearson

The dreary autumn afternoon matched my feelings, dull, grey and sombre, as if it too were in mourning. My heart heaved like a lead weight as I looked down at the mound of earth before me and tried to make sense of what had happened. Was this all that remained?

I read the writing on the stone plaque:

Alexander Matthews
1932 - 1992
Dearly Missed

Dearly missed. That wasn't enough. That didn't account for all those years we spent together, the happiness we shared, the love we had.

'Come on ol' girl,' I jumped as a soft hand patted my back. 'We've got t'go now.'

I looked up at Old Corry. I'd forgotten he was here, but then how could I, he was the one who brought me here, who stayed by my side all through the service. Yes, he understood. He knew what Alec meant to me.

'You come on home wi'me girl.' I stood up slowly, my old bones feeling heavier than usual and silently said my last farewell to my love, my friend, my life!

Corry and I walked through the streets that held our memories, both deep in our own thoughts. Everything reminded me of my Alec; the streets where we walked on our daily strolls, the Barn Inn, our local pub, where we would sit for hours with his friends. He would play dominoes or cards or just talk about the good old days while I would watch and listen, full of admiration, so proud to be by his side.

Behind the village were the beautiful heathery hills where we discovered our love. We both younger then, of course. We'd chase each other through the heather, then he'd call my name and I'd jump into his outstretched arms as we fell to the ground, me smothering his face with wet kisses. Yes, those were the days, our days. How I wish we were there now, that time had stood still for us and we could have run in those hills forever.

Fellow villagers were amazed at how attached we became to each other, at how much feeling there was between us and the devotion I had for him.

65

We met fifteen years ago, both lonely, both in need of love. His wife had just left him and I just happened to turn up, right when he needed someone. We hit it off straight away. I would sit for hours listening to him talk about his life, his problems, what went wrong. I never judged him, that wasn't for me to do, I just listened, understood and forgave. Then, when the tears came, I'd comfort him, cuddling into him and softly kiss his tears away.

To repay me, he gave me a home, food and the warmth of his heart, more than enough to keep me satisfied. He never rowed me, he didn't need to, we had a deep understanding. There was no need for words. I understood his every action and gesture, sensed his every feeling. I'd run to obey his silent orders to the astonishment of his friends.

Some, those who couldn't understand, said he must be cruel to make me so obedient. They didn't know I did what I did not out of fear but out of loyalty, a loyalty I expect they were jealous of.

'Here we are then.' Again, Corry's words brought me back to reality. He opened the door for me and I stepped into the aroma of fresh baking and stew cooking.

'We're home, May,' Corry called. May, Corry's wife, came out of the kitchen, her motherly figure coming towards me with wide arms.

'Hello there, Fran,' she said as she gave me a hug. 'Come in and get a heat at the fireplace, love.' She led me to the sitting room. As I went in, I heard her whisper, 'Poor old dear.'

'Aye,' Corry replied. 'She's going t' really miss him.'

I sat by the fire while Corry brought me some stew. 'Get this inside ye girl, it'll do ye good.'

He left the bowl beside me and went away. Although I loved May's cooking, I left the stew and went over to the window. Life in the village was carrying on as normal. Had only my life stopped, mine and Alec's? I walked back to the fire. Life was normal for us too for a while. I'd sit by the window waiting for Alec to come home from work. He worked nearly all day although I wasn't alone all of the time, he made sure of that. Gracie, from next door popped in a few times to see how I was. I enjoyed her company but was always glad when she finally left as it meant Alec would be home soon. I'd go to the window and wait, watching, listening until I saw the familiar walk coming down the street. I'd run to the door and when it opened I'd throw myself into his arms, drowning him in my loving kisses.

One day he came home early. Gracie was still with me. He didn't greet me the same; said he was ill, then Gracie helped him into bed. When she left I went to see him, unsure of what was wrong. My lovingness didn't seem to ease this pain. I knew in my heart something terrible was happening .

He slept for a while with me by his side. When he awoke he turned and stroked my face, 'My dear Fran,' he said softly, 'I think this is the end, girl.'

In the next few days, many strange people came and went as well as a few familiar ones. Everyone seemed worried and upset, all hugging my Alec and saying goodbye. Alec stayed in bed and I stayed constantly by his side, bewildered and confused. Unable to help as I watched my love slip away. The strangers didn't seem to like that, they said he needed rest and peace not some old . . . 'Watch out girl,' I leaped back to my senses as Corry brought wood to the fire.

'Thinkin' about Alec, are ye. Aye we're o' gaun 'ti miss him, lass.'

Corry had known Alec all his life. They had grown up together, served in the army together and dated girls together. Next to me, Corry knew Alec's feelings the best. That's how he understood our relationship, while others made a mockery.

Corry was rambling on about his memories with Alec but I was only half listening. I was in the heathery hills again, young again, running and playing. Oh what I'd give to go back. Suddenly, I felt my old self once more and it was last week. Alec was sleeping again, he was never awake for very long. I was, as usual, by his side, begging for a miracle to return the Alec I knew to me, the one so full of energy and happiness. Slowly he stirred and reached his hand out towards me. He held me gently, stroking my hair and face.

'I have to go now Fran, old girl,' he spoke so quietly I could barely hear him. 'Can't take you with me this time . . . sorry . . . be good, my lass.' With that, his hand slipped off my head as he let out his final gasp of life.

I lay my head on his chest pleading for him to wake up, to come back to me. It shouldn't have ended like this. I should have gone first, not him. I felt drained of all life and energy. The pain in my heart hurt so much I thought I was dying. Perhaps I was just wishing to die, so we could begin our love once more. I fell asleep listening to the emptiness of his heart, straining my ears for a beat amongst the silence.

I was abruptly wakened by Gracie coming in for her morning visit. She burst into the room humming a cheerful tune.

'Good morning, Fran. How's our patient today then?' she smiled brightly as she opened the curtains. 'Come on Alec, time for breakfast.' When Alec didn't respond, she tapped his shoulder, 'Alec . . . Oh no, Alec.' The shock and realisation of what had happened came over her face, pushing away the cheerfulness. 'Fran, why didn't you come and get me, eh? We could have saved him,' she cried as she ran out of the room. Alec didn't want that though. I knew. He wanted to pass away here, with me, without any fuss.

'Fran, are you listening to me. Alec always said you were a good listener.' Corry's familiar voice came floating back to me. There was a knock at the door. May answered, 'Oh, hello Miss Hutton. Come in, come in, just go through, Corry's there with Fran.'

Miss Hutton was one of those who never understood Alec and I, always looking down on our relationship. I knew she never really liked me. I knew she wanted Alec for herself but I stood in the way!

Corry stood up to meet her. 'Hello there Miss Hutton.'

'Hello, Corry, wasn't it a nice service today for Alec.'

'Aye, it was that, a nice send off, wasn't it Fran.' I looked his way to show my agreement.

'Is Fran staying here then?' Miss Hutton asked half-heartedly.

'Aye, I promised Alec, I'd look after her,' he replied in a whisper.

'I don't know why everyone's making such a fuss,' Miss Hutton snapped. 'If Alec had found himself a good wife to look after him instead of her, he'd still be here today,' she sobbed pretentiously. I took no notice and looked away.

'Quiet now, she'll hear you,' Corry whispered.

'The way you all act,' Miss Hutton continued, 'as if she's human. She's only a dog, for God's sake, she doesn't understand,' she shouted.

Corry led her into the kitchen out of my earshot.

Perhaps I was only a dog, but I understood more than she'll ever realise, especially about Alec.

'Fran, my lass,' he used to say. 'You're better than any wife, ye know that, better than any wife.'

'Yes Alec, I knew.'

The Millionaire

by

Elizabeth Wilson

It was gossip that the Englishman was rolling in money and was mad. Mad, because what possessed a man to leave a fancy life in London for a place like Burnside? 'yon bit fairm at the back o' beyont,' . . . 'He surely needed his heid looked at,' . . . 'He kent nocht aboot it ava,' . . . 'He'd spent a fortun' on sic' a muckle shed,' . . . The talk had drifted back and the newcomer, John Grey, did his best to explain that he rarely set foot in the capital city and was not a rich man. His truth was not so easily spread or believed: sometimes he felt that every penny he spent was noted and added up by others as well as himself.

One evening late in October John put his tractor under cover and went to look at his cows. Their shed was large and sturdily built and had cost him a lot of money. Its new-ness was stark against the dour greens and browns of the Scottish hills.

'It fairly stauns oot,' he was told, 'like a sair thoom.'

'It will weather' he had answered. The roomy cattle courts were on either side of a broad passage stacked with straw and hay and mineral feed for winter was closing in, his first winter on the high farm.

The cows ranged tightly at wide, concreted troughs, feeding with a concentration which always amazed and pleased him. 'It is like being in a church!' his wife Charlotte said when she witnessed this intensity and heard the soft sounds of eating rising to the vaulted roof. Stout barriers separated the higher centre passage where he could walk to check every animal. They were similar in age and breeding: he had learned to recognise the markings on each long face reaching for piled-up hay. Troughs below the hay racks were emptied of turnips, always downed quickly and with relish. They pray for everlast-ing turnips, he reckoned, in this church.

Taking a last look, he spoke aloud, 'That's it girls,' he told his cows, no longer feeling it ridiculous to talk to them and it amused him to search their mild eyes for any gleam of response. 'Everyone's gotta eat and it's my turn now,' he informed the watchful faces nearest the door, and left the steading.

Better for man and beast, inside there, he thought, huddling into his coat against wind blown straight from Lochnagar; it would be the heart of the farm. He loved the mixture it offered - from hay, something of summer, the cows breathing it out; their warmth, the dryness of straw, fresh dung, not offensive at all, a faint antiseptic from the mineral

69

powder. He could hardly believe it was his reality rather than the dream he had for so many years, but there were things he had not foreseen.

He forced a purposeful stride towards the farmhouse where light beamed from every room and powerfully from halogen lamps outside intended for use in emergency only. It was, he knew, a generous welcome for him at the end of a day's sheer slog but he resolved to stop the extravagance of this.

It began one evening when they came back late from a shopping trip to Aberdeen, thirty miles away. He had driven with great care on the rough farm road back to the silent dark house and courts beyond, where cattle waited to be fed.

' A house on a hill should blaze with light,' Charlotte decided then, 'like a beacon, a beacon of hope in a naughty world,' she ended, only half-seriously. He had not demurred but even then had visualised the surge of glee at Hydro-Electric.

The need for economy weighed heavily on him and the tale of his riches seemed less of a joke: they must cut down, rein in somehow for his money was draining away - it went out and as yet nothing came in. They had to survive until it did. No room for the fantasy of light but he would tell her gently and not tonight.

It was his birthday. Neither of them mentioned it when he left at first light for the far boundary of the place, to make the fence there tight against his neighbour's beasts, clever at poaching his grass when they could. Sandwiches and fruit eaten as he worked were as nothing as he thought of supper. Charlotte was sure to mark the day somehow, cook something special. He hoped to God she had not spent money on a present.

Their back door opened into a narrow lobby and then into a hall used differently now to contain smart new washing and drying machines, deep porcelain sinks and an ironer on a stand: an old-fashioned larder next to the hall had become a roomy shower. Charlotte had planned it, suggesting that the best way to combat farm mud and worse stuff threatening to a civilised way of life was to curb it at the very door. She was right, of course, but civilisation carried a price which he sometimes found too much: tonight, slumping into a chair just as he was would have been luxury.

He hung his waxed coat against a wall covered as were all walls in the house by a very nasty green-coloured gloss paint, somebody's bargain buy of long ago. An unfortunate one and also unfortunate that Charlotte had scoured everywhere so fiercely, the film of grime had been easier on the eye. One day, he vowed, they would start on decorating the house, when funds were in. Whenever!

He stripped and stood under the shower letting hot water course down his spine to reach the core of his tiredness. He noticed that his hands were becoming calloused and a bit engrained but did not scrub at them. Being 'water-sweet' is enough, he decided - I will avoid a shine. He dressed in the clean clothes put ready for him and added an old warm sweater. He would have preferred whisky to the wine he guessed Charlotte would offer. He felt one hundred rather than the forty-four years of his life.

The AGA, another costly addition, made the kitchen warm and pleasant, the food from its oven sending delicious signals to his yearning insides. He saw the best china, glass and silver on the fine old table from their other life and registered that Charlotte looked very nice but was smiling rather oddly. Then his mouth fell open, his eyes incredulous of what had been done to the walls.

Hardly any bilious green was visible between animals deftly outlined, balloons coming from their mouths wishing him 'Happy Birthday!'. Cows with smiles and flirtatious long-lashed eyes cavorted from skirting to ceiling, each one named, his favourite, Lucy, prominent and accurately coloured. St George, the black bull, stood four-square and belligerent offering 'Congratulations but tak' care.' A flock of curly ewes slanted marble eyes to Boris the ram, and from their tight little mouths lines led to a joint message of goodwill. From a puddle she had been unable to contain his young sheepdog splashed 'Love, Love, Oops . . . Sorry!' Geese stretched long white necks and orange bills gabbled best wishes. Hens clucked and little chicks cheeped. Cats in the process of catching mice turned aside to wish him well; their unfortunate prey expiring uttered 'Happy Birthd . . . ' 'Happy B . . . ' or tragically merely, 'Hhhhh . . . !' An old cat asleep in a basket snored kind thoughts oblivious of skylarks soaring in bonhomie overhead. Space in between sketches was filled by turnips, turnips with smiling faces and fluttering leaves atop them - 'Dinna' forget us neeps!' they chorused.

John Grey began to laugh as he had not laughed for a long time, tears running down his face into his recently grown beard: the weariness of the day lifted.

'You are one crazy woman!' he told Charlotte, taking the crystal glass of good malt whisky from her hand, and held a plate for a slice of succulent paté. He started to laugh again. 'How could you?' he managed to ask, 'how could you cover up that beeyootiful paint?'

Before he went to sleep that night John remembered the day in the spring of the year when he and Charlotte first saw the farm, its small fields and crumbling drystone walls. They had made their way to a high point, crossing a burn with primroses clustering on its banks and yellow, scented musk spilling into the water. Moorhens were dabbling in a shallow pool made where the stream was choked by weed.

At the top they looked down at the farm, the little grey house, the few tumble-down buildings, all caught as in a bowl of sunlight among hills which seemed to roll into infinity. The air was cold and the clearest he had ever breathed.

Walking down they had disturbed a flock of tiny birds and heard the soft beat of many wings as they skimmed overhead and up and up into a cloudless sky. Charlotte had remembered. He felt sure that all would be well.

Congratulations Mrs Robinson

by

Agnes L W Berry

'Would someone, please, answer the phone! I can't leave the kitchen.'

'Got it mother!' came Jane's quick response, as she bounded down the stairs. 'Mother, it's for you!'

'Take a message can't you! I am up to my elbows in yeast.'

'But the caller insists he speaks only to you!' persisted Jane.

'Then he shall have to ring back, won't he?' I retorted impatiently.

'If you say so mother!' as she swept into the kitchen to witness the drama.

'Ah! I see what you mean, you are busy, but mother, that phone call did sound urgent.'

'Did he leave a message?'

'No!'

'Then he shall have to ring back, won't he?'

'Alright, I must be off to work now. I will try and get home early.'

The baking had been getting on top of me all morning and with dinner guests arriving in the evening, time was precious. It was almost lunchtime before I had everything under control in the kitchen, then I flopped into a chair with a cup of coffee. No sooner had I done so, when the doorbell rang, and rang, persistently.

'Goodness me! is there no rest for the wicked? Alright! Alright! I'm coming!'

A middle aged man stood in the doorway, a big grin lighting up his face. 'Good day! Mrs Robinson?' he ventured, raising his hat in greeting.

'Yes.'

'I phoned earlier, but you were otherwise engaged.'

'So your the mystery caller!' I interrupted. 'Sorry about that, but I was preparing for a dinner party tonight and just could not come to the phone. What was so urgent, that you could not leave a message with my daughter?' I asked.

'I am the bearer of good news and you had to be the first to know that you have in fact, won top prize in a recent competition you entered.' He said with pleasure.

'Who me!' I gasped, 'but I never win anything! I enjoy the fun and the challenge they give me, then I forget all about them. Won't you come in?' I asked, after the initial shock.

'Thank you! my name is Gerald Nicholson.'

'Now tell me I'm not dreaming.' I said at last.

The man chuckled. 'I can assure you that yours is the normal reaction we find with winners. But to get down to the nitty gritty Mrs Robinson, brace yourself, for you have just won a four berth houseboat.'

'A houseboat!' I blurted out. The words sounding more like an accusation than an exclamation. 'What on earth would I do with a houseboat and where is it? I'm sorry, could I offer you something to drink? coffee perhaps?'

'Your very kind, but no thank you. I have other calls to make today and can only stay a few minutes. The houseboat is moored along the broads and one year's rent, which is included in the prize, has been paid in advance as from today. These are the papers signifying sole ownership of the vessel, but we would require you to come to the broads tomorrow afternoon at 2pm to be officially handed occupancy, keys etc, and perhaps give a short statement to the press. Will you do that Mrs Robinson?'

'Yes, I expect so.' I stammered, finally regaining my composure. 'Then it is true? it is not a hoax? I really have won a major prize, I can't believe it.' Emotion took over and I began to cry.

'You can certainly believe it, so don't upset yourself. It's a wonderful houseboat and we shall see you tomorrow at 2pm, when we will be happy to hand it over to you. Oh! and Congratulations! Mrs Robinson.'

With these last few words still ringing in my ears, he doffed his hat and said goodbye.

I decided to wait till all the family were gathered just before the dinner guests arrived, to break the news . . .

'A houseboat!' chorused the family in unison.

'Yes! these were my sentiments too, when I was told.'

Then suddenly, the whole household seemed to erupt with peels of laughter, as each in turn, hugged and swept me off my feet . . . saying what a clever mum they had.

Needless to say, the dinner party was a huge success. My win became the topic of conversation for most of the evening, consequently, for the first time I was able to appreciate my good fortune.

The great day arrived and my husband John and son Grant escorted me to the broads. When we arrived at the quayside, a few people were gathered there including Gerald Nicholson, a Photographer and Reporter. Mr Nicholson introduced me to the sponsor Mr Stewart and his secretary.

'Now can we have a photograph of you and your husband together Mrs Robinson? thank you!'

John squeezed my hand for moral support. 'Hang in there, it won't be long now!' he said reassuringly.

I don't know how I got through the speech and I can't remember a word I said.

'You did well mum,' encouraged Grant.

When all the formalities were over, I was ushered to the waiting houseboat. I shed a few more tears when I saw it, but they were tears of happiness.

'It's all yours now Mrs Robinson,' said Mr Stewart, as he and Mr Nicholson shook hands with me in turn and handed me the keys. And soon they were gone, leaving the three of us staring at the prize in wonderment.

John squeezed my hand. 'It's really lovely and you deserve it dear.'

'It is something that the whole family can share and can you just visualise the holidays we will have John.'

He smiled in agreement.

'C'mon then,' Grant said at last. 'Let us get aboard to get the feel of it and dream of the lovely summers ahead.'

As we clambered aboard, I felt on top of the world . . .

Heatherlands

by

Tommy Mackay

'Over on BBC 1 now, the first showing on British television of the acclaimed blockbuster 'Heatherlands' - a groundbreaking innovative masterpiece which enthralled audiences and critics alike on its initial release. Marlon Brando and Robert De Niro are just two of a host of stars giving Oscar-winning performances in what many commentators have described as the definitive work of 20th century cinema. That's except for viewers in Scotland.'

'What?' Scanning the small print at the bottom of the newspaper TV page I noticed, under 'Regional Variations', that we were to be treated to something which I couldn't even pronounce. I flicked channels and, sure enough, there was a homely, pasty-faced country lass in an Arran sweater, gargling Gaelic and smiling benignly. I hit the on-off switch with a vengeance and headed for the pub.

As I stood at the bar reading the tariff notice, I toyed with the idea of working my way through every brand of whisky arrayed before me. I checked my wallet and decided I might just make it to the 'Glenmorangie'.

"Bells' please.' I smiled at the barmaid who disconsolately jabbed a glass into the optic.

'Anything in it?' she droned.

'Just ice.'

The pub was half empty. Glancing round I noticed a table of four teenage lads apparently amusing themselves by aiming mocked adulation at the two young girls sitting on the other side of the room.

'My God! Pink stilettos!' quipped what appeared to be the leading wit of the group. His fellow raconteurs contributed similar cutting barbs, and their wild delight at their collective repartee reduced them to peals of laughter.

Apparently unaware of the excitement their presence was occasioning, the girls, wrapped up in their own company, completely ignored the explosion of mirth around them.

I turned back to the bar. "Haigs' please.'

In another corner of the pub sat two slightly older males. Not for them the trendy designer-labelled lager bottles sported by the *bons vivants* across the room; their nectar was of a darker hue and encased in straight pint mugs: vessels of incredibly tough, thick glass, judging by the fierce grip each clung on to them with. It was a testimony to the manufacturers of these pint glasses that they could withstand such intense pressure. Even from my standpoint, a few feet away, I could see the whites of their knuckles. Their faces had that classic hard man look - rock-face serious brows and murderous eyes. They sat opposite each other in complete silence as if their aggressive demeanour compensated for the lack of conversation, their rigid masks communicating more than words - a badge of mutual understanding.

And yet I detected a hint of annoyance in their disgruntled features, an annoyance I suspected they felt at the audacity of others having such a good time whilst they were obviously engulfed by their indoctrination and lifetime subscription to the harsh grit of reality. Or maybe not.

I ordered another: "Whyte and Mackays' please.'

Beside me at the bar, though not encroaching on my elbow space, an old timer nurtured his half pint of 80/-. He seemed to have been observing me.

'You're fairly knocking 'em back,' he said.

'I need it,' I answered. 'You know, I was just going to stay in tonight and watch a film, and what do I get? Bloody Gaelic!'

'You're easily driven to drink, aren't you?' he laughed. 'Any excuse, eh? Besides, you shouldn't knock the Gaelic you know, it's a dying language.'

'It certainly smells funny anyway. Do you speak it like?'

'No, but that's not the point is it? You can't just let old Scotland die because of this. . .' He gestured round the pub. 'What are they going to replace it with, eh? Juke boxes and space machines? This used to be a proper pub before they done it up. It looks like a restaurant or something now. No atmosphere. Are you from around here?'

'Just up the road. I don't usually come in here though. D'you want a drink?'

'Oh I can't see you right son. Don't get my pension till tomorrow.'

'That's all right, what you having?'

'I'll have a 'Grouse' then.'

'Two 'Grouse' please.'

'You're mixing it, aren't you?'

'Eh?'

'Different whisky every time. I've been watching.'

'Oh, yeah. Just soaking up our heritage, doing my bit, preserving the past like you said. Do you want ice in that?'

'No, nothing. It's just a wee chaser. I'd better head home after this - the wee woman will be wondering where I am. Cheers!'

As another whoop escaped from the teenagers, the two girls simultaneously rolled their eyes upwards and shook their heads, obviously unimpressed. The hard men clenched their teeth even tighter and the old man stared blankly in front of him. The barmaid, though, seemed to be slightly amused by the young bucks' antics. Me? I felt somehow apart from it all, as if I'd tuned into the wrong channel. And what is the badge of the chronically indifferent? I checked my couture - a slight fraying in the left knee of a black pair of denims. The high culture starts here, except for viewers in Scotland.

One of the hard men sidled up to the bar. 'Two special,' he grunted. A huge roar erupted from the young pretenders' table.

'Aw shut-up,' growled Mr Hard. The teenagers didn't hear but my drinking partner smirked. The hard man obviously didn't appreciate this apparent approval of frivolity. He scowled at the old man:

'What you laughing at, grandad?'

The old man looked slowly up, disdainfully. 'Nothing. . . much.'

'Is that supposed to be funny?' The hard man's eyes glared as he knocked the old boy's half pint over the bar. 'Now, *that's* funny,' he sneered.

I couldn't let it pass, and I knew I'd regret it, but I piped up anyway: 'Hey, come on, he didn't mean any harm.'

The next morning my head was thumping as I slowly opened my eyes. A blurred white figure crossed my limited horizon. I called out,

'Nurse! Where's the television room?'

'Ah, Mr Dewar! How are you feeling this morning?'

'Bloody awful!' I ran my fingers over the bandage round my head. The memory of the stitches made me wince, and as I tentatively prodded my puffy eyes, I felt they were almost level with the tip of my grazed nose. 'Never mind that, where's the telly?'

'I can wheel one in for you if you like.'

When she switched it on it was showing 'Postman Pat' in Gaelic. 'Jesus! Switch it off,' I groaned, and lay my head back on the pillow.

Shadow Of The Past

by

Louise Lauder

The first thing Marissa Frances Lennox seemed to remember, were faces peering down at her, making cooing noises and one voice remarking, as the baby's hands were open and not closed tight like some infants, it was a good sign. The child would not be greedy!

It was the voice of her mother's Auntie Moll, one of these wise old ladies. In later years, Marissa always thought she looked very much the old maid type, but this lady had been twice to the altar although never blessed with children of her own.

By the time she was five years old, the little girl had three brothers namely, Frederick Joseph, born fourteen months after her, then Henry some eighteen months later, who incidentally did not get any middle names as the feeling was that at the rate they were going, they might run out of names. Well it was always a joke in the family. Lastly, there came Ronald, two years younger than Henry.

Marissa could never understand why she did not get the little sister she wanted. Before the birth of Ronald, she was sent on holiday for a month to St Andrews, some fifteen miles from her home town of Dundee. She had been to this particular convalescent home before. She was such a thin child; her mother worried about her, so she was taken to the children's clinic, which at that time was in Isles Lane. The doctor was very kind and sympathetic, and usually prescribed malt to build the child up, or sometimes advised St Andrews. Mrs Lennox had to pay something towards the cost, but never seemed to mind even though with four mouths to feed, she had little to spare. Marissa did not like going away like this. At this home they were dressed alike with tweed coats and blue berets and taken for walks by a Governess along the cliff tops and down to the beach where it could be really freezing.

This time, however, she was promised there would be a wee sister when she got home, so her disappointment was great indeed when she first gazed into the cot and asked the baby's name only to be told 'Ronald'. She felt badly let down.

After much crying and performing, she had to accept things as they were, but through the years she kept hoping.

As Marissa grew up, she was expected to help a lot with her three brothers, with her mother out working full time as a weaver in one of Dundee's many jute works. When the girl was around eleven years old, there came the threat of trouble with Germany. On

August 29th 1938, the Treaty of Munich was signed by Neville Chamberlain of Britain, Deladier of France, Adolf Hitler of Germany and Mussolini of Italy.

Neville Chamberlain came back waving the paper to prove to the nation that everything was fine. However, the rumblings went on. Local authorities decided that with the threat of war, everyone would be issued with gas masks. These were bad enough, but babies were put into a monstrosity which completely covered them, and so everyone went around with this cardboard box slung over their shoulders held by a piece of string.

Mr and Mrs Lennox decided for their family's safety, they would be evacuated. When the offer came along, many parents would not allow their children to go, but one morning, the four little Lennox children set off for the railway station with their mother in attendance complete with a few possessions and gas masks. They were duly boarded onto trains not knowing where they were going amid many tears. The train pulled out leaving most of the mothers behind.

They travelled for hours, all these children with helpers watching over them, and Marissa all the time keeping an eye on her brothers. The train broke down which delayed things even more. It was night time when they finally arrived at their destination, just a very small place with one main street called Laurencekirk, where they were bundled into, of all places, the cattle market. This was to last for hours, as people kept going around looking for the evacuees they had agreed to take under this scheme. Most would take two children of one family, even three at a push, but nobody wanted four, so Marissa huddled there with her brothers refusing to be split up as some had suggested. Her mother had said, 'stay together' so that was it - Marissa would not budge.

They were the only ones left. Then, finally, after much discussion, one of the councillors said that he and his wife would take the family. It was a happy decision for the Lennox's. As well as being a councillor, they were business people in this small place, and in spite of being such busy people, they did everything they could for those children. In fact, they had two boys of their own, one at university in Edinburgh, the younger one a few months older than Marissa, so they really had big hearts to take the evacuees.

On the Sunday morning after arrival, the children were called into the sitting room to listen to the news on the radio. No television in those days. Poland had been invaded by Germany on the 1st September 1939. They were told to be out of that country by the 3rd September 1939. Neville Chamberlain, then Prime Minister, informed the world, 'We are now in a state of war', as they had not conformed to that order.

The children took it all in their stride, soon settling down to village life and school. It was all very different from what they had known, but they enjoyed the change doing things like going to the potato gathering and taking part in plays in the village hall, learning to knit squares from odd bits of wool for soldiers' blankets. Their parents visited from time to time, but this just seemed to unsettle them. However, after several months, Mrs Lennox was not happy without her children and decided to take them home to Dundee.

In wartime Dundee, the Lennox's lived in a tenement block, which these days are known as flats. It was two stairs up with a communal toilet on the stairs landing. This was shared by five families - sheer torture if anyone needed to go places in a hurry! Their house was known as through going; it consisted of three rooms, you entered from a tiny square known as a 'lobby'. First room was a kitchen cum sitting room, bathroom - no bath, just a black cast iron sink in which you washed as best you could. In those days, most people used the public baths once or twice a week. The second room, a bedroom, was used by Mr and Mrs Lennox, then the small room through again, was Marissa's' room. With her being the only girl, she was privileged. The boys slept on a sofa bed which was folded down at night in the kitchen. This had to be folded up early in the morning or there wasn't much room to move about at all.

After a short time, John Lennox volunteered for the Royal Navy, was accepted and sent abroad with the rescue tugs. He was never on leave for over three years. Sue Lennox was left to cope with four kids on her own, plus a full time job which was very heavy work indeed and besides all this the shopping which she did more often than not in her lunch hour, coping with food and clothes being rationed. It was coupons for most things, then many an evening spent in the public wash house. For this a basket was placed on an old pram with a wash board, a bar of Fairy green soap, a small scrubber for stubborn marks on shirt collars etc., then wheeled through the streets to the wash house.

On arrival at the cash desk here, you received a key for a wash stall which contained two deep sinks and a small boiler for the white clothes. After everything was duly washed and rinsed, these sopping wet clothes were dragged in the basket down a passageway to the machines known as extractors, then onto the dryers which were frames with hot pipes which pulled out from the wall.

You noted the numbers on these frames, always leaving someone to watch them as it often happened clothes disappeared in the drying process. There was another room which held irons and mangles, should you wish to do the lot on the premises. Then to the cash desk where the assistant counted your time and charged accordingly. Marissa hated the wash house, but again being the daughter, it fell to her to help her mother.

So the years passed. When Marissa was fourteen, she left school to work in the factory beside her mother who had decided she was to be a weaver also. The girl was not stupid and would much rather have done something else, however, in those days you had respect for your parents, and did what you were told. Her mother was always good to her, and very rarely lost her temper. She was a patient woman with her daughter, but of course she was that bit firmer with the boys who were now at an age to need a father's hand.

They seemed to be doing well at school, Henry had even won a bursary, which meant that he attended an academy instead of just a secondary school. Quite an achievement at that time. Fred was quite clever also; the youngest Ronald was much in demand as a footballer in his spare time.

Winston Churchill was Prime Minister by this time. A very tough man known as 'The Bulldog', he was determined never to give in to the Germans. Many nights were spent in the air raid shelter at a nearby school, where they sat shivering often hearing enemy aircraft overhead, but luckily, only two bombs ever fell on Dundee, killing one person when one fell on a tenement block in Rosefield Street. It was always a great relief when the 'all clear' siren blew.

In those days you could walk in the streets at nights, although the blackout was in force which meant that not even a chink of light must be seen or the ARP (Air Raid Precautions) would be yelling 'Put that light out,' and banging on your door.

However, after five years, the war was over. Victory in Europe or VE Day, 8th May 1945, the celebrations were wonderful - dancing, parties and bonfires in the streets went on for days. A happy time, yes, but for so many a deep sadness for those loved ones who would never return.

For Marissa, a new life was beginning.

The Birthday

by

M Stewart

June 1917.

Maggie, sitting on the back doorstep looked disconsolately across the drying green. There was nothing 'green' about that arid patch. The windows of the miners houses seemed like so many sad eyes looking out on the higgelty-piggelty poles which held up the clothes lines on which the miners' clothes were pegged.

World War I, nearing its end, had failed to touch Maggie's family in any serious way. Her brothers were too young for active service, and her father, a miner, was more valuable at the coal face than in a dugout in France.

It was Sunday - a day of rest? For the miners' wives it was the only opportunity to hang out to dry the moleskin trousers caked with coal dust mud. Maggie and her sister had the hated task, sometimes, of hanging out the wet moleskins prior to having to scrape them when they were dry.

Normally Maggie was a happy child - secure in her family and her many cousins all living in the same community. But today her horizon was clouded. She had fallen foul of her brothers. They had brought home in glass jars some minnows guddled from the stream which ran close by the coal mine. Maggie, anxious to curry favour with her brothers had tried to put fresh water in the jars, but had forgotten to put the stopper in the sink. The minnows all disappeared.

How hateful brothers could be! Maggie had only one sister - fourteen years old - who had no wish to be bothered with a six year old sister - going on seven - especially when it was her tedious chore every evening to brush Maggie's thick, unruly hair. She was anything but gentle with the hairbrush, but Maggie was resigned to the nightly torture.

Yes. Tomorrow she would be *Seven*, and she had seven brothers - four older than she, and three younger. Having a birthday next day held no happy prospects for her. Birthday presents were not expected - nor were they given, when the priorities were new boots and warm clothes. No. She would receive, as all the others did - thumps on the back (or posterior) according to the number of years one had attained.

Maggie sighed, then brightened. Ah yes. There *Was* something to look forward to. - A Clootie Dumpling - rich and fruity, boiled in a cloth over an open fire for about three hours - if her mother had time from her many chores to prepare it. Her mother? Source of all wisdom - her homespun philosophy solving family and neighbours' problems.

Maggie couldn't remember ever seeing her mother taking her ease. If she wasn't knitting or re-footing socks, she was altering some garment to fit someone else, or baking girdle scones over the open fire. But if the boys stepped out of line she could handle them according to their guilt - or need. Very rarely had she to refer them to their father who seemed always preoccupied with his 'penny' tin-whistle or his draught board. Heaven help the boys if their father was summoned. They were marched into the 'room' which housed the beds for six of them. Off came their father's belt and appropriate punishment was meted out.

Tomorrow - her birthday, she faced with mixed feelings. Her brothers had retired to the 'room'. The baby was snug in his rocking cradle and Maggie crept into the recessed bed which she shared with her sister. The curtains were drawn across the bed so that the gaslight would be shut out. But this did not shut out the drone of her father's voice as he read to her mother, her knitting needles seeming to punctuate every sentence.

Sunday. Her birthday at last!

The typical miner's breakfast of stew that had been slowly cooking on the hob of the open fire all night. No stew ever tasted so good. Birthday gifts? None! Thumps? Plenty. Surprisingly Maggie's father suggested she should take a walk with him in the afternoon, and off they went to the public park and sat themselves down near some gorse bushes. Her father produced his clay pipe and proceeded slowly and methodically to cut thin slices from a wad of thick, black tobacco. Having filled his pipe he sat back and puffed away.

Maggie sat in silence. She wasn't having such a bad birthday after all. After fifteen minutes watching the smoke curling upwards her father asked her to pick a few daises for him. Puzzled, but with unquestioning obedience she did as she was asked. When she returned with her apron pretty full she found her father had cut a large piece of gorse into a shape resembling a Christmas Tree. He propped it up in some earth and then carefully impaled a daisy head on each thorn. Maggie watched in silent delight. Her father had guessed that his little daughter wanted to be seen as a little girl longing for the finer things of life. Her aspirations were different from her tomboy brothers. She gazed from the gorse-daisy tree to her father's smiling face.

'Thank you, father.'

'Happy birthday, Maggie.'

Another Springtime

by

Seán Costello

It was his move. It was his move but he couldn't concentrate on the board. Chess often had that effect on him. The more involved he got in the game, the less he wanted to study the pieces. The more he pondered all the available moves the less inclined he was to make one. Sometimes it was enough just to know the options. Choosing the best one was another matter. He couldn't always summon that kind of energy, that conviction.

He made his move.

It was still light outside but night was approaching. At what pace it was hard to tell at this time of year. The train sped southward. Did it stay lighter later further south? Were they seeing more daylight from the moving train than they would have if they'd got off further back up the line, or if they'd never left home at all? Were they in some sort of impossible race against the darkness? And what if . . . ? And so on.

She'd made her move. She too had taken her time but had seemed more purposeful about where she positioned her piece. It didn't mean hers was the better move. He didn't know what it meant. That she had more of a sense of purpose?

He made a quick move, probably a bad one, but his was the sort of game that allowed for the odd bad move. He couldn't play it any other way. He made a quick move because he didn't want her to get impatient and tell him to stop staring out of the window. Because he was staring out of the window with a purpose now, if that's not putting it too strongly, he was staring out at the lambs. They were new-born. How new he couldn't tell. How much can you tell from the window of a speeding train?

It all depends. Trees and telegraph poles flash past in an instant. Signs on stations where the train doesn't stop might just as well be blank. But something like a flock of lambs can stay with you as if you'd walked right through the field, not hurtled blindly past it. Perhaps because you can't so much as catch a glimpse of a field of new-born lambs without remembering all the fields of new-born lambs you've known before. Their first faltering steps. How they're left to get on with it, with at best a cursory lick from the ewe. Not like that familiar scene he'd witnessed the Sunday before, by the riverbank. A woman pushing a child in a buggy. A man calling out. She turning around to see a little boy on a bicycle emerge from the shadow cast by the giant arch of the Dean Bridge. The man right behind him, his hand on the saddle, guiding him. 'On you go, son. Go to your mam.' The boy wobbling, his lip quivering. The man smiling back encouragement. The boy wanting to give up. Knowing he's got to learn sometime, but not now, any time but now. He shuddered inwardly, knowing the boy had to fall. He did not want to witness that.

But this was different. This was something he could hardly tear himself away from, though he'd seen it all before. This was another springtime come. It had come to him when and where he least expected it - on an inter-city train journey with night falling and the reflection of a chess board gradually taking the place of the world ourside . The funny thing was, the more he strained to look, the less he saw of the world and the more the board loomed out of the night at him, reminding him of what he mind was supposed to be on.

'It's your move.'

Already! What had changed since he'd last looked? He didn't have the nerve to ask to see her last move. But he noticed a difference all right. Only it was nothing she had done, it was a move he'd made earlier himself that he only now saw the implications of. It was to this, rather than any move she might have made that he responded. He took his index finger of the knight. Good or bad, he was stuck with his move now. Only this was neither one nor the other. Just necessary.

Beyond the lone-standing facade of the ruined abbey chapel the field was dotted with white bodies, some motionless, others moving. There was even the odd black one to be seen. And no, not moving, gambolling was the only word for what they did. Some didn't move at all, while others gambolled. Still one second, then for no apparent reason, momentarily airborne, kicking out with their legs in wild ungainly little leaps. It made him feel giddy, strangely elated at the mystery and inevitability of the scene being played out before them. He could sense her and her mother's quiet pleasure in the field and the antics of its recently arrived inhabitants, although they spoke of something else entirely. They belonged to this more than he did, but he felt included and it felt good to feel included.

The feeling didn't last long. She and the mother chatted away as before. Up ahead he had spotted a small, black, recumbent form. He was too far away to see if it was merely resting, or if . . . But he knew all right, before he got close enough to know for sure, before he saw the mad spasmodic twitching of only three of the lamb's upraised legs, kicking out in a sickening parody of its gambolling fellows. He had known it as long ago as last year, or was it the year before, when her mother had taken them to see the school she had gone to as a small child and the old Saxon church beside it with a flock of sheep grazing in its graveyard. They had heard the bleating of the lambs and shared the same strange elation. Except that from one of them this tremulous cry was a cry of pain, the poor dumb animal having become ensnared in the barbed wire fence.

It was hard to tell how long this present lamb had lain there, how newly-born it was, when the ewe had given up on it. They stood watch together while her mother crossed the field towards the farmer's house.

They were in the next field now, beyond the stream with its little island where they'd stopped in the hope of spotting otters. The dog now safely off its lead ran madly to and fro as if intent on wearing itself out. A ruined stone cottage reminded him of other, far off fields and the remains of homes abandoned in famine times.

The rain came. From the slope they could hear, then see, the farmer's tractor approach the spot where the lamb lay.

'About bloody time, too.'

But they knew it was already too late to do, or undo anything.

A Tearful Situation

by

M J Wells

When Rachel, my four-year old niece, suggested we visit the zoo, I had no desire to be an Uncle Killjoy. After all, it was the right place for a couple of animal lovers to spend an hour.

Also, as Rachel quickly pointed out, we had a camera - at least, she had. And what finer starting ground was there for a trigger-happy photographer?

So without thinking deeply how much the excursion was going to cost me, I agreed, even managing to sound enthusiastic. My enthusiasm didn't wane, even when it came to buying a new film for the camera - in fact, it was a day for enthusiasm.

The sun shone warm and bright, and the flowers in full bloom made it a joy to be alive. The peacocks were parading up and down, showing off their beautiful plumage. Then, all of a sudden, I didn't notice these things any more.

My attention was captured by a young woman standing near us. She was really pretty, as anyone who could distract me from the peacocks would have to be .

Then a party of giggling schoolgirls temporarily got in the way, causing me to lose sight of the vision.

The giggling was something I had to contend with every now and then, depending on what was showing at the local cinema or on television.

Girls kept mistaking me for some actor, Robert Redfern, or some name like that. Once a girl had even asked for my autograph. I'd obliged, if only to get some peace, though I doubted the name Alistair Campbell made much impact.

I put on my sunglasses, hoping this might foil them, but it only seemed to make matters worse.

Fortunately, the teacher supervising these girls was a man, and presumably not a movie buff, for he quickly herded the party along to look at the monkeys.

I felt there was probably a joke there somewhere, but my mood was not jocular . . .

I could see the girl again, and she was crying. Tears were streaming down her cheeks, and she had taken out a handkerchief, trying, not too successfully, to dry her eyes.

There was a tug at my sleeve. 'The lady's crying,' said Rachel, all concerned. 'Why is she crying?'

'Oh, yes, so she is,' I replied, feigning mild interest, and thinking about the possible reason.'

Maybe she'd just had a disagreement with her boyfriend, if she had one. Maybe he'd gone away. If so, was there just the chance he wouldn't be coming back?

I found myself wishing so. I'd certainly have been glad to fill his place.

Knowing that Rachel was not inclined to drop an unanswered question, I fell into the trap of expressing a theory. 'Maybe she's just said goodbye to her husband.'

Rachel did not explore the unlikelihood of a romantic parting at the zoo, but switched to a related channel. 'Has she got any children?'

It was a question I scarcely cared to contemplate, having just swapped a supposed suitor for a hypothetical husband. 'They'd be with her, wouldn't they?' I said, with a leap of logic that seemed to satisfy her.

In the meantime, though, I simply couldn't stand there and offer no assistance. Crying ladies always upset me.

But what could I say to comfort her? Teething puppies and moulting budgerigars and balding hamsters were more my forté.

I glanced at my watch. It was two, and in one hour's time I had to be at the station to meet Sam Grant.

Roderick, my brother, senior partner in the veterinary practice, had sent me into the city to meet the new student. The roads back home were pretty confusing, and it seemed like good Scottish hospitality to meet the student part way.

Roderick and his wife Carol had been promising for weeks to take Rachel to the zoo, and when the news of my trip into the city fell upon Rachel's ears, she didn't hesitate to pressgang me into service.

I had driven down to meet Grant, although I had initially wondered why Roderick was bending, or more precisely, bending me over backwards to meet him.

Maybe I should take a leaf out of his book and be similarly kind to this crying girl.

What was she doing here all alone? Ah, yes. I'd answered that before. Her boyfriend had left her, hence the tears. Perhaps she'd sent him packing, and perhaps these were crocodile tears, even though she was standing by the peacocks.

Rachel, at this stage, commenced her habit of jumping up and down, alternating from one leg to the other, a practice I have observed in her and other girls of her age. I suspected this would preface some request.

'Uncle, would you take a picture . . .?' This was followed by a perfectly timed pause, after which she added a beseeching, *'Please . . .'*

I really did not welcome the distraction from the crying girl, but I did dutifully enquire, 'What do you want me to photograph, Rachel?'

'The big birds,' she replied. 'Will you do it, Uncle Alistair, please?'

Rachel really had a way of asking favours that made you want to comply, and I would normally have snapped the peacocks without the slightest hesitation. There was just one distraction - the sobbing stranger. I couldn't really photograph the scene without getting her in it, and it did seem most ignoble to take her picture when she was in such an unbecoming state.

The schoolgirls were returning from the monkey house and I didn't want to be made a fool of again with this Robert Redroof business, so I had to make a move somewhere.

I decided I'd cross over to the crying girl and get a good shot of the peacocks. I'd be pleasing Rachel, and could get into conversation with the girl, too.

'May I help you?' I asked her. 'You obviously seem to be in some kind of - ' I stalled, trying to think of a tactful word or phrase.

'Trouble?' she suggested.

'Well, that's about it, I suppose,' I agreed. 'But the main thing is, can I get you out of it?'

My back was to the sun, so I took off my sunglasses. She looked surprised.

'What's wrong?' I asked.

'You'll never believe this,' she started, 'but you have a double called - '

'I know,' I interrupted wearily, 'Robert Redrum.'

She laughed, very infectiously, and I was glad this resemblance business was at least cheering her up.

'That wasn't quite the name I was going to say,' she told me. 'And in answer to your kind offer, I don't think you could help me, not unless - '

I was hopeful. She need only name it, I was sure I could do it. Tame the tigers, outrun the cheetahs, grasp the sunlight in my hands - anything! She had that effect on me!

'Go on,' I prompted.

'Unless,' she replied, with a twinkle in her eyes, 'you have a cure for hay fever.' Then she sneezed.

I laughed. 'I'm sorry. I'm not laughing at your hay fever, running eyes and so forth - I really sympathise, but I thought your tears were much more serious. As it happens, I'm a vet, and we don't get too much hay fever with our patients.'

She looked interested. 'Where do you practise?'

'Oh, about forty miles from her over in Inver-rossie.'

I really felt drawn to this girl, even though I knew virtually nothing about her except that she was upset by a high pollen count.

I was about to try and change the course of the conversation when Rachel, who had been keeping a low profile, introduced a fresh subject.

She had resumed her jumping up and down, but much more urgently.

'Uncle, I need the loo,' she sobbed.

I was panic-stricken.

'The loo at the zoo . . . ?'

The girl smiled, although I hadn't intended a capricious phrase.

Roderick and Carol had said nothing about my supervising such a delicate matter, a very grave oversight.

'Well, I don't know,' I mumbled, trying to figure out how I could accompany her.

But now there was a remedy. It was a case of the damsel helping the knight in distress.

'Don't worry,' said the girl, 'I'll take her for you.'

I was so thankful; she really had saved me.

They were gone quite a while, and I began reviewing what I'd achieved. Precious little, really. Mainly, I had found her, possibly Miss Right, but had less than an hour before I would meet this Grant fellow. How could I forge some deeper relationship with her in that time, apart from making medical history and curing hay fever there and then?

I wondered if this Robert Redfield ever had difficult problems like this one in any of his movies.

The girl and Rachel were returning now, and I knew I had to come up with a fresh development. Maybe if I suggested having coffee in the café it would help.

I knew it seemed a contrived suggestion, but heroes in stories always managed to get away with it. But, to my dismay, as I started fumbling about in my pocket for coffee money, I discovered I had only five pence left. The admission to the zoo had cost me more than I'd anticipated, plus Rachel's film.

I then discovered that in my rush to leave home, I'd forgotten my cheque book; I could be thankful there was plenty of petrol in the car. Another grim financial fact lumbered across my mind.

What if the girl had had to fork out two pence on Rachel's behalf? It was a sorry state of affairs if financing a trip to the loo would reduce my assets by almost a half. I decided I wouldn't enquire into reimbursing her.

What a situation, I thought. Finding this delightful girl but having so little time - and even less money - to spend on her. Roderick would never forgive me if I missed Sam Grant at the station.

And I really couldn't ask her to get the coffee and make out an IOU. It would be one way of getting her name and address, though, I thought, and I could always add on the two pence, but it really seemed a bit too risky.

The girl glanced at her watch when she reached me. And I didn't notice any rings on her fingers.

'It's two-fifteen,' I told her, needlessly, and the reference to time was like the start to a countdown.

'I really must be going now,' she said, out of the blue.

How could I raise the cash in a hurry? - I wondered, not responding to her exit line.

Perhaps I could charge those schoolgirls for Robert Redfield's autograph. I voted down that idea, too, as a bit of a cheat.

I knew that people often threw coins in the pools nearby, but the idea of submerging fully clothed for a few moments was obviously not on. Besides, I'd be sure to wind up with something more serious than hay fever.

'I must be going now,' she said again, more urgently. 'My hay fever seems to be clearing. I think it's psychosomatic.'

She was about to wave goodbye, when Rachel chimed in. 'Please may I take your photograph?'

The girl blushed a little, and looked at me as if awaiting my reaction. I felt like a film director about to call the shots, although Rachel's camera technique was very much in its infancy.

'Why not?' I coaxed. 'I'm sure you'll make a pretty picture.'

Rachel executed the shot quickly while the girl was still blushing, and I knew the glow of her cheeks would come out well on the colour film; that is, if Rachel had, in fact, managed to include her face.

And I thought here was a golden opportunity to ask her name and address so we could post on the photograph. But before I could ask, she waved goodbye and she was off . . .

I felt desolate. And Rachel, who had obviously come to like the girl, looked like I felt.

It soon became time to drive to the station for my meeting with Sam Grant. The name suddenly brought to mind a picture of Grant's Tomb in New York which was doubly appropriate, for that was how my spirit felt, entombed . . .

And then the optimist within me started proposing a storybook solution. What if the girl was rushing to the station, too? What if I met her there again? Surely then I could devise some way of getting her address or telephone number?

And then I realised how I was deluding myself. Making these plans when the girl had probably gone for good.

Rachel still seemed to be in the doldrums.

'Uncle, will we see the lady again?'

There was no point in being abysmally frank, I thought, so I tried to soften the facts. 'Who can say, Rachel,' I replied. 'Maybe some day.'

Rachel, of course, did not drop the matter. 'When, Uncle, when?'

'I don't know when,' I said, defensively. 'Maybe some day when we don't expect to see her.'

Rachel was giving my vague comments careful consideration. 'Did you like her, Uncle?'

I gulped again, braked at the traffic lights and looked at her. Cars, buses and lorries pulled up behind us, and the din of the traffic faded as if all were awaiting my reply. I

91

wound up the window, to isolate ourselves from all the ears of the city, and turned again to Rachel.

'Yes I liked her very much,' I said.

Then there were horns blowing from behind and I moved off, seeing the signal had changed.

Within minutes we reached the station, but all the parking places there were occupied. That left only the parking meter zone a block away.

I drove there quickly, for time was running out, and then came the finishing blow. The greedy meter demanded my one and only five pence.

Roderick had written to Sam Grant, specifying the news-stand at three as the rendez-vous. I swiftly surveyed those there for someone who would match my impressions of him and Rachel, of course, did the same, twirling round on one tiny foot.

'Look, Uncle,' she exclaimed, 'there's Mr Grant.'

Why I took that observation seriously I'll never know, she'd got me in enough com-plications already by reducing me to a state of financial ruin for the day, and even though she had brought me close to the girl of my dreams, she'd ended up stealing her away into the loo, of all places.

I followed the line of her pointed finger which led to an Indian gentleman wearing a Sikh's turban; an unlikely Sam Grant, I thought.

'Don't point,' I rebuked her, mildly, re-directing the offending finger inadvertently to-wards a more likely Sam Grant, a young man wearing a kilt.

I managed to dissuade Rachel from the idea of taking a snap of the kilted stranger with some argument about not wasting good film on strange men at railway stations, and tried to convince her she'd seen men in kilts before, although at that moment I couldn't catalogue any.

'Maybe he's Mr Grant,' she suggested.

It was a possibility, I agreed, but one would have thought he'd at least have been wearing the Grant tartan.

And then I spotted a young man in his twenties carrying some suitcases towards the news-stand and looking very bewildered and in search of someone.

'This must be him,' I declared.

'Why him?' asked Rachel, and it was amazing just how much disappointment, disap-proval and dejection she could inject into two words.

How much happier we'd both have been if we had lost this chap at the zoo and met the girl here instead.

We were about to make our way over to him when I heard something above the hub-bub of the station. It was a sneeze.

I stopped in my tracks, tightening my hold on Rachel. It would have sounded ridicu-lous, I know, to say that the sneeze sounded familiar, but there was no harm in wishing.

I glanced over my shoulder, forgetting about Grant for the moment. Approaching us, struggling with a couple of suitcases, was the girl.

'Uncle, it's the pretty lady,' cried Rachel, bobbing up and down again.

This time I wasn't going to let the girl get away. I'd grab her before she set foot on the platform, if that was where she was heading, because now my pockets were completely empty I couldn't even afford the platform ticket.

'Maybe she's meeting her husband,' suggested my irritating niece.

'She's not married,' I asserted, though I did not explain the ringless finger clue and just hoped my eyes had been focusing correctly.

'Hello,' I shouted, running towards her.

She looked quite happy, which bothered me. I'd hoped she'd have looked at least slightly miserable at our parting and that, save for this chance second encounter, we would never likely have met again.

'Oh, hello again,' she said casually.

And that bothered me even more. I'd expected some hint of surprise. Now, with her lack of misery or surprise, I felt dubious about my approach.

Well, I'd chance it, I decided, checking that Sam Grant was still waiting at the news-stand.

'About your hay fever,' I began, feeling a complete idiot, 'I think - ' And suddenly was lost for words.

She waited attentively.

And then Rachel came in with a question of her own.

'Have you got a husband?'

The girl laughed good-naturedly, while I froze.

'Actually, I haven't,' she replied, and I was delighted to get confirmation of that.

Rachel looked very bewildered. 'Is that why you were crying at the zoo?'

This was my chance to come in again, and I seized it.

'Yes, about the hay fever,' I babbled. 'I think I know what's causing it or, at least, ag-gravating it.'

She smiled. 'I think I know, too,' she said.

'Really?'

'Yes. I have this theory that it's brought on by some emotional tension, like meeting someone for the first time, being tested out in some way, like an exam or a new job.'

'That's what you meant by psychosomatic?' I asked. 'Or even a train journey to some distant destination?'

She smiled, but this time I suspected the joke was on me.

93

'But I'm not taking a train journey now. In fact, I landed this morning on an earlier train. I left my luggage in the cloakroom, had a quick look around the shops, and found myself near the zoo.'

I thought the light was filtering through, but I was still ninety per cent blacked out.

'So you're a local girl, are you? But no, why would you wander around your own city, leaving your luggage at the station?'

Her cheeks flushed slightly, as if embarrassed at some revelation she would make. Then she handed me her suitcases.

Delightful as it was to be her porter, why and where did she want them taken was the two-pronged question.

'There's a simple explanation,' she said softly. I looked at Rachel for support, but her mouth was open in surprise.

'Try me,' I responded. 'I'm pretty simple.'

'The simple explanation,' she disclosed slowly, 'is that we're meeting each other here at three at the news-stand.'

My grip on the cases slackened considerably. 'But that's impossible,' I replied. 'I'm meeting a Sam Grant.'

'Oh, that.' She laughed. 'It happens all the time - like your Robert Redfire business. What would you say if I told you I'm Sam Grant?' Her pretty mouth was curved into a smile.

I thought for a moment. 'I'd probably say something like, Sam Grant must be the best looking guy in town!'

She blushed again and, laughing, said, 'Well, I am Sam - Samantha!'

Suddenly it all clicked into place. Now I knew why Roderick had been so considerate and secretive, the sly fox.

'So you knew all along, from when I told you at the zoo I was a vet from Inver-rossie.'

She nodded. 'Even before you told me that, I was about to say you had a double called Alistair Campbell. Your brother sent me a photograph so I'd recognise you at the station.'

I laughed.

'But why did you let me suffer all this time?'

'Life has its surprises,' she said, 'and it's nice to pull a few of your own now and then, isn't it?'

Rachel's jumping up and down intensified. 'Are you coming home with us?'

'Yes - that is, if your uncle isn't too angry with me.'

Rachel turned to me with soulful eyes. 'You're not angry, Uncle, are you? You told me you liked - '

'No, I'm not, Rachel,' I broke in quickly.

We still had about fifteen minutes before the parking meter would move into the red, and I was still thinking - among other things - that there was still time for that quick coffee before we drove away. This time I had a golden opportunity to raise the cash.

'How about a coffee?' I proposed.

Her eyes lit up.

'And since I've both hands tied up with these cases, maybe you'd be treasurer. I'll pay you back when we get to Inver-rossie,' I added.

'I thought you'd never ask,' Sam said, turning towards the buffet.

Then I hesitated.

'There's just one tiny detail that bothers me,' I confided. 'If you're Sam Grant, who's that lost-looking guy at the news-stand?'

She stopped, turned, and shrugged her shoulders.

'Maybe he's Robert Redfield,' she said, demurely.

The War Criminal

by

Robert Davidson

Gonna changa ma name tae Penkowski an gie masel up as a war criminal. Everabody knows there weranae oany Tally war criminals, jist poor bloody edgits gettin kill-ed; figures o' fun maist o' the time. Poles tae, until they getta the Polish Pope insteed o' a good Italian. Poles are taken serious noo its aw Solidarity. So Ah changa ma name tae Penkowski an jist walk intae the polis oaffice an say, 'Pitt oan the hauncuffs, Ah'ma commin quietly.' Add a bitta class. Make a nice change fur them efter drunk an disorderly, breach a the peace, olla the time.

Seen oan the television lasta night a man livin in Emburra, inna big big hoose, nice gairden, verra respectable area, wis war criminal inna Poland. Minded me o' the Pole inna the shoap next door tae the cafe, an Ah coulda believe! Didda lovely leather work. Pole's deid noo an no needin his name orra recommendations, but didda beautiful work! People a come fae aw ower furra the leather bags. Lasta furever, Rosina still goat the wee school bag we goat furra the grandaughter. Could afford then, jist. Oor ain weans hud tae cairry their books inna piece a string. Butta the grandaughter didanae want. Must a hav Andy Pandy on a wee canvas bag insteed. Onaly mistake the lassie ever make. Verra clever girl, wenta the university an merrit an Inglishman. Donna see noo, but Rosina keeps the school bag. Lovely work everyb'dy alwais say.

Butta the Pole he never pleased, never a word oota the man in twenty year. Goat a his breakfast from the cafe twenty year!

'Good a mornin Mister Penkowski, nice day furra the ducks!' Ah sais.

'Good morning Mista Luca,' an notta other word. Points tae whit he wants first aff, then disanae even dae that fur it alwais the same. Sits with the tea an a fried egg roll starin inta the distance. Didanae bite it, cuts it up neat. Real craftsman wi the fried egg roll as well as a leather, but never a word. He nivir hadda the good Inglish like me, runs inna the faimley. The grandaughter didda languages atta the university. Shoulda heard her! Saida Dante like a Angel. Butta the Pole? He sits an looks inta space.

'Displaced person!' sais Rosina.

'Butta naw,' Ah sais, 'perfectly legal Polish officer, metta nice lassie here an gotta merrit. Gotta a faimley. Sometimes I see his wee boay.'

'So how a come the breakfast?' sais Rosina.

'How a come 'how a come'? Ah'ma supposed tae know the ins anna ootsa a nother man's household? Nuff trouble wi ma ain!' God forgive Ah say tae Rosina! Onally ever the wanna trouble! Onally ever money! Nivir a nuff! An when we finally gotta the cafe oorsel's alla the teenagers lookin furra coffee bars, then itsa weans wantin twinty six flavours ice cream! Onally twenty six! Whit's wrang wi a slider? Used tae think the 99 wis the height o' luxury! Noo itsa wee packets inna back o' taxis! Where they getta the money, ehh? Me an Rosina worka, worka, worka, an finally the cafe jista disanae cover the overheids. Disanae feed me an Rosina never mind gie the boays employment iffa they wish. They no wish oanyweys an jist as well, but onally furra wee while. Then it's shuttings an redundancies an a staunin furra dole. Widda been pleased a nuff tae staun behind a coonter then.

'Least there is a dole,' sais Rosina. But Ah hadda big plans. Gonna be a nother a Corolla, a Valvona. Nae such! Gotta a nuff tae bury. Gotta the grandaughter tae university while Rosina say it spile her chances. Not so! Merrit tae the Inglish man, livin in a London inna fine hoose worth quarter million pounds. Notta bad furra man whose granfaither hudanae shoes tae his feet his hale life. But it wisanae whit Ah wanted! Came tae Scoatlan wi the big ideas. Gonna make a big money. Jist gettin oan ma feet an it's Isle a Man: interned. There Ah committa ma war crime.

Can believe the Pole ehh? Aw black a brows an black a silence! Canna believe wee fat Tomaso, jist a bletherin, lettin his tongue run away. Not so! Held a ma tongue since 1946. Canna look in the face an say. Onally thing Ah don't tell Rosina aboot ma hale life. Fur eighteen month Ah eata the rations o' a dyin man. Uppa sterrs fae me inna the auld hoose Senor Toghneri lived since a 1920. First a man in Scoatlan tae gie me a start. Treated me like a his ain, couldanae staun the Isle a Man an tattie howkin. Wisanae the work that kill-ed him, wis disgust. Lived here since a 1920. Respectable citizen goat a wee cairt oan a bike an went roon a sellin pokey hats tae the weans. Well a loved man! 'Here's Mr Toghneri!' aw the weans wid a shout. Didanae know Fascisti fae Frascati! An a comes the war an he's interned. Well interr-ed shoartly efter, an his two boays commended tae ma care. Wan has a the consumption. Shoulda eat, disanae want. His brother an me eat. Shameful! The brother's jist a boay; there's excuse! Furra me nane! His dyin faither tells a me,

'Tomaso, ti prego dal fondo del mio cuore di proteggere figli miei!'

'Non disturbarla, mio caro,' Ah sais, 'detto e fatto!'

No everabody die o' the TB. Ah know good food, rest an fresh air's whit's a needed. Well he's a gettin the fresh air okay. Ah should say, 'Eata up! Eata ma rations as a well orra yer faither's ghost he haunt me.' But he sais disanae want, an the brother an me eata the boays tatties. Isanae aw, we didanae smoke his fags! Gie him oors insteed! Think it pey him back furra food he disanae want! Gie the fags we widda kill-ed a nother man tae get fur oorsels. Think we're daein him a favour. Dies a happy man, mair or less; knew his brother an freen ready tae gie up their fags tae him. Ah kin hear him coughin yet! Thought the fags gie'd him a bitta pleasure; atta least steadied him a bit. Noo aw ye hear aboot's smokin an health hazards, an ye kin a be jist sittin next tae sumb'dy smokin an a ye die o' lung cancer. Wella the boay dies inna Isle a Man o' TB. Breaks his Mamma's heart an she die. The young Toghneri comes hame 1946, nae faither, nae mother, nae brother, an a his uncles faimley aw kill-ed inna the Blitz. No even a roof tae the auld hoose. Starts a drinkin!

Thatsa ma war crime! 'Well it's a no in the Treblinka class,' Ah kin hear the young polis sayin. Iffa he's heard of! 'Notta the slaughter o' Warsaw is it? Mair goat kill-ed at Stalin-grad,' you say. Ah hear, but inna the night Ah hear 'detto e fatto,' an Rosina breathin quiet an a also the babies when the boays were wee an still inna the bedroom.

'Nae worse than a Nazi!' Ah say tae cheer a masel up. 'Nazis were the wan aff real worst a guys inna hale history o' man.' Ah wis tellt at a the time. Repeated tae the boays inna the school, an the grandaughter goat a the same. Ah tell ye not so at all. Huvanae goat an education so Ah cannae prove, an couldanae aska the grandaughter ehh? 'Thin-ka yer Papa's a war criminal Beatrice?' Ah think!

Inna Isle a Man the Tallies havanae goat machinery. Like a 1840. 1740 even. Could a been ma ain granfaither, a contadino! Hadda boots but that wis aw Ah wis aheid oan. The Nazis are inna the twentieth century. They've goat a trains. Iffa nae trains, cannae transport a population tae the gas ovens. Can turn a Jews intae soap onaly if a ye've goat the equipment twentieth century! Cannae turna them intae pizzas iffa alla ye've goat is a breed oven! Getta ma point? All a ye need is a the goods. Gie me a the tools an Ah'll dae a the joab. Onna Isle a Man nae tools so is a the Beast o' Buchenwald inna the history books, an no Tomaso Luca inna the Isle a Man. He jist a poor bloody Tally didda nae hairm tae oanywan. Cept the wans he goat a his hauns oan.

'Naw,' ye say, 'he kill-ed them wi ignorance.' But Ah widanae swear. If Ah hud a been an educated man Ah widda known ye didanae gie fags tae man wi TB. Ye didanae eat a his food whitever he sais. But wid Ah huv done different? Ah don't a think. Ah think a like the Nazis Ah'da dae exact same again! Shoulda pit me oan a trial fur it.

Also, Ah wonder whit wis Mr Penkowski a lookin at aw they years, no talkin, no smilin, when he wis a well fixed wi a fine wife, the wee boay, an the good a business?

Brass Tacks

by

Drew McAdam

Helen Peterson cowered into the armchair under the angry gaze of her husband. 'But Edward, this metal figurine is so beautiful . . . I couldn't resist it. It's wonderful.'

'It's a waste of money, that's what it is.' He crossed to the window and glowered out into the garden. 'We have more important things to spend our pension on than brass knick-knacks. Look at this place, it's nothing but a dust gathering junk shop.' He waved his arm around the room.

It was a small, gloomy living room with little in the way of furnishings or luxuries. But the room was remarkable for the fact that brass objects littered every horizontal surface, including most of the floor.

Brass bells and buttons vied for space with souvenir ashtrays, miniature vehicles, pots and animals. A rearing horse on the mantelpiece rose above a platoon of soldiers, who in turn pointed their tiny rifles at the Eiffel Tower. Even the settee and armchairs were littered with brass items waiting for the attentions of Helen's yellow polishing cloth.

Any light that entered the room reflected from the burnished surfaces, glittering like banks of fairy-lights.

Edward turned on his wife and growled, 'This fixation with your brass collection has got to stop. Do you hear me? I won't stand for it any longer. You just sit there all day polishing the things. And when you're not polishing, you're buying more.'

'But I find it so relaxing . . . and the doctor says relaxation is the key to the healing process. I have to think about my heart condition, you know.'

It was on Edward's lips to tell her that thousands of other people were recovering from heart attacks, but none of *them* filled their houses to overflowing with brass objects. He would find a way to put a stop to this. One way or the other, he would stop her.

'There's an antique fair in town this afternoon, Edward. I hear there's a selection of brass-framed mirrors for sale. Will you drive me there?'

Edward spun round on his heel to face her. 'Mirrors? For goodness sake, haven't you been listening to me? You've got brass trinkets in every inch of this room, now you want to hang the things on the wall? Mirrors indeed . . .' His voice was a roar of fury.

Helen clutched the figurine in one arm as though it was an infant she was protecting from some terrible fate. Her other hand patted her chest. 'My heart, my heart,' she mumbled.

Edward drew himself up short. 'I'm going out,' he said. 'I may be late. Don't bother waiting up.' As he strode towards the door he stumbled over a large brass pot. Aiming a vicious kick at it, he threw a withering glance at his wife and then, with a slam of the door, was gone.

Helen stared at the closed door and said, 'If you feel that strongly about it, I'll get a taxi.'

Edward drove into town and had been walking the streets for almost an hour, gazing idly into shop windows, when his eye caught sight of a large box in the window of 'Pranks'. He pushed the plate glass door open and entered.

He had stepped into an Aladdin's cave of fancy-dress costumes and practical jokes. For a few moments he drifted from one display cabinet to another until the sales assistant approached and asked if he was looking for anything in particular.

'That monster box in the window. Can I see it?'

The assistant spilled the contents of the box onto the wooden counter. There was a wig, fake scars, bolts that fitted onto either side of the neck, make-up, plastic boils and vampire fangs. 'Do you have anything more realistic?' Edward asked innocently.

The assistant nodded. 'We have a deluxe set, but it's rather expensive.'

'Let's have a look.' Edward rubbed his hands together with glee.

He spent the next few hours visiting second-hand clothes shops around the town. By the end of the day everything he needed had been crammed into two plastic carrier bags which he stowed on the back seat of his car.

Darkness had fallen when Edward's car rolled silently into the driveway, the headlights switched off so as not to give Helen any warning of his arrival. He peered out the windscreen to where the bedroom light burned behind closed curtains.

In his mind's eye he could see her, sitting up in bed with a selection of brass vases and horse buckles lying in the folds of the duvet, a yellow cloth in her hand.

'Poor old girl,' Edward grinned. 'You're about to get the surprise of your life. . . or death.'

Reaching into the back seat of the car, he hauled over the carrier bags. From one he took a long black coat and slipped it on. He was not a small man, and had difficulty manoeuvring himself in the space between the back of the seat and the steering wheel. Even so, the coat was several sizes too large for him.

Next, he pulled a jersey from the bag and stuffed it up under the shoulder so that it formed a hump, unbalancing him and giving a grotesque outline to his frame.

He pulled a latex rubber mask from the other bag and tugged it over his head, fitting it snugly to his face with his palms. He could feel the warmth of his breath and the clamminess of rubber on his flesh. He tried to see the finished result in the rear-view mirror, but could only make out the outline of his head and the glint of his eyes in the darkness.

The effect would be horrific, he knew that. The mask had been horrible enough when it had lain limply on the shop counter. It would certainly give Helen a shock, enough to make her heart skip a beat - forever.

He pushed his hands into a pair of clawed, leather gloves, pulling on one talon at a time. The effect was complete.

Edward pushed the front door of his house open and slipped inside. Closing it silently behind him, he leaned against the door for a while to let his eyes become accustomed to the dark. He could hear the hiss of his breath trapped behind the rubber of the mask, and could feel the steady thump of his pulse in the hollow of his throat.

'You are in for such a fright, old girl,' he breathed into the darkness. 'Your old ticker will never stand the shock. The perfect murder.'

He crept forward, listening for any sound of movement from the room above. His tread was light upon the carpet as he padded past the dark form of the telephone table and came to the bottom of the stairs.

Placing his toes on the first step, he transferred his weight forward. The wooden boards creaked slightly. He leaned forward and started to climb the stairs on all fours, like a toddler, spreading his weight.

Step by step, he climbed. Hands splayed, feeling the coarseness of the carpet through the palms of the gloves.

As his head rose above the top step and came level with the landing, he moved into the circle of light cast from the brass lampstand outside the bedroom door.

In that moment he saw the dark, deformed figure crouching in the far corner. Torn, fleshy face; gouged eye; tufts of hair and an evil sneer below the wildest eyes he had ever seen.

A cold ball of terror punched him in the chest. It was as though he had been hit with the full force of a sledge-hammer. He teetered on the edge of the step, then he was suddenly falling backwards, his hands flailing in a frantic attempt to catch hold of the banister.

On hearing the scream and the series of bone-crunching thumps, Helen pulled herself out of bed and cried, 'Is that you, Edward?'

She moved towards the door and peered through the open crack, but could only see the empty landing.

Gingerly opening the door, she stepped into the darkness and called her husband's name. Moving onto the landing she saw the body lying in a twisted heap at the bottom of the stairs, limbs twisted at impossible angles.

A gasp came from her lips. Reaching out for support, her fingers grasped the brass frame of the full-length antique mirror she had bought that very day.

The Potato Peeler

by

K O'Brien

The kitchen smelled of grease and burnt toast. A bowl of peeled potatoes sat on the draining board next to the sink. On a small, wooden table - its surface scarred and peeling - lay a bag of groceries.

Margaret Brennan sat in an armchair in the tiny sitting room. She was watching television. A cat purred and rubbed against her fat legs.

She sighed. 'C'mon, puss.'

The cat followed her into the kitchen where she emptied the remains of a tin of cat food into a saucer. She placed the dish on the dirty linoleum floor. The feline gulped down the meat.

Margaret wandered into the hall, rubbed a finger along a small, glass fronted display cabinet and inspected the dust. She studied her reflection in the brass framed wall mirror. Absently, she touched the mole on her cheek and tugged the long black hairs that sprouted from the blemish. A few came away in her fingers but many more remained.

Shuffling back to the kitchen, she pulled a sack from under the sink. She dropped a few potatoes on to the draining board and began to peel them. When each was finished, she let them plop into the bowl beside the others.

'I'm going to peel about fifty today, Puss. What d'you think of that?'

The small, black and white cat sniffed the air and meowed.

'Yes,' she crooned, 'fifty of dem.'

As she carried out her task, she studied the world from her kitchen window. She watched women struggle from vehicles of all shapes and sizes, carrying large bags of groceries, scolding tantrum torn children. Toddlers, their faces smeared with jam or ice cream and imprisoned in their high tech pushchairs, looked on witlessly as older brothers and sisters showed them the way towards the complete demoralisation and subjugation of the adult species.

Margaret jerked in surprise at the sudden rap on the front door. She dropped the half peeled potato into the sink and went into the hall.

Someone had stuffed paper and dog excrement through her letter box. She swore and opened the front door. A crowd of youths were standing by the stairwell of the building.

'Spider!' they called in unison. 'Spider!'

Margaret scooped up the paper and faeces, throwing it at the crowd. 'Piss off ye little sods.'

'Fuck off yersel, ye ugly bastard!' yelled a curly haired boy.

Then, still shouting obscenities at the woman, the crowd disappeared into the stairwell.

Margaret stood, panting with fear, her legs quivering, by the door. She listened. Silence. When she was satisfied that they had gone, she went back inside, locking the front door.

She paused at the mirror, stroking her mole. It looked like a spider crawling over her face. They're right, she thought, I am ugly. She stared in disgust at her own reflection, straight, shapeless hair, pig-like eyes behind thick lensed spectacles, cheeks like livid, red welts. She wondered what it would have been like if she had been attractive enough to get herself a husband. Wiping tears from her eyes, she returned to the kitchen.

Her mood brightened as she peeled her twenty sixth potato.

'Past the halfway mark, Puss.'

She watched the grey clouds gather in the sky. Soon, large spots of rain streaked her window. Through the glass, she watched people running for cover, wrestling with umbrellas as the wind grew in strength. The street traffic now glided past, lights ablaze and windscreen wipers beating back and forth. A puddle was forming in the weather beaten grooves on her window sill and, as it grew dark, Margaret could see the whole universe of stars reflected in the watery murk, a few feet away from where she stood.

'Thirty peeled now, Puss. You never know who might drop by. I need to be ready to cook something.'

The cat purred and jumped on to the draining board, stepping lithely between potato peelings.

Margaret laughed. 'Feeding time again? Oh you hungry puss, you.'

Margaret opened another tin of meat and tipped half of it into the saucer for her pet. She continued with her task of peeling.

She sighed as she finished the last potato. 'All done.'

She picked up the cat and carried him to the sitting room. She sat in her old armchair and the black and white tom fell asleep in her lap. She watched television.

She woke with a start. She had fallen asleep in the chair. Grimacing at the awful taste in her mouth, she glanced at the clock. It was midnight. It looks like I won't be getting a visitor tonight, she thought as she tipped the unhappy tom cat on to the floor. Then she remembered, nobody ever came. She did not know of anyone that might want to visit her.

Before she went to bed, she tipped all of the potatoes into a black, plastic bag and put it outside her door with the rest of her rubbish. Tomorrow, she would peel some more.

Artifice

by

Gary McAdam

Chemical analysis of the hair proved it to be dark brown. Cells from the follicle belonged to a male. The root was grey.

'So, were looking for a forty to sixty year old male Caucasian with dark brown hair who knows the area. That narrows the search to about fifty thousand people.' The DI said in a cocktail tone of sarcasm and disgust.

The forensic technician, however, remained unperturbed, save his habitual finger drumming.

He spoke tiredly to his superior. 'We're looking for a clinical madman who hates leaving tracings of his comings and goings, maybe extending this. . . trait to everything he does in everyday life. Why else do you think he shot that bomb? Any detonator would be reeking with dabs, even after use.' He said. The technician was a close friend of DI Andrej, and thus felt he had every right to give an un-heeded conversation stopper in his usual, obnoxious style. But the technicians words practically landed physically onto Andrejs ears.

DI Andrej was not ordinarily squeamish, but the record of the high street bombing captured on a high speed anti-crime closed circuit TV system still filled him with horror. Looking for the source of the bullet that had ignited the bottle stuffed with high explosive on slow motion also gave Andrej a clear, uninterrupted view of the Saturday shoppers in the precinct being torn to shreds with shards of concrete and metal. Horrific frame by horrific frame.

Although it was a memory that Andrej would rather not harbour, the endless playbacks and scrutinization of the bombing proved to be valuable to the case - it was Andrej himself that had noticed the gun-flash, eight frames along, in the window of a disused building. This led the investigation unit to search the disused building which in turn had led to the discovery of the hair in a disused flat.

Unfortunately, that was all they found. One hair.

Preliminary analysis of the hair was compared to the Eco-Caution on the day of the bombing. Carbon dioxide matched. Carbon monoxide matched. Lead, chlorine, sulphur dioxide, tritium . . . The percentage of all airborne contaminants matched the contaminants lodged between the scales of the hair - and had proved that the hair had come from the assassins head.

'Got something, boss. I've done a rundown of the shampoo he uses.' The forensic technician said seriously.

The DI sniffed. 'Well. That's us got our man, then.' Again, dripping with sarcasm.

'Actually, it helps us no end. One of the ingredients here looks like a flora extract.' He continued to tap the keys on his console. 'That's affirmative. Computers matched it with . . . well, there's a definite link between this stuff and honeysuckle sap. Some genetically engineered strain.'

The DI paused and thought out loud. 'Hardly be much honeysuckle in the UK anymore, never mind high-grade engenetics flora. What am I saying? Hardly much free growing stuff like that since around 2020. Must be expensive shampoo.'

'Oh, it is, Steve. The best. And here's something else. I think this ought to clinch the deal - electron microscope pictures.' The technician, said, smiling.

The investigator was presented with the electron image on the main monitor. The hair looked more like a phosphorus green tree-trunk. The technician zoomed into the tip of the hair. Andrej noticed that a ridge stretching across the flat surface of the hair-end was causing the technician most interest.

'See that?' the technician said, pointing out the ridge to Andrej. 'That ridge appears when the hair breaks in two, where the two blades of a pair of scissors meet.'

'So?' The DI said, more confused with every passing moment.

'Watch this.' The technician said, zooming in further to the pinnacle of the ridge. Dead microbes were now apparent, and the further the technician zoomed in, the more those microbes looked like gigantic slug-like beasts. And there were other light areas as well. .

'See them? Between the bacteria.' The technician said.

'What?'

'Crystals.' The technician quietly, but passionately said, happy to have found something useful on his own.

'Crystals?'

'Crystals.'

'So? What about them?'

The forensic sighed. 'Minute shards of crystal that have dislodged from the blades of a pair of scissors. A special type of crystal that makes the scissors razor sharp. It's unusually expensive, and I believe that this sort of thing is unique to posh barbers and hairdressers. So were looking for a very rich man.

DI Andrej smiled. 'Great . If we could get PR onto all the high class hair joints and get them to collect and index samples of their clients hair . . . I mean, sooner or later our bombers going to have to go to his local for a trim.'

He stared at the electron microscope pictures for a few moments before turning to the forensic. 'Could we match the DNA of this hair to another of the bomber's hairs?'

The technician nodded.

Andrej clucked happily, patted the scientist on the back and returned to his desk.

It had taken all of two weeks for a positive DNA match to turn up. It had taken all of ten minutes to rush the luxury mansion and arrest the bomber after positive identification. It took less than ten seconds for a Mister Robert Simpson to collapse with shock after his arrest.

'You'll get nothing more from this one, inspector.' The cardiology doctor said, switching off the life-support apparatus. 'Heart attack and brain haemorrhage rolled into one. He didn't' have a chance. Sorry.'

Andrej looked at the body.

'What will happen to him?' Andrej asked, an uneasy feeling of concern sweeping over him.

The doctor began filling in an LCD tablet form and momentarily looked up at the policeman. 'Spend a couple of days on a slab before autopsy. He isn't on the organ or limb donor list, but his pacemaker makes good salvage.'

'He had a heart attack despite his pacemaker?'

'Yeah. Happens sometimes. Course, that haemorrhage didn't help matters either. But, his pacemaker's one of those high-tech state of the art things. Japanese, I think. Good haul. Could go to someone less able to afford it than him.'

Andrej studied the man. Fat. Fifties. Bald. A suit that cost the same as Andrej's car. Richest man in the city, easy. What could his motive be?

'Look, doctor,' Andrej said cautiously, 'when this guy's wife turns up, do you mind if I break the news?'

'No. Please do, makes my job easier.'

'Good. There's something else I want you to do for me. Police business this time.'

Andrej stood at the entrance of casualty ward and watched as the navy blue Bentley skycar glided over the rooftops of the houses on the horizon. The tritium powered limo then descended, manoeuvred towards casualty and hovered between two road cars at the roadside. Mrs Simpson then more or less erupted from the side of the vehicle and kept running towards the casualty entrance. Andrej then stretched out his arms and caught her in mid-sprint.

She was the same as her husband. Repulsively rich, and not afraid to show it either. Silk suit underneath a shammy leather and mink coat. Sickening. The price of her coat could easily feed a family of four for a year. And, either money had preserved her youth artificially, or she really was in her mid twenties.

'Mrs Simpson, I am your husband's arresting officer.' Andrej said calmly, despite the womans frantic struggling. 'I'm afraid your husband died ten minutes ago.'

She abruptly stopped trying to haul herself away from Andrej and stared at him disbelievingly. Too disbelievingly, Andrej thought.

'How?' she asked.

'Heart attack. There was nothing the doctors could do.' Andrej replied in his self-taught and well rehearsed 'I understand' tone. Then he cleared his throat. 'Mrs Cheri-Ann Simpson, I am arresting you on the suspicion of the murder of twelve people by bombing on the twenty third of December 2033 last year. You do not have to say anthi. . .'

'What? You're arresting me? But it was my husband's hair you found!' she protested, this time in true disbelievement.

This time, Andrej wore his fake 'puzzled' expression. 'I don't remember telling you about a hair? The press weren't informed about any forensic evidence either, under the anti-terrorism Act. And nobody was told about the search on the derelict flat. Now, how did you get to know about the hair, Mrs Simpson?'

She didn't answer. Uniformed policemen joined Andrej.

'Why did you do it?' Andrej asked, again, in his 'understanding' tone. 'Money? Crime of passion? What?'

Finally she broke her silence and looked at the ground. 'A lot of reasons.'

Andrej was emotionless. 'Go on.'

'At first I wanted a divorce, but later I decided I wanted the house and the money and the car too.' She gave a sweeping look towards the Bentley before continuing. 'I used my husband's hunting rifle and laser sight. I thought that if I set him up, I could keep everything if he was in jail. Having a heart attack was a risk, but also a bonus, I suppose. How did you know I did it?'

'His pacemaker had a built in polygraph, in case you didn't know. We recovered and studied the polygraph record chip. There was no increase in pulse, blood pressure, respiration, perspiration, electrical skin resistance or temperature at the time of the bombing; he certainly didn't do it . . . besides, I just couldn't find a motive, and then you walked into my life, see?'

Andrej smiled sarcastically. 'By the way, why did you want a divorce?'

'He was a stiff. Dull, straight, boring . . . only cared for his mining company. He drove me mad,' she said. 'Can you imagine being married to a man like that?'

'Yes,' Andrej said, 'Every pay-day.'

He clicked his fingers at the uniformed policeman. 'Take her away.'

The Drawing

by

Kevin McInally

Paul Jenkins was a second year Art Teacher at Johnstone High. A strange and almost unusual event happened to him in the year 1991. A young girl with cool, ice-cutting eyes turned up for the first class that term. The other children were the usual pimpled-faced kids. This girl stood out a mile, (a hundred!) from the other children. Forget it he told himself. As a treat he would let them draw whatever they wanted to.

He gave them all a sheet of A4 paper. As the pimpled kids drew M C Hammer and other things he watched the young girl drawing. Her name was Nicola Stirling. He knew because it was written on the drawing paper at the top. The square piece of paper was turning into what looked like a 15th Century sailing boat on the edge of a lagoon. He bent over her to get a better look at the 'ship'. She looked up and he asked her where she had seen such a ship. The reply hit him like a Frank Bruno punch.

'That is the ship on which I travelled to get to the New Land.'

She said this in a *I'm - not - telling - a -lie - voice*. Paul Jenkins bent over her more to get a better look at the ship. The name of the ship was carved on the side. *S S Long-hurt.* His eyes looked at the pale moonlight which seemed to light the night up in the drawing. A strange sense of sudden *deja-vu* crawled over him as the bell went for end of class.

He took all finished drawings in one hand and sat behind his desk. He looked at the drawing (drawing, drawing, drawing) and began to shiver for no reason.

The next time he had that class for a lesson was on Wednesday. He asked the class to finish their drawings and write an explanation about what they had drawn.

Nicola Stirling was looking at him intently. It made him uneasy. . . very uneasy. A great many pieces of paper lay in front of him but he was holding Nicola's drawing in his hand. A master drawing was what warmly greeted his eyes. The ship was anchored just off an island. A small breeze hit his face. *He* was in the drawing! The ship's mast was blowing. The water wrinkled in the moonlight, the trees made sounds in the wind. He turned round and saw a girl no older than fourteen screaming. That girl was Nicola. A cannibal was putting - or trying to put - her into a steaming pot. Then he was in his chair. He was in 1992 not 17 something. He turned the paper around and read the explanation to all this madness.

I drew this from my memory of when we went to the New Land. I was killed that night and this is what I saw before I died.

Kathleen Turner

Paul got up and ran to the records' room. He looked up 'ships'. He found what he was looking for. It was the file named S S Longhurt. He read the trips it had made. When he reached the end his heart stopped.

LAST TRIP: 1792   America: 'The New Land'

LOST: One girl killed by cannibals on a
                        Monday night.
                        Two more were lost.

NAMES OF
THOSE LOST: Kathleen Turner, Steve McKinn,
                        Sir Edward Kuig.

No Title

by

Malcolm Milne

Friday, 4 p.m. Pleased at the prospect of no more work until Monday, I assemble my collection of books, pens, envelopes with hastily written notes on them, and bundle them all into a ridiculously small folder. I am now ready to embark on my weekly 'adventure'. That's right, I'm, going to the library.

I park my car directly outside the library entrance and walk briskly in. Upon entering I am cheered by the familiar sight of two old worthies in their customary places at the newspaper lecterns, perusing the local paper. As usual they have split the paper into two parts: she assiduously scanning the births, deaths and marriages section, he engrossed in the sports supplement. Occasionally the foreboding silence of the main hall is pierced by the woman remarking in a chillingly harsh voice, 'I see auld Wilson's deid then.'

'. . . Oh aye,' comes the half-hearted reply.

Strangely reassured by the old couple's presence, I slowly make my way past shelf upon shelf of extremely musty smelling reference books, all arranged in perfect chronological order. Adjacent to the shelves are two flea-bitten armchairs, placed back to back, which are presumably provided for the use of the public to browse the reference books. However, they are currently occupied by two scruffy looking gentlemen who are fast asleep, seemingly propping each other up like book-ends. The smell of stale alcohol hangs suspiciously heavy in the air. Their down at heel appearance almost suggests that they have brought the decrepit chairs with them. Idly considering this thought, the combination of odours of decaying books and the equally stagnating drunks becomes overwhelming, and I decide to move on, presently arriving at my intended destination: The South Reading Room.

Ostensibly provided for reference purposes of valuable books and manuscripts, the small and compact reading room exudes an air of Victorian elegance, richly furnished with a very grand walnut veneer table, which is inlaid with a smooth matt green Basil leather. Surrounding the table are twelve large, commodious chairs, which only adds to the persistent air of exclusiveness. Silence reigns. I sit down quietly at seat A3 and wait patiently for one of the library staff to attend, and in the process manage to drop my over-laden folder. Amidst the mournful calm, the ensuing din seems to be amplified ten fold, bringing disapproving stares and 'tut-tuts' from the other three studious occupants.

Inwardly cringing with embarrassment, I am approached by a rather demure librarian, dressed conservatively in a brown tweed skirt, matching brown moccasins, and a fair isle pattern sleeveless tank-top. 'Can I help you sir?' she enquires, timorously.

'. . . Y Yes, can I see the bound volumes of The Scotsman newspaper, 1914-1918 please?'

'Certainly sir, do you have your reader's ticket?'

'Oh yes I've got it here somewhere.' More audible fumbling ensues as I search in my jacket for the elusive ticket, finding it in my breast pocket. She gives it a cursory glance, then whispers, 'That'll be a couple of minutes,' before scuttling away to some darkened recess deep within the bowels of the library.

Soon she returns with three weighty tomes and lays them carefully, one on top of another, on the table in front of me. This act of seemingly effortless strength belies her thin waif-like appearance an assumption which immediately makes me feel rather guilty, prompting me to blurt out loudly, 'Oh thank you very much.' She peers at me rather oddly through her half-rimmed spectacles before swiftly walking away. It is at this point I am aware of the feeling of three pairs of eyes boring a hole in the back of my head. Once again I've incurred the tacit wrath of my reading room companions. Deciding that dumb insolence is the better part of valour, I throw them a sickly apologetic grin/smile and proceed to intensely study the text in front of me.

Soon I am lost in the fragile, yellowing pages of the newspaper, immersed in articles referring to the First World War, my own particularly favourite subject. Tales of heroic endeavour are recounted, such as 'the advance to Passchendaele' and of 'the enemy's precarious hold on village'. Reports are decidedly sketchy, and the columnist is always referred to as 'our correspondent', alluding to the secrecy and caution that was inherent in war-time Britain. Lower down the page there are further perfunctory reports of 'British success in Palestine - Bersheeka occupied, eighteen hundred prisoners and nine guns captured'.

On a lighter note there are various advertisements with olde-worlde slogans such as, 'Quaker's Oats satisfy the children's needs, much more nourishing and economical than bread'. Another ad asks, 'Are you anaemic, run down? A martyr to indigestion? Then try Wincarnis, it's the wine of life'. In the extreme right-hand corner is the 'money and commerce' column, which reports that, 'the markets are very dull and inert'.

Thinking to myself that sub-heading could easily be describing today's economy I muse over another advert for 'Woodbine cigarettes, 20 for 9d' when a voice suddenly stirs me, politely saying, 'Excuse me sir, but we're closing now.' It's my friend the petite assistant. Glancing at my watch, and amazed to find that two hours have elapsed since my very public entrance, I hurriedly gather my belongings noticing that my three colleagues have vanished without even saying good-bye. Smiling at this mildly amusing observation, I make my way out. Next Friday can hardly come soon enough . . .

The White House

by

Patricia Flanders

As the engine spluttered and then stopped the woman looked round her, wondering what to do next. She did not know this place and the snow had worsened steadily over the last hour. Already the windscreen and windows were covered in white and the eerie glow made her even more nervous. She knew she would have to leave the car. She hoped there would be a house nearby with a telephone and she could decide then the best thing to do. She looked down ruefully at the high-heeled gold sandals, so right for a cocktail party, so wrong for tramping through the snow. She pulled her thin elegant coat more closely round her and opened the door. She gasped in shock as her foot sank into the soft snow. She had no idea it was so deep. In town of course it did not settle but here, in the country, it could have lain undisturbed for days. A brief look round showed no traces of tyre marks. She suspected she had missed the signpost in the poor light and turned on to a side road. However it must lead somewhere, she thought, a farm-house perhaps. She thought wistfully of her friends in the bright warm room, laughing and talking. Perhaps someone would ask where she was and then be distracted, as they were offered another drink or a sandwich and she would be forgotten.

She walked on and on, losing all track of time. Once she pulled back the cuff of her coat with stiff clumsy fingers but the watch face was only a blur in the swirling snow. The poor sandals were saturated and her feet and legs felt numb as she stumbled on. The thin coat clung to her, wet and cold, and her soaking hair was plastered to her head. There was nothing to be seen except the trees flanking the road, and she stopped, un-certain what to do. She doubted if she could make it back to where she had left the car but surely she must soon come to a building of some sort.

On either side of the white fields stretching into the distance dazzled her eyes and misty shapes formed and reformed, coming closer until, peering into the whiteness, she could distinguish two figures. A little girl skated cautiously round the edge of a glittering lake, looking back occasionally for approval. A voice rang clearly through the cold crisp air, each word striking her like a stone.

'She is only one of twins. The other died as she was born. They showed her to me and I held her in my arms.'

The little skater stumbled and fell. As she clutched her bruised knees she saw the other girl in the centre of the lake, an ethereal dainty figure, sweeping gracefully across the glittering ice, her silver hair streaming behind her. She smiled gently, her eyes warm and friendly, and seemed about to speak before she dissolved in the coldness of the evening.

It was almost dark now and the soft snow still fell relentlessly. Panic swept over her as she trudged on, her feet sinking deeper into the snow with each step. Her breathing sounded ragged and uneven, and there was a sharp pain in her chest as she drew in the freezing air. She knew her strength was failing and unless she found shelter soon she would collapse. Perhaps if she rested for a few minutes she would feel better, and she stumbled to the side of the road, leaning thankfully against a tree trunk, closing her tired eyes to shut out the glare of the snow.

'Did she have a name, Mama?' the wistful little voice asked again, although she had been told so many times.

'Yes, I called her Angel, because she looked so beautiful, lying in my arms, so pale and peaceful.'

As always tears formed in the sad eyes and the little girl wrung her hands in despair. Too far away to touch, yet near enough to see clearly, the dainty creature in her silky white dress, her hair adorned with trembling pearly flowers, turned her impossibly beautiful face towards the little girl and smiled in compassion.

The woman was really frightened now. She must not drift away into dreams again. She must get to her feet and struggle on although her limbs felt heavy and useless, and unwilling to obey her commands. She stumbled on for a few yards, her wet clothes encasing her body like an icy sheet. She strained forward hoping to make out something, anything, but the wind had risen and the snow was beating into her face.

As she looked down at her stiff whitened coat she remembered her reflection in the mirror of her bedroom, her mother's face behind her.

'She would have been a lovely bride,' her mother said, pushing the girl's hair back from her ears in a gesture of hopelessness. A cold hand clutched at the girl's heart and that day too was spoiled. She moved through her wedding day, unmoved and unfeeling, as if she had no right to claim happiness or affection that belonged to someone else. The colour had leeched from the roses she carried and their sweet perfume faded away. The other girl walked beside her, unbearably lovely in clouds of pearly lace, holding out her frail white hand as if to comfort her,

She shook her head to dissolve the memory of that April day when the trees had been burdened with white blossom above her head, moving slightly in the gentle breeze.

'Please help me. Somebody help me,' she whispered in despair.

She thought she could hear someone answering her but it was only snow falling from the smaller branches. It had sounded like his voice that very last time, hushed by grief and hopelessness.

'Nothing makes you happy,' he had said, 'I don't know what it is you want. I would do anything for you but you seem to be looking for something I cannot give you.'

She had looked long and wonderingly into his eyes but she knew she could never believe him and so she let him go. Better by far than suffering the terrible pain when he turned his head and saw his real love beckoning, and he must follow her. She had seen the other girl, lovely beyond words, looking at her, not him, with a sorrowful smile that gave her a tenderness which made her irresistibly beautiful, before the memory faded from her mind.

She knew she could not go on any longer. She was exhausted and the darkness was closing in on her. She felt herself slide to the ground without being able to save herself and her eyelids felt so heavy she had to let them close over her aching eyes.

When she opened them again she saw the outline of a large house ahead and her heart rose suddenly. Everything would be all right now. No hurry, just one step at a time. She put one hand out to push open the tall white wrought iron gates and made her way along the straight path to the porch with its glistening columns. The heavy door swung open soundlessly at her touch and she walked slowly into the lofty hall across the white marble tiles, which felt like silk beneath her feet. Above her a dozen chandeliers glittered and dazzled blindingly. She knew she must climb the sweeping stairway that led upwards, disappearing into a white haze far above her head. Each stair seemed to grow more steep than the last but she kept going, not curious because she felt she knew this house and questions were no longer necessary.

Finally, she reached the top and made her way along a corridor. On each side of her, door after door swung open to reveal white-walled and white carpeted rooms, inviting her to enter but she knew she must not stay. She walked on and on until finally she came to the room at the end of the corridor. In the far corner she could see someone lying, as if curled up in sleep. As she made her way across the room, the walls and ceiling seemed to disintegrate into a million white glistening flakes that swirled about her head but they were warm and comforting as they brushed against her cheek. She glided forward through the feathery mist until she reached the still figure in the corner. Desperately tired now, more weary than she could ever remember, she knelt beside the other person and brushed away the white flakes that covered her. Without surprise she recognised her own face gazing up at her, so pale and wan that her heart contracted in pity. She knew then her ordeal was over and she need struggle no more. She lay down, taking her other self into her arms in loving forgiveness and sank thankfully into endless peace.

It Reminded Me Of Rome

by

Stuart McDonald

(brmng, brrnng. . brrnng, brrnng. . brrnn) 'Falding 661 - Barbara Ritchie speaking . . . Oh hello, Mrs Price, how nice of you to phone. How are . . .?'

' . . . on duty at the hospital canteen?' Should I've been there?'

' . . . Oh dear, I am sorry - but I'm sure you managed to find someone to . . . '

' . . . Oh, you had to do it yourself! When was this, Mrs Price?'

' . . . The sixteenth? Oh but we were away on holiday then . . . '

' . . . yes, we decided to go on the spur of the moment . . . To Florida.'

' . . . Yes, Florida.'

' . . . Well, d'you know my friend Cathy . . . Cathy Woods? . . . no, well her husband Malcolm had just retired and I said to Steven 'what d'you think if the four of us go away for a holiday'? and we managed to get this trip to Florida almost at once! Steve's very senior now and can take time off when he likes . . . Yes, isn't he lucky!'

' . . . No, we didn't stay in the one place, we were on one of those coach tours from a place called Fort Lauderdale to New Orleans and stayed in different hotels. Normally, of course, Steven and I would've hired a car but, as we were with our friends, we didn't have to mix much with the other tourists - you never know how comfortable you would be with them, do you . . . '

' . . . On the coach? No, there's not much chance to talk over the high backs of these seats, is there? I did see Malcolm speaking to them a few times - but then, with his position on the Council, he was used to dealing with all kinds of people!'

' . . . Yes, we were near the Kennedy Space Centre. Malcolm went there but I wanted to see the shops in Orlando - beautiful shopping area, it reminded me of Rome! - and of course Cathy was with me.'

' . . . No, Steve came with us, he didn't seem to want to see these space things after all. He's such a tease! He said he'd better be my cashier and keep the travellers cheques and credit cards.'

' . . . Yes, they're all in his name, he says the Bank Manager said that's the safest way.'

' . . . Yes, we were at Disney World - you sound as though you know all about there?'

' . . . oh, you've been!'

'. . . Yes, I found it very nice but, I'd soon seen enough so we were only there for the morning. I wanted to go back to the Shopping Mall that Gary - he was the courier on our coach - had told me was worth a visit. He was so good! Gave me lots of addresses of good shops and told me just to mention his name and I'd be taken care of! I must write to the tour company and say how helpful he was.'

'. . . Yes, you do hear of some but we must've been very lucky. As I've said to Steven, 'if you're nice to them . . .' Gary even told me about Bentley's who make wonderful luggage.'

'. . . Yes, I had to buy another case to hold everything - I did get a bit carried away, but Cathy is so good at telling me what I look best in!'

'. . . I really didn't notice if she bought anything for herself, but - well, between you and me, I think they have to be, um, - a little careful with the pennies.'

'. . . Oh, she's such a good friend - I've known her for ages.'

'. . . I could've bought more but Steve said the customs wouldn't let any more through this year.'

'. . . Funny you should say that, but Steve didn't seem to take to Gary very much. And he was such a nice boy - there was only one time he was - well - just a little forgetful, but it had been a long day and he'd had to answer such a lot of silly questions from some of the others about history and stuff! We were on a tour which took us all day down the Florida Keys - that's a string of islands over a hundred miles long - to a place called Key West.'

'. . . Oh, you've heard of it?'

'. . . Yes, very nice with such expensive houses but, oh it was a long day! Well, when we set off in the morning, Gary said over the coach microphone that we were going on to the next hotel next morning and had to have our cases out of our hotel rooms by six-thirty a.m. sharp so that the porters could collect them. The group was in two coaches and we were on the second coach. Gary said he would give us sticky labels with '2' on them to put on our cases so they'd know which coach to put them on.

'Well, at the end of the trip to the Keys, we didn't get back to Fort Lauderdale until after eleven at night.'

'. . . Yes, I was very tired by then. Well, as the coach got near to the hotel, Gary said, 'Don't forget you're to be up sharp tomorrow for an early start', then one of the other people on the coach, a Welsh lady sitting at the back, shouted out, 'But Gary, what about our 'number two 's'? And d'you know, everybody laughed, which I thought was un-fair, because I was wondering the same thing as I didn't want my new case with all the things I'd bought to get lost!'

'. . . Oh dear, Mrs Price, that's a nasty cough - have you choked on something?'

'. . . Yes, you go off and have a drink of water. And remember, anytime you want me to do a spell at the canteen - or anything else - just let me know. I'm always willing to help other people as you know very well, it's no trouble to me.'

'. . . No, don't say anything else, dear, you'll be fine when you've had a drink.'

'. . . 'Bye.'

'. . . 'Bye.'

(. . . nnng)

Balloons On A Taxi

by

Margaret Stoddart

The sun shone brightly on Scotland's capital city. The streets of the centre of Edinburgh dominated by the castle, high on its rock, were awash with tourists. An air of gaiety prevailed. A day to enjoy oneself.

An upmarket, chauffeur driven limousine purred softly as it crouched awaiting takeoff at the traffic lights, the junction presently controlled by traffic wardens.

'I wonder what is causing the hold-up?' remarked one of the car's two passengers, an expensively suited executive. His companion, several years his junior, was similarly garbed; the two were obviously engaged on business rather than pleasure.

'I think it is the taxi drivers' picnic sir,' the immaculately liveried chauffeur volunteered. 'The day they take underprivileged children out for a treat.'

At that moment the procession came into view; a long line of gaily decorated cabs festooned with brightly coloured balloons and streamers; smiling children waving to the passers-by, some clutching flags, their happy faces framed in the assorted reds, blues, greens and yellows.

'Does your heart good to see it, doesn't it sir?' The chauffeur returned the wave of one of the excited little boys.

As the pageant passed in front of the windscreen like a scene from a movie, a strange transformation crossed the features of the older man. He was good-looking in his mid to late forties with that air of dynamic life-force which marks the successful tycoon but at this moment a soft sadness crept into his eyes, almost misting them over. He fell silent and still.

'Everything all right sir?' the younger man enquired. The only thing which differed between the two men other than age was speech. the senior man's deep, pleasant voice was decidedly regional, local Edinburgh, whereas the other conversed easily in what is generally referred to as received pronunciation.

'What? Did you say something? I am sorry. I was miles away.'

'I said is everything all right sir?' the younger man repeated as the last taxi disappeared from view and the car moved smoothly forward.

'Yes, yes of course,' Another silence followed then with a wistful little smile the older man turned to his colleague. 'Do you know Graham, I once went on that picnic.'

'You sir?' Graham's eyes widened.

'A-ha! Yes I went twice actually.' He gave a soft chuckle. 'You have realised that I am what is laughingly called a self made man but I doubt if you know just how underprivileged my childhood was. My father never got over the war, my mother got T.B. and I was cared for at the Childrens' Shelter. That is how I got my invitations to the picnics.'

Graham made no comment as his superior gazed thoughtfully ahead again, steeped no doubt in his personal memories but an odd little smile played around his own lips as some amusing thought occurred to him.

'I think Graham,' the self-made man said, jerking out of his reverie, 'I owe much of my success in life to those picnics. I remember feeling such a mixture of pleasure and gratitude and resentment. I knew the taxi owners and drivers meant well, that they acted from kindness of heart yet I felt it was charity and I hated that. It won't come as news to you that I possess a rather fierce pride. I promised myself then that one day I would own a taxi and I would be the person handing out pies, sweets and ice-cream,'

Graham laughed aloud. 'You have done somewhat better than that, eh sir?' A small sweep of hand and eye took in the luxury of the opulent car.

'True. Very true but it still leaves a boyhood dream unfulfilled.' He turned to look at his companion and noticed the impish grin still lingering on his face. 'You find it amusing? I hope you are not laughing at me?'

'Oh no sir,' Graham assured his boss. 'I wouldn't dare to laugh at you, but I do find it amusing.

The tycoon raised his eyebrows. 'Your reason had better by good,' he rejoined.

'I think you will be amused sir when you hear my story. You know my background was a great deal happier than your's. I also lived in Edinburgh but I had a nanny and one day when I was out with her, the taxis went by. I so wanted to join in and wave a balloon. I was very upset when she said I couldn't go I could not understand why we could not hail another taxi and follow. I had quite a tantrum in the street. I poured out the story to my mother when we got home screaming about how bad Nanny had been to me, how unfair not to let me run after those taxis. Mother tried to explain why I could not go but I would not be consoled. I cried and cried and was still crying when my father arrived home. I think that was the first time my parents tried to explain privilege to me. My little mind had to accept that I was too well-off to share in that treat. I recall even at that early age offering to swap some of my best toys but I finally got the message that my father's money could buy me lots of things but not everything. So, you see, your privilege influenced my thinking in later life. It's funny how our formative years stay with us.'

The pair sat in mutual silence for a short while, each mulling over the other one's unexpected revelation. Suddenly the older man sat up straight and addressed the chauffeur.

'Jack, turn round and follow those taxis. We'll catch them up and stop at a good quality sweet shop on the way.' He reached for his car phone and keyed out a number.

'Miss Taylor? Ross here. Graham and I will be a little late. What?' He glanced sideways at Graham and the men exchanged mischievous grins. 'Tell them two naughty boys are about to gatecrash a picnic.

Time Expired

by

Stuart McDonald

By the end of the meeting I knew that Roddy Fraser had to die. It had started weeks before, a knowledge that things were not right, and the climax came in my office. I made the decision with reluctance for over the years I had built up an affection for him. But then, decisions are my business and personal regrets cannot be allowed to influence them.

Roddy is a character. Tall and lean, with one of those raw Scots faces that go with long service in the Regular Army and shaving in cold water, he could be, by turns, totally charming or a cantankerous individual with a biting line in sarcasm. A difficult person to handle at any time and not universally liked, although some of his opinions seem to find favour.

I first came across him about three years ago when he was taken on as porter and handyman at the local electronics factory. I knew his background of course. He had some money from his pension and had supplemented it by doing odd jobs, simple building repairs or gardening, around the small Fife town, where he was a well-known figure. At first he seemed to do well. He was willing and always helpful, good for a bit of homespun philosophy or fatherly advice. He went to church on Sundays and supported the town's football team in winter, the cricket team in the summer. In fact, the only things marring his otherwise exemplary behaviour were an outspoken intolerance of those he considered fools, and the occasional drinking bout - of impressive duration. These sprees, once over, had no apparent effect.

Then about six months ago things began to change. His sharp tongue seemed to become more bitter and was heard more often. He snapped at people for no reason or totally ignored them. Gradually he became more withdrawn and his time-keeping increasingly erratic. His drinking intensified and the effects were beginning to show. No one could approach him without being brutally rebuffed and his indifference showed how little interest he had in them or in his job.

There was no particular reason why he shouldn't be wandering round the factory after everyone had gone home. After all, security was part of his responsibilities. But when he was discovered in the Research Office by the Managing Director, removing pages from project files, it was realised that the problem had reached a crisis. I knew that things had gone far enough. A meeting was arranged.

After he left I sat, idly fingering the onyx-handled paperknife on the desk. My room has that unnatural quiet that is a characteristic of modern offices. Strip lights and deep carpets, triple-glazing, and air-conditioning so efficient that you risk pneumonia just coming to work, pastel walls and oak panelling, tasteful displays of pot plants. Not what one might expect behind the facade of the Victorian mansion the company used as a headquarters perhaps, but pleasant enough. And I had my own possessions around me, the paperknife, photographs in silver frames, a couple of rather nice water-colours, and the huge blue and white Spode bowl that had been my grandmother's, to make it my special place. The bowl was filled with hyacinths that almost matched the deep blue of the pattern and their fragrance filled the room. A private world, cocooned from life's bustle, and therefore the ideal place in which to contemplate someone's death.

I considered the options. I had already decided on Roddy's demise and it was now surely only a means of finding a convincing way to achieve it. There would no doubt be an uproar when the news broke for he was something of a celebrity but I was equally sure that there would be satisfaction in certain quarters.

Could I hire a killer? No, perhaps not. There was no way I wanted to become involved in a murder investigation. So that ruled out guns and knives or things like poison unless it was so obscure that it would be untraceable. That thought was quickly discarded. First of all I had no idea if there was such a thing and secondly, if it was so obscure, how could I obtain it, far less set the scene for it to be administered? No, his death had to be either accidental or the result of illness. His recent inconsistent behaviour might indicate the latter, but how could this be brought about in just a few weeks? Painkillers perhaps, and an apparently self-adminstered overdose. It could be put about that Roddy had recently learned that he had some terminal disease. His altered behaviour pattern, which was becoming known, would reinforce this idea and his death would no doubt be interpreted as him taking the quick way out. Yes. Definitely a possibility.

Accidents were trickier. Either it had to be something that went tragically wrong during the routine of Roddy's life, like brake failure on his old banger, or a faulty electrical appliance in his cottage, or else he had to be given a logical reason for him to do something out of the ordinary which would have disastrous consequences. It would have been handy if he had done a bit of rough shooting. Accidents do happen when guns are being cleaned. Unfortunately Roddy was not one for countryside sports.

My secretary popped her head round the door to say goodnight and as I gathered the papers for that evening's meeting into my worn, old briefcase, I wondered how she would have reacted had she known that she worked for someone who was plotting a man's death.

The meeting, a golf-club affair, was long and boring and, after I had said my piece, I found my mind wandering to Roddy Fraser. His deteriorating conduct had even been discussed before the meeting started. Naturally I didn't join in but it confirmed my opinion that I could probably get away with the overdose idea. The more I thought about him though, the more I felt that an accident would be better. Perhaps, to do him justice, and as a sop to my own feelings for the Roddy I had known in the past, it would be good to make it an accident in heroic circumstances. But what? I still had no notions on that when the meeting broke up and, after a drink with the Secretary, I drove home.

As we prepared for bed, my wife and I chatted about tomorrow's programme and plans for the weekend. She was shopping in Edinburgh and I had a conference. We were meeting up at the golf-club for lunch. A bedtime conversation as normal as any between husband and wife. I never take work home.

The conference, a fortnightly affair, was due to start as usual at ten but, in practice, it never got going until nearer half past so I had about an hour to myself or, rather, for Roddy Fraser. No inspiration had come in the night. In fact I had slept so soundly that I was even late reaching the office. Settling myself down, coffee conveniently to hand, I let my mind wonder. Something dramatic. A spectacular end. Gratitude of the town. Roddy a hero - but definitely dead.

An idea began to form. The barn near Roddy's cottage could go on fire just about the time Roddy normally gets back from the pub. Knowing him, his sense of duty will prevail. He will do what he can to put out the blaze and to release the frightened beasts kept there. If the whole blazing roof fell in on him that would be that. Only an outline, a bit vague still, but it had possibilities. I looked at my watch and realised it was well after ten. My half-drunk coffee was cold and I had used up a whole hour almost without knowing it. Still, I had made progress.

Everyone else was there, coffee cups, books and piles of paper littered the long, polished mahogany table and the air was blue with cigarette smoke. It really was time these meetings were no smoking. Exchanging greetings with various people I eased my way into the chairman's place and called the meeting to order.

'Right everyone. I've got some news. As you know Martin has wanted out for a while and we've been paving the way. Well, he came to see me yesterday. He's just heard he's got the part at Stratford and he wants to leave the show by the end of the month. That means we're going to have to write Roddy out pretty well right away. If we make it something spectacular - his death would do, and I've had an idea about that - it would certainly help our ratings.'

There was silence - and then everyone started to talk at once.

The Walled Garden

by

Patrick Conway

Stella and Kenneth Sim were woken by the dawn chorus of birds in their Perthshire garden. Stella was reminded of tropical mornings when birds woke her to a busy day of office work and social life. Such days ended eight months earlier when Kenneth gladly took early retirement from the international mining company which had employed both of them. The chorus reminded Kenneth of happy boyhood wakenings in his Aunt Meg's house in Dunkeld. As it faded, he drifted back to sleep. Stella got up, to work in the garden before breakfast and to cut some deep blue cornflowers to give to their daughter, Gabriella, when they met for lunch later at the Atholl Arms Hotel in the village.

She hoped Gaby might be ready to talk about her future, now that her divorce was nearly complete. Gaby had never explained why her marriage collapsed. It had also ended the couple's partnership in hotel management. Stella was burning to suggest that Gaby should continue in the same line, perhaps with a little help from herself. She also wondered how and when some of Aunt Meg's estate might become available for the purpose. Auntie would be 91 tomorrow in the St Catherine Hospice. Her mind was frail but, anticipating her decline, she had already signed a power of attorney for Kenneth and the family's lawyer, Henry McNair, the junior partner in the practice, was dealing both with Aunt Meg's estate and Gaby's divorce. Lawyers seemed to be getting younger every day, Stella thought.

Among the envelopes in the morning post was one for Kenneth with the imprint McNair & Co. W. S. on it. Stella put it on top of his pile on the breakfast table, but he started with the others. When she returned with some fresh coffee, Henry's letter was open on the table.

'Well?' she asked, 'what's the trouble?'

'No trouble at all, dear, why do you say that?'

'You look very thoughtful at the least. What is that letter about?'

'It's the draft advertisement to sell Number 10 which Henry and I discussed last week.'

Number 10 Avondale Road was technically well described, Kenneth thought. 'Stone built Georgian town house in excellent condition and quiet location . . .'

Arriving in that quiet location to visit Aunt Meg had always been a step into a land where voices were soft and the sharpest sounds were the calls of jackdaws from the dovecote in the garden. Only in the night, when a yet deeper peace descended on the

125

Cochrane residence, did voices have a higher, disturbing pitch and Uncle James' cough surprised between the opening and closing of a door.

'Oh good!' Stella brought him back to what she had rightly guessed as trouble. 'If you give him a ring today it could be in the Scotsman next Thursday.'

'Yes, that it is so, but I will have to check it first for errors or omissions.'

Stella looked at his averted face. 'Best of luck then, I'll let you get on with it. You remember, don't you, that I'm lunching with Gaby? I am leaving you a salad and you can choose between the mackerel and the ham to go with it.'

'Porch, panelled entrance hall . . .' Kenneth's eyes outran the text through the baize door into the back passage, out past the coal shed onto the lawn, past the entrance to the walled garden, back through the conservatory, up the stairs . . .

'Yes, I remember, I'll be fine.' he said to the empty breakfast room.

He remembered the winding-handle and linked levers which opened the conservatory windows, and how one summer he and Aunt Meg had made a climate more memorable than Burma's. He remembered the treasure hunt clues to the cupboard under the back stairs where she hid the bicycle which was her present for his eighth birthday, and how she taught him to mend the first puncture and tighten the chain.

' . . . a second stair to the rear is fitted with a stairlift . . . ' He remembered when she asked him to obtain information about devices to help one up a staircase; how she had selected a make, checked the plans he drew up and, accompanied by the 1812 overture from her gramophone, made her first ascent.

When he visited her last week the technology which supported her life was not of her own choosing, and she gazed without comment at the security camera on the ivied wall of the hospice garden.

He put Henry's letter back in the envelope and picked up the newspaper.

At the Atholl Arms, Stella sent back the undercooked saddle of lamb and opened the campaign.

'Your father had a letter from Henry McNair this morning. It was an ad for Number 10 which I am sure will be perfectly satisfactory but Kenneth will agonise over it for a week at least.'

'I remember Daddy was expecting it.'

'Have you heard any more from Henry about your divorce?'

'Not since I saw him earlier in the week, Tuesday wasn't it? It shouldn't be long now.'

After learning from Henry that she would soon be free, Gaby had enquired about progress on Number 10. Henry, to his later surprise, had shown her the draft advertisement. She had gone on from his office to the hospice. Mrs Cochrane was asleep, the Sister said, but had enjoyed her birthday cards except for one which she kept throwing to the floor. Sister's smile said that such behaviour was quite OK. Gaby picked up the card. It was from Kenneth and portrayed a paradisial walled garden. She watched her sleeping conspirator for a while, thinking about the secrets they shared: how much they had loved Uncle James and now loved Kenneth, and how they detested Stella's pushiness. Their secrets had never been spoken, but Auntie had brought out Gaby's talent for intimacy as she had Kenneth's for engineering. So only they knew that Uncle had died in the walled garden where he should not have been allowed to wander, and each knew of the other's unconsummated marriage.

'These flowers are a lovely colour, Mummy, I think they are my favourites at this time of the year.'

Stella felt sufficiently encouraged by unusual warmth to hint her thoughts about Gaby's future.

'Yes, I know, I've got to make some decisions, and you may be on the right lines. It's difficult to concentrate but I'm seeing Henry again tomorrow and once that's all over I'll be ready to talk about things.'

'Gaby dear, we would both love to talk when you are ready. Look, could you come round this evening and help your father with the ad? You could take it with you tomorrow.'

'Sure, you can expect me between six and seven, I'll come on my bike because the car is in for a service and the ride will be nice anyway.'

Kenneth had found no faults in the advertisement, but could not yet admit to himself that planning to sell No 10 was as grievous as watching his auntie die. He was glad when Gaby made a few innocuous suggestions and took responsibility for finishing the job with Henry.

Next day, when the telephone rang, Stella was watering the flowers in the hanging baskets and Kenneth, watching the golf, was nearer to the instrument.

'Daddy, I'm at St Catherine's.'

'Rather late dear, without your car?'

'It's all right, Henry is with me and will take me home.'

She reached behind her and grasped Henry's hand.

'Oh, well, that's good. Did he accept our changes to the advertisement?'

'Better than that Daddy, we brought it with us and for a while Auntie was lucid enough to read it.'

Henry tensed, and she squeezed his hand.

'Good heavens, thank goodness, I mean, was she, well, all right?'

'Yes, for long enough to,' she pulled Henry's arm round her, 'say that she did not want to have the walled garden mentioned.'

'The walled garden? Why was that?'

'She did not say, and of course we did not question her.'

Henry put his other arm round her and took the phone.

'Mr Sim, this is Henry McNair.'

'Good evening Henry, it is kind of you to help my daughter, I am sure Mrs Sim will be grateful also.'

'I shall be glad to help at any time, and at this moment I think Gaby would like me to speak for her.'

She squeezed harder.

'Mr Sim, your aunt slept for a while after talking to Gaby. When she woke she asked for soup.'

'Yes?'

'Sister Marian advised us to wait, she evidently knew what to expect, and Mrs Cochrane died peacefully not long afterwards. I am sorry to be the bearer of this news.'

Stella was standing at Kenneth's shoulder. She gave him a nudge and said, 'Tell him we are very, very grateful and that we look forward to seeing him a great deal more when everything is all over.'

Kenneth looked at her smiling face, understood, and told him.

Goodbye Mrs Ellis

by

Allison Milne

You sit with your peroxide head bent low over your bible. It's the only book you've requested since you came in here. Not, perhaps, the sort of publication the press and people might expect you to be reading. You - the bleached blonde night-club hostess. You - as one judge in all his impartiality, called you, common little West End tart. You with the gun.

But there's a lot about you they don't know - how you have been, here, with us in these endless days and nights that must be filled with such terror.

Not once have you begged or pleaded that it's unfair. You have done this thing and accept the price that you must, in law, pay.

You have received your few visitors calmly, and have not cried when they left. If you have cried at all, it has been in the night hours in your sedated dreams, and even then, your innate good manners dictate that you don't cry out loud.

Only three requests from you - bleach for your roots, paper and pen to write to Mrs Blakely, and materials to make soft toys destined for children somewhere. Not your children - to them you are already gone, and that's best. Your small hands work tirelessly on those soft toys, or hold your bible, or one of the ten cigarettes you are allowed each day. Those tireless small hands that, hours from now, will be tied in a strap behind your back, lest they swing free and render the whole business unseemly. And your ankles, in their West End seamed stockings, will be tied too.

Don't listen now, don't think, it's best that you don't know this final humiliation, but your pale body, once loved by David, and many others. Once desired by patrons in your night-clubs, well kept and clothed in silk, will be stripped of its camiknickers and you will be sewn into a garment of leather, designed to catch your inner woman's body when you fall. And your blonde head, now bent low, will be raised, and a hood placed over it.

A final prayer, Mrs Ellis?

And then the trap - the trap that will launch you into eternity.

No more prayers. No more cigarettes, no more soft toys, no more anything - for you. But memories, for us, of your quiet and continued dignity in your last lonely hours. And the knowledge, although it will never be yours, that you have helped pave the way to the end of all this.

Goodbye, Mrs Ellis.

Mists Of Time

by

Lorna Whelan

'Come on! You'll get left behind!'

Fiona hitched her rucksack to a more comfortable position and hurried to catch up with Rob.

'Pay no attention to him, Fiona. This is supposed to be a fun walk.' Mary left her brother to walk on and waited for her friend. Fiona smiled, looking around her at the bare hills and shivered despite the morning sun.

'Eerie, isn't it?' Mary commented. 'This glen is so atmospheric. I always fancy it's watching me; have you noticed there are no birds?'

Fiona had. This was her first visit to Glencoe, and she found it impressive. True, there were no birds, or any living thing apart from the odd sheep, but that was the essence of the place. Fiona stood for a moment, savouring the silence.

Rob shook his head, amused. 'Watch it Fiona. She'll be trotting out her ghost stories next!' Mary thumped her brother affectionately on his back.

'Save your breath for walking Rob, or it'll be *you* who gets behind.'

Fiona threw her rucksack onto the ground, leaned against a huge rock and allowed her body to slide down till she was sitting. Squinting up at the blazing sky, she wriggled out of her sweatshirt and tied it around her waist.

Mary grinned at her flushed face. 'Scorching, isn't it? We don't get too many days like this around here - make the most of it.'

'Beats rain and midges any day,' Fiona giggled. She was rummaging about in her rucksack now, and finally found what she was looking for. 'Ah. . . my water bottle. . .' Fiona's face fell comically as she realised it was empty. 'Have you any water left Mary?'

'Finished it off ages ago.'

'Me too,' sighed Rob. 'Pass them all over and I'll refill the lot.'

'I'll do it,' offered Fiona, 'or else I'll fall asleep sitting in this heat and sleepwalk back down! Which way to the burn?'

Rob looked at her, smiling. 'You really are a city girl aren't' you? Can't you hear it? Over there.' Rob jerked his thumb.

Fiona smiled back, refusing to rise to the bait. At fifteen years old, Rob was out to prove himself leader of the pack.

Fiona found the burn without difficulty and refilled the bottles. Gathering them up, she made her way back to Mary and Rob.

It was not until Fiona had walked completely around the rock she had been leaning against that she realised something was amiss.

Mary and Rob had gone. Fiona set the bottles down and looked around. Nothing stirred.

'All right! Very funny!' she called.

There was no reply.

Fiona walked slowly around the picnic site. There was no trace of Rob or Mary, no rucksacks, not even flattened grass. Increasingly nervous, Fiona began to shout again, close to tears.

'All right, you win. Stop fooling. Please . . .' Her voice petered out to a whisper.

Fiona sat down by her rock again and bit on her lower lip. She had expected better of Mary, but Rob . . . well, he was still a schoolboy, really. Ten minutes later, Fiona was too angry to wait any longer. This had gone on too long for a joke; she made her mind up to find her own way down the hillside and wait in her car.

Jumping to her feet, Fiona set off in the direction they had come from. Perhaps if Mary and Rob saw her leaving they'd stop this silly game.

Fiona's skin was tingling now, and realising she was cold, pulled her sweatshirt back on. The sun had gone, and a light mist was beginning to swirl around the hills, adding to her discomfort. The peace she had found that morning in the stillness of the glen was replaced by foreboding.

Fiona was not confident of the route they had taken that morning, and began to feel frightened. Had she taken a wrong turn on the way back from the burn? But even so, Rob and Mary would have heard her shouting! Deep inside, Fiona knew something was very wrong. Mary wouldn't have let her leave by herself.

Fiona stumbled on through the thickening mist, gaining speed on the descent, and couldn't prevent herself from tripping over one of the many rocks that littered the hillside. Falling heavily to the ground, she cried out as a sharp pain shot through her ankle.

'Blast!' Fiona hugged her leg to her chest, foot dangling. The pain subsided and was replaced by a dull throb.

At that moment, Fiona heard a footfall and her body tensed. Peering in front of her she saw two figures looming through the mist. 'Rob and Mary!' she thought, relief washing over her, and began to shout.

'Over here.'

As the mist before her dissolved, Fiona realised it wasn't her friends; it was two men, tightly wrapped up in plaids, their feet and legs covered in woollen wrappings tied on with leather thongs.

Seeing Fiona on the ground, the men turned to each other and spoke in a quick light tongue.

'Gaelic!' thought Fiona. They must be local, then she smiled, ignoring the throb in her leg. 'Can you help me? I've . . .'

One of the men moved towards her, dropping to the ground to squat beside her. He spoke gently, then paused waiting for an answer.

Fiona shook her head regretfully. 'I don't speak Gaelic. I'm sorry.' The man sighed, smiled, and spoke over his shoulder to his friend, who joined him on the ground beside Fiona. Still smiling, the man reached for Fiona's leg. Sensing he meant her no harm, she allowed him to examine the swollen ankle and bind it with a strip he tore from the bottom of his plaid. When he had finished he pulled Fiona to her feet. Using their sticks to steady them, the two men helped Fiona down the hill, each with an arm around her waist.

At last they reached the foot of the hill. The men lowered Fiona to the ground.

'I wish I could thank you properly. You've been very kind,' she began, but the men had turned back towards the hill, and were soon out of sight. Fiona was puzzled. Why had they left her here? She was no better off than when they found her on the hillside! And then she heard the voices.

'Fiona! Fio . . . na!'

Sitting up as far as she could manage Fiona shouted back.

'Over her, I'm here!'

Rob and Mary appeared less than a minute later.

'Where on earth did you get to, you silly girl!' Mary scolded, her relief at finding Fiona giving an edge to her voice.

'What do you mean, where did I get to?' Fiona stared at Mary resentfully. 'You both had disappeared when I came back with the water bottles. Some joke.'

'Fiona, we waited for half an hour before we started looking for you. You must have mistaken the way back. In fact, we came off the hill to raise the alarm! Thank goodness you found you own way down. Oh!' Mary noticed Fiona was having problems standing. 'What have you done to your leg?'

Swallowing her indignation, privately worried that they might be right, Fiona explained what had happened to her. Her voice tailed off as she realised Mary and Rob were staring at her. Mary broke the silence.

'Fiona, what mist are you talking about? It's been glorious all day!'

Suddenly, Fiona realised Mary was speaking the truth. The sun was beaming down.

Rob saw the distress on Fiona's face and acted sensitively for once, gently pushing her to a sitting position on the ground. Mary swallowed, then asked, 'What did these men look like?'

132

As Fiona spoke, Mary nodded her head gently and took her friend's hand.

'Fiona,' she began carefully, 'there are no locals who dress like that any more. And no one from the village speaks Gaelic who does not also speak English . . . ' Mary stopped and looked at her friend, seeing the hurt on her face. 'I'm not doubting what you say. This is a strange place. Rob and I have grown up with the tales of the glen and we tend not to take them seriously, but some of the old folk in the village . . .' Her voice gained strength. 'Old Hannah for instance. She calls them the 'ancients' - these men, or others like them, have helped out more than one lost walker. But they're not from our time, Fiona.'

Rob made a last stab at jocularity. 'What are you talking about Mary? Fiona probably knocked herself out when she fell and has dreamed all this, isn't that right Fiona?' Rob turned to Fiona. She was ashen white.

'I don't think so Rob,' she whispered, pulling back her trouser leg to reveal the brownish tartan binding torn from the man's plaid. 'Look.'

The Murder Mystery Tour

by

Ken Peebles

'Iain this tour sounds different, let's try it while we are in Edinburgh.' Iain looked up from signing his wife Marjorie and himself into the register of their Princes Street hotel. Iain read from one of many leaflets at the reception. 'A Murder Mystery Walking Tour with a Guide, leaving late every evening round the historic parts of Old Edinburgh - yes, that sounds too good to miss - let's grab a few leaflets and we can plan our week in Edinburgh.'

Marjorie and Iain Fraser were from New Zealand and had saved long and hard for their holiday of a lifetime in Europe. They had spent a week in London which they enjoyed, although they found the pace and bustle a little overpowering, then a few days at Stratford on Avon, which although enjoyable, seemed to be mainly populated by Japanese photographers.

The Scottish part of their holiday, they were hoping, would be the highlight, as both were of Scottish parents and Marjorie was a Fraser before marrying Iain; although her side was from the Inverness area, while Iain's from Aberdeenshire. At home they had gone as far as they could with compiling family trees and had written to many relatives in Scotland telling of the forthcoming visit and that they would 'phone on arrival.

After an excellent meal they settled down to a smooth single malt whisky and worked out their tours for the week. They decided the Murder Mystery Tour would be on their last night and replenishing their glasses got down to the business of 'phoning the relations.

As the evening wore on, while it was very nice chatting to people who were previously only a photograph or signature on a letter, it appeared that everyone in Scotland was going to be busy that week and it would be on their second week, when they were hiring a car and touring, that the relatives could be visited. While feeling slightly peeved that they had travelled so far and others didn't seem to be making the same effort, they agreed to enjoy their first week in each other's company only.

The week flew by as they took bus trips to the rolling border hills, bringing memories of reading Sir Walter Scott, the majestic mountains and lochs of Perthshire; roaming the streets and shops of Glasgow and its mighty river Clyde where you could almost see the ghosts of the great Queen liners slipping down-river on their way to America. Before they knew it the last night was upon them and they prepared for the walking tour. 'Wrap up

134

well' the leaflet said and it was late Autumn, also a mist had been drifting in all day from the Forth.

As they walked up to the High Street the mist was turning the lights of Princess Street and The Mound into soft damp, glowing orbs. Iain thought it an ideal night for a Murder Mystery Tour, while Marjorie thought it to be a little too authentic and gave an involuntary shiver.

Just before coming to the Castle they saw a group of people with someone who was obviously the guide. He was dressed entirely in black, wore a swirling black cape and wide brimmed black hat; on his face was a black mask over his eyes and nose only. When he had ascertained that everyone was present and after telling the party to try and stay together as far as possible, he moved off with a remark to have a glance back at the castle, as from now on they would be in dark closes, courts and alleyways and would not have any more views of the castle on the great rock. By this time the top of the castle could hardly be seen as the fog had thickened. Iain thought the scene now looked more like Transylvania than Edinburgh.

As the guide took them through the stairways and closes of old Edinburgh, through Boswells Close and down Semples Close and Milnes Court he told of the murders and of the murderers who had lived in these parts, of the body snatchers Burke and Hare who stole bodies so that the surgeons of Edinburgh could learn their trade. Of Mary Queen of Scots and the murder of Rizzio in Holyrood. The Auld Tollbooth where the head of the Duke of Montrose was impaled on a stake in 1650 and how eleven years later it was the turn of the Marquis of Argyle.

In one particularly low and narrow close, where by now the walls were dripping and the cold was seeping through even warm coats, Marjorie and Iain were at the back of the group when the guide invited them to read the plaque about the legendary Deacon Brodie. After reading it, they turned to join the others, to find that they were totally alone; it was as if the rest of the party had drifted into the stone walls with the fog. Marjorie's grip on Iain's arm tightened appreciably and she let out a gasp -

'Where have they gone Iain?'

'Oh! they must have moved on while we were reading and probably they are just round the next corner, we'd better get a move on if we are to catch up, or maybe you'd rather go back?'

Marjorie would much rather have gone back; but she didn't want to spoil it for Iain, so she just gripped him tighter and moved forward. They carried on round the next corner but the close ahead was empty, about fifty yards ahead was another corner which had wisps of swirling mist blowing round it. Even Iain was beginning to feel apprehensive. They increased their pace, when about five yards from the corner a heavy, studded, black wooden door creaked open and a figure in black leapt out! Thank goodness, it was the guide; but something wasn't right - he was taller and thinner than their guide.

'I know what you're thinking! I'm not your original guide! It's true, we always have a spare guide who walks the tour after the party to collect stragglers, as there are some very dangerous steps and stairs in these closes.' Iain thought this strange as surely he should have appeared behind and not in front of them.

'Right,' said the guide, 'let's continue,' he opened the door further but not a glimmer of light came from the door, only a smell that was impossible to place, it was a dank, putrid yet sweet smell that could have been a combination of old ale and perhaps even older bodies.

'Be careful of the steps in here, its barely lit and they are well worn.' Just as they were about to turn into the door, Marjorie let out a scream! Two pigeons, unseen by them had been perched on a ledge and decided to take off; although Marjorie ducked at the last moment the wing of one pigeon brushed through her hair - the close was filled with a flurry of wings, noise and feathers as they disappeared into the fog. Marjorie was really trembling by now and her grip on Iain's arm was like a vice.

The guide led them slowly down the stairs. At the bottom it was almost completely black and they could distinctly smell beer and dimly make out barrels scattered around the floor. This room he said had been the actual cellar of the hostelry where Burke and Hare used to meet and wait until the Old Town clock would strike midnight, when they would leave to begin their hellish nightly task. The guide stepped back and said to Iain,

'If you feel your way along that wall you'll come to the actual door they would leave by.' Iain felt the wood of the door and as he moved further the door creaked open about an inch and the hairs on the back of both Iain and Marjorie's necks rose in horror. Through the gap in the door they could see grey ghostly figures moving about and what looked like a ghoulish ghostly apparition of a piper raise his pipes to his lips. Seconds later the air was rent by the wail of bagpipes. Just at that the door was wrenched from Iain's grip as it opened inwards and he was pulled into the room. As light flooded the room from all angles and as Iain and Marjorie shielded their eyes from the glare, a great cheer went up and when they could see properly, the room was full of their relatives from all over Scotland, who had set the whole thing up with the help of the tour company. The rest of the night was spent in a much more relaxed atmosphere, stories were exchanged, new friends were made and it was the perfect end to the Fraser's first week in Scotland.

Half A Mouthful Of Phlegm

by

Stewart Morrison

Haymarket was deserted save for a few idling midmorning travellers. Outside a wooden fronted pub, grip bag at his feet, Arthur Wood lit his first cigarette of the day. With an abrupt cough he ejected half a mouthful of phlegm, placing it with ease in the gutter some six feet away. A pigeon dipped its beak in the shining ectoplasm, then flapped off. Arthur turned and headed off up Morrison Street's hotting pavements. Across eager one way traffic a pub ejected its first drunk of the day. Over beyond, a massage parlour and the police station. Near the fire station an unexpected twist of the cross-contra flow system almost sent him to his death as he carelessly ambled over West Tollcross. He walked slowly behind a large dog as it dragged its owner into The International. Passing a low hedge Arthur looked over to the playground. A child pushing an empty swing, a roundabout still.

On a bench nearby, two squirrels were procreating in a wild frenzy of tails. Pausing a moment, he watched them closely and changing his mind about sex altogether, wished he and Christine still saw one another. Around Arthur deep black bark on aged trunks. Dark victorian earth scattered with bald grass and caked starling shit. Frightened sparrows broke fluttering from unseen perches above, startling him with their queer chatter, and vanished into the empty grey ceiling of chestnut boughs like a blurred impulse toward Newington.

Beyond the children's hospital he climbed to the attic floor in a victorian block. Within the dark hallway he passed the kitchenette and unlocked the door to his room. At the far end of the hall, the vague outline of a naked body could be seen through the awkward glass of the bathroom door. He backed gently into his room trying to figure out whether it was Fiona or that boyfriend of hers. The crinkly glass made any decision arbitrary. He closed his door and dropped his bag.

The room was furnished in the style of the lesser junk shops of Ratcliffe Terrace. A bed against one wall, and on the opposite, a table and two chairs. Sunshine spread broad bars of dust down the length of the room. Two casement windows were set halfway down the sloping ceiling. Had anyone ever been tall enough to see out of them, they would have been rewarded with a fine view over the treetops, across the meadows to the Royal Infirmary and a mess of old town roofs.

Some hours later Arthur, fragrant and suffering some digestive discomfort, closed the door and made his way down ninety two steps. An entirely unsatisfactory lunch of frozen pizza and black tea, had been followed by an equally unsatisfying bath. Fiona, her boyfriend, or possibly both of them, must have used up all the water. He'd soaked for an hour or more in tepid suds, staring at the aged tiled walls, it's corners dotted with tired spiders. An ache in his stomach became more acute as the water cooled. He rose dripping, shivering and groaning simultaneously. Sitting in his underpants, he smoked a cigarette noticing with some surprise twin arching paths of fade on his carpet. Slightly worse than the rest of the wear, it had been traced by the direct sunlight through the casements. Leaning forward, he touched the faded sunlit patches. The wool was quite warm. He felt it was strange he had not noticed before.

At the street door, the cool stairwell gave way to a heat of quite unexpected intensity. Arthur Wood stepped into the sunlight. Above him trees seemed to buckle in the heat. Tender leaves trembling on immature stalks. He crossed the road and walked under the Jawbone Arch, touching the aged green white whalebone. Pale touches of chestnut sparking high above Melville Drive. A listless breeze carried the last drifts of cherry blossom in great eddies across an ocean of shaking grass. Over the Meadows the sun screamed down on a few adventurous walkers, while scalded sunbathers lay coaxing their melanin into action. A gap in the trees bared the finely ridged gills of Salisbury Crags and a bus heaved silently through the traffic lights toward Marchmont. Whether by fault or design, it's of no consequence which, Arthur Wood found himself wandering through the gates of a churchyard some ten minutes later. He crunched his way along dark paths through scatterings of old leaves, crisped in hopeless decay. Deep in the wall's shadowed ivy cold grey stone. Some distance away, a dog tore silently at the ground, its face a grimace of murderous jaws. At the end of a leash the dog owner stood gazing at the skyline in a pre-occupied kind of way. High above, a figure stared out over the city. A rooftop statue strangely visible atop a muddled scree of slates and guttering. Arthur figured it perched somewhere around the High Street. The courts probably. As he turned his head, a seagull drifting high on an effortless thermal dropped a white package from its feathery arse. As it fell, it stretched and swirled, separating into two discernible loads for a moment before rejoining some seventy feet above the unsuspecting scalp of Arthur, now nervously contemplating the approach of a large, playful canine and its bored owner. The dog owner spoke.

'Beautiful day.'

As Arthur prepared a suitable reply two assaults were made upon his person. The first, a pale greeting from a fowl of the air showered his head and shoulders. The second, an over friendly advance from an alsation, stretching its lead in attempted coitus with Arthur's leg. Flexing his toe through the restraining leather of his brogue, Arthur put paid to the canine's passion. Arthur felt an inexplicable compulsion to respond to the dog-handler's greeting. And an irresistable urge to flee. Anywhere.

'Yes. Beautiful day.'

Arthur stopped running a short distance beyond a statue of a small dog. A bus was pulling up at a stop a few yards distant. He leapt on and put a fifty pence piece in the box in front of the driver. He was quickly carried over the High Street and down, gliding gently past an ecclesiastical book-shop and the mighty bank of the Mound. The bus purred at a set of lights, and Arthur looked down on a group of Japanese tourists await-ing the cuckoo on the flower clock. The sounds of the city seemed muffled and indistinct. Noises strangely distant. Placing a finger in one ear, Arthur was disgusted to find it clogged with a cold wet slime. He glanced at his shoulder. An emulsion of seagull crap peppered his black tee shirt, and an odour not unreminiscent of mushrooms filled his nostrils. The bus sailed up Hanover Street and begun its descent into the New Town. He turned to a disgusted looking old lady seated behind him and enquired as to the number of the bus he was travelling on.

'Twenty-three.'

A few short minutes later he descended the stairs and pressed the bell. The bus pulled up just after Canonmills.

The Royal Botanical Gardens entrance lay up a short lane. He breezed through the gate in no mood for looking at plants. Or even the dull fish which are found drifting feebly through the leafy municipal ponds of the hothouse complex. Stopping only to purchase a couple of filled rolls he strode purposely across the wide lawns and sat down on a warm bench by the lake. A chicken salad roll was torn savagely into small pieces. Arthur cleaned out his ear with the clingfilm packaging. He sat for a few moments in silent con-templation then cast his bread upon the water. A flurry of water fowl approached. Reach-ing a hand towards his foot Arthur lifted a stone the size of an egg. A convoy of mandarin ducks, avocet and a mute swan had begun drawing the soggy picnic into their bright bills. He raised his fist slowly. The stone felt beautifully hard. The birds were very close now. He smiled.

'Good ducks.'

Jeanie's Faither's Leg

by

L Jenkins

'Aw, come oan Jeanie - take us up to see yer faither's leg!'

Katie jostled Jeanie's elbow in an endeavour to persuade her to take her up the stairs to peek at her faither's artificial limb which was always kept beside his bed as a spare, equipped with a boot which was so well polished that you could almost see your face in it. It was in the middle 1930's during the Depression in Edinburgh in a street located just behind Edinburgh Castle. Jeanie's father had lost a leg in the 1914/18 war and walked with the aid of an artificial limb and a walking stick. He had been picked up, presumably dead, amongst the littered dead bodies in the bloody battlefield and tossed into the 'death cart' to be disposed of with the other bodies. He was ultimately found to be still barely alive and was taken a prisoner of war, his severely wounded leg being of necessity hacked off below the knee at one of the emergency field hospitals where the hoards of young men, some barely 17, were being carried in to join the other wounded and dying. Jeanie had only once seen her father's stump which strangely enough filled her with no feeling of revulsion at all. With it being roughly hacked off instead of a clean break, it looked like a sawn-off shotgun, all ragged and rough.

The children never heard their father talk of that traumatic part of his life but Jeanie, the dreamer of the family, had gleaned some of the poignant story from her mother, of how through the war years she had been informed that her husband was missing and presumed killed in action. Prayers had been said in church for her and her grieving family. Then after the war was over her mother had gone to the door to answer a knock and found a tall thin gaunt man with a long beard standing there on crutches and . . . minus a leg. She couldn't believe that this gaunt stranger was, in fact, her long lost husband believed dead. Jeanie loved to hear this story and hung on to her mother's every word.

The job of polishing his boots was a very much sought after one which the young Mackintosh family took it in turns to do for the princely sum of six pence a week which they received when he came home from work on a Friday night. A number of the children nearby knew exactly when he came home on 'pay night' and it was some time before Mrs Mackintosh found out that her husband normally would dig into his pocket and give them a penny each. His tired face would break into a smile as they greeted him.

'Hello Mr Mackintosh, that you hame fur the night noo?' The greeting would ring out loud and clear as they eagerly awaited the proffered penny.

Some of Jeanie's friends just wouldn't believe that her father was minus a leg, not understanding how he could walk so well with only a slight limp.

As young Katie persisted in wheedling her, Jeanie reluctantly made excuses. Her mother usually washed her floor at this time and didn't like a hoard of kids messing it up especially as it had just started to rain.

'We winnae be a minute. Please . . . Jeanie!!' Katie coaxed. Her pleading little face was hard to resist, and the other youngsters chorused together strongly in support of her.

'Oh, alright then, but mind - you jist come in for a second to hae a quick look!'

They threw up their arms joyfully in glee and ran giggling up the four flights of stairs behind the still reluctant Jeanie. As they approached the door she held her hand to her mouth.

'Wheesht' she admonished them and the giggles were hastily smothered as they followed her into the large kitchen. There was no sign of Mrs Mackintosh. Jeanie had whispered that she must be in the parlour making up the beds. The huge parlour had to be utilised as a bedroom too as the only one small bedroom had to be kept for Jeanie's big brother. The four little girls slept in two beds in the parlour and Jeanie's little brother shared the small bedroom with his big brother.

The eager children stole up to the bed recess where Jeanie's parents slept. It was a high bed blocked up on four chocks with a freshly washed bed-pan drawn round the bottom with a drawstring. Mrs Mackintosh didn't like to keep anything under the beds although in most of those old Georgian tenements, with even larger families, there was no other place to store anything and could easily be a harbour for the rubbish collected over the years.

The only thing that Mrs Mackintosh kept under her bed was a big wooden chest, or kist, where all the important documents were kept such as Insurance policies, birth certificates etc. On the few occasions when this was opened Jeanie loved to peer at some of the old dog-eared photographs of the Great War days. One of those never failed to intrigue her as it was not of her father but of a dashing sailor lad sitting in a field covered with daisies and on the back an almost indecipherable scrawl. Her mother just laughed coquettishly when Jeanie questioned her about it.

As the children scanned the room for the sight of this wonderful leg, the bed was pounced upon. On one chair a huge pile of books were ready for Jeanie or her sisters to return to the library. Their father was an avid reader and it fell to the girls in the family to return them when finished - a veritable nightmare - for he had read so many books that it was the most arduous of jobs to remember the ones he hadn't already read. He was so strict with them that woe betide the unfortunate one who brought him home one which he had already read. Although he never lifted a hand to chastise any of his children, his biting sarcasm and choice vocabulary was perhaps worse. If one was not quick enough to duck when a polished boot came flying through the air, it was just too bad. However, the sisters were far too agile to be on the receiving end of their father's missile which possibly he knew but, nevertheless, the saga of the library books was a far from pleasant one. On the other chair beside the bed the youngsters abruptly stopped, taken aback momentarily as they spied it.

'Aw, it disnae look like a leg at aw, it's a funny looking auld thing!' Katie's mouth was opened wide in disappointment.

It was indeed a strange object, propped up against the bed, all straps and leather harness. If it wasn't for the shiny black boot firmly placed on the artificial foot it would have been difficult to recognise it as an artificial limb at all.

'I jist cannae understand hoo yer faither can walk in that thing and climb aw thae stairs tae!' She turned to Jeanie as if she could produce an answer to this questioning challenge.

'Aw I can say is yer must hae an awfy clever daddy.'

Jeanie perked up a little. Yes, she thought rather proudly - she supposed her father was rather special but she had never thought of it before.

'Well then, whit's aw this aboot?' Mrs Mackintosh came bustling through the door, her thin little frame swathed in a hessian apron, sleeves rolled up past her elbows.

Kate and her wee pals were still standing there, mouths agape at the object in question.

She blurted out. 'We didnae think it wid look like this Mrs Mack.' Then she added, making Mrs Mackintosh's harassed face break into a smile. 'Jist fancy him haeing to work aw day wi' that thing oan!'

'Aye!' Mrs Mackintosh retaliated. 'Jist ye think yerselves lucky that ye hae a quid pair o' legs on ye!' She laughed at the awe-struck young faces.

As Jeanie drew the girls away from the bed, Katie turned to her mother.

'Ta, Mrs Mack for letting us hae a look - we'll be able to tell the ithers noo that we've seen Jeanie's faither's famous leg!' And they clamoured noisily down the stairs.

Mrs Mackintosh wearily brushed her hair back from her brow, but she had learnt something today from 'thae per wee lasses'. She was smiling to herself as she went back to work through in the parlour. She'd have something to tell to her Bill tonight. 'From the mooths o' bairns indeed!'

Brothers

by

W McMaster

We were both ten years old at the time and life was a lucky dip of adventure. The out-side world knew Fallas as a wee mining village in the midst of Scotland's industrial belt but to Jim and me, who knew better, it was all there was. To the south was a moor, packed with places exciting enough to arouse tinglings of anticipation even now. There was a working sand-quarry which ensured that the wee burn from the moss had beaches of gold. The beauty of the Highlands was recreated in Muldren glen, scene of organised family picnics and attended by most of the clan of around fifty adults and children. It had a miniature white-water torrent which hurried its way through the glen, creating small waterfalls and deep pools which delighted small-fry and watchful parents alike.

Over where the miners played pitch and toss in amongst the coal bings were yet more moors, peppered with the remains of long ago. There were ruined mine-head buildings, small grass-covered coal bings and murky ponds, some of which hid pit shafts. The whole area was the subject of parental warnings and boyish legend; the horse and driver with cart which disappeared one stormy night; suicides of demented woman; the children who fell down hidden shafts in the gorse and heather. Each site had its share of notor-iety, and while no-one knew the truth of these stories, passers-by tended to hurry past. You could never tell when an unspeakable thing was going to materialise to punish the doubter.

There was also an old quarry which was the most wonderful place this side of Ziggy's pond. Down a long slope into its bowels was a set of rails with several old bogies which could be levered on to the track by a couple of determined lads, and after a failsafe brak-ing system was formed by placing large boulders at the end of the track, the bogie was inched to the top. Once there, with a stone under a wheel, the bogie was poised to begin its run.

One would jump into the bogie while the other kicked away the stone and leapt in as the chariot gathered speed. The length of the track must have been a couple of hundred yards, and just before reaching the bottom, a decision had to be made; to jump before the vehicle crashed into the pile of stones, or steel every nerve and sinew, stay put and take the buffeting that followed. Strangely, I cannot recollect any bones being broken, or indeed any ill effects at all. Some Being must have watched over us in our innocence.

Also in that quarry was a rock face where the earth and heather had been stripped away by blasting, laying bare the very intestines of the moor, and when bogie runs palled, the next great venture was to cross that cliff. This was via an ill-defined track with crumbling rocks underfoot hanging precariously over a sheer drop of thirty or forty feet to the floor which was littered with boulders and had an evil-looking little pond lurking at the base of the rock. The magnetic attraction at the other side of the cliff was what appeared to be a small cave dug into the wall, and young imaginations endowed this with all kinds of magical possibilities. It had never been reached, and the usual outcome was that fear overcame curiosity, although of course the *real* reason was that the day was too hot or it was nearing dinnertime.

Now I should explain that we were, in the words of our families, 'thrawn wee objects', and one day it got into our heads that this was going to be *the* day, so off we set and after many heart-stopping close shaves managed to reach our goal. As it turned out, the cave was a big disappointment. It proved to be a hole used by some animal or other, but, feeling proud of the achievement, we began our return.

It was not long before we discovered the truth of the saying that the last lap is the longest. As the day wore on and the heat from the strong summer sun seemed to flatten us against the wall of the quarry, we tried to inch our way back to safety. Small stones, dislodged by feet searching for a secure hold, arched out into the void taking ages to finally plunge into the green pool at the foot. The bottom of the cliff seemed miles below and I imagined how long it would take before my body hit the water and wondered if the water was deep enough for me to survive. Jim said nothing but followed me in grim determination. The sun was gradually swinging round to the west, telling me that at home my tea was being prepared, coinciding with my father's return from the coal mine where he worked in impossible conditions. The mine did not have pithead baths and I thought of him, unbelievably filthy, undressing in the porch of our house before having a long hot bath. I found myself thinking of my sister, not in the way I usually did as a nuisance and a girl, but as someone who would be quite nice to see and above all, I knew that I badly needed the presence of my mother who scolded me often but failed me never. A few sharp words from her right then would have been worth more than all the honeyed tongues of creation.

I was brought back to our situation by hearing Jim say in peculiar voice, 'I'm stuck!' He had always been the strong, silent type, the closest of many cousins, and I had long envied his ability to box well and play football with much skill since I had severe limitations in both directions. I had never thought of him as anything other than a brother, for I lived with his family for some time when my mother had been taken seriously ill. He didn't look at all like the Jim I knew, and repeated, 'I'm stuck! I can't move.'

Curiously, I didn't think of the very important fact that Jim was my elder . . . by a whole fortnight. 'Come on,' I said, 'take it slow and put your feet there, and there,' indicating the more solid-looking sections of the path which had, at that point, crumbled away to nothing.

'I can't,' he repeated, looking very odd indeed.

What happened was that he had 'frozen' and needed a jump start of some kind to get him going. I didn't understand this although I was well aware of his stubbornness, amounting at times to blind, unreasonable pig-headedness. He had stopped speaking to me for ages after I had scored more points than he had done in a school exam, and on another occasion had said, with pride, that after falling out with anyone, he would never be the one to speak first.

This new side of Jim puzzled and exasperated me. I pleaded with him without success until I suddenly realised, quite calmly, that the whole thing was in my hands. Lowering myself into the gap in the path, I found sound footholds and said, 'Climb over me.' After some hesitation he did so, and I carefully followed him on to the track. Without further incident, we edged slowly off the cliff and went home in silence.

That day was never spoken again, but we both knew that our relationship had changed. We were brothers no longer. When we meet, we behave in a civilised way, just like casual acquaintances.

Life, Death And Syncopated Thinking

by

James A Walker

They'll come for you with a yellow van and take you away, Joe Forbes, if you don't watch yourself. The boy could've been run over, and what would you have known about it, eh?

'You mustn't run out into the road like that, Tommy. There might have been something coming.'

'It's all right, Granddad. Your're with me. I knew you were watching.'

I was miles away sonny. Miles away. I was with your Granny at the back of the beach at North Berwick in among the marram grass, kissing and cuddling and carrying on, and I was only fifteen years older than you are now.

'I can't be watching you all the time, son. Keep a hold of my hand, there's a good lad.'

'Can I have an ice cream please?'

'Son, you could have the Earth, the Moon, the Sun and the stars, if it was in my power to give them to you - but yes, you can certainly have an ice cream to be going on with.'

'You're funny, Granddad!'

Funny in the head, and getting funnier.

'Here you are, Tommy. Get one for me too, will you?'

Could've been killed, for all the watch you were keeping on him. 'In the midst of Life we are in Death'.

I remember this promenade just before I went off to France. They had these great concrete blocks set down there. I wonder if it would've stopped the tanks landing. And there was barbed wire too. Thank God it never came to invasion here. How the sappers in Normandy managed to deal with the barbed wire under the cliffs and on the beaches on 'D' day, I'll never know. The Jerries nearly turned the air into metal the first day. Aye, a lot of good lads were left on these beaches. I'm lucky to be alive.

Just a wee twinge in the knee, and my thoughts go scampering off. Maybe it's going to rain. I always feel it before the rain starts. Instead of going out to the rocks, maybe it'd be better to walk back the way and look at some of the shops.

'Here's your ice cream Granddad - and here's your change.'

'Thanks son. Tell you what. You look after that change for me, like a good lad. Stick it in your pocket, and then if I don't remember to ask for it back, you can keep it. All right?'

'Mum says you're not to give me money.'

146

'Well you tell her I haven't given you money. I've only asked you to look after some for me. That's all right, isn't it?'

It hurt like Hell at the time. I thought I'd never walk again but the medics did a grand job. Just that little twinge now and again.

'This ice cream's good.'

'Why're we going this way, Granddad?'

'Seeing that I'm not allowed to give you money, I thought we might go by the shops, and I could maybe buy you a wee present.'

'Wow! That'd be ace.'

'Easy now. Just a *wee* present. I'm not a millionaire, you know.'

Far from it. Still, it's only money. Easy come, easy go. Not like life, is it? By heavens, going was hard for some. Jock Nisbet died screaming, and Chalky White was too weak to scream, but the scream was in his eyes. I held his head and watched him die. Machine gun - rat-tat-tat - like that. My knee got it, and his insides were falling out. God, my leg hurt, but I held him until he died. Chalky. I don't know if I even knew his first name.

'You got a cold. Granddad?'

'No, it's just that my eyes water a bit in the wind. But don't go so fast, Tommy. I'm an old man, you know.

'Look Granddad. Look at that in the window.'

'What's that, son? Where?'

'See? That black gun. You pull the trigger and it makes a noise like a real machine gun.'

'What about that car there, son? It's radio-controlled.'

'But it's £10, Granddad, and you said a wee present.'

'Aye. I know. But we could have fun with the car. Somehow I don't fancy playing with the gun.'

The Dress

by

Meg Paterson

She was glad when it began to rain. It suited her mood somehow. December shoppers opened umbrellas. Bright mushrooms, dancing along the busy pavements.

Outside Marks and Spencer's, a bearded youth thrust a leaflet in front of her. She gently pushed his hand away, noticing the fingerless gloves, the broken front tooth, the practised shrug. Glasgow supports the homeless.

Good for Glasgow, she thought.

Light-headed, she crossed the road, brake lights swimming in puddles around her like blood clots.

The window display in a classy, designer dress shop caught her eye. Even the central figure of Santa was made of huge scarlet scarves. The whole window was wreathed in silk scarves. She opened the plate glass door. Two chattering bearded matrons held it to allow her through. The door shut behind them with a dull thud, putting an audible full stop on a sentence. It was then that she saw it. The dress. Black, sexy, seductive and silly.

It was backless. From shoulders to waist a deep V plunged, the material held together by the delicate tracery of a spider's web. She was like a child now, needing the promise of a treat to swallow the bitter pill.

It fitted perfectly, and despite the signs of utter weariness which she saw in the fitting room mirror, she knew she looked good.

Madonna's twin sister carefully wrapped it in tissue paper before laying it in its box

No, she wasn't going anywhere special, not really.

Outside it was still raining.

Further down Sauchiehall Street, a damp Salvationist stood on the kerb, waiting for his little army to announce to a disinterested Glasgow that a Child was Born.

The familiar words brought tears to her eyes and salt water rain drops rolled off the end of her nose

Not today thank you.

But she rolled an offering into a perfect cylinder and pushed it into his can.

Glasgow supports the needy.

The dress in the box felt heavy now, another weight to carry around. The box, her guilt, his son.

She bought him a book he wanted in Smith's. It felt good to be buying something for him.

He was probably still in his bath. She had been right to leave him in the steamy closeness of the hotel bathroom. That way there had been no opportunity to hold him, to cling to him. She knew he wouldn't want that. His way was best.

She was far too early, yet managed to arrive in the foyer looking and feeling flustered.

An Irish nun wrote down her particulars. A doctor came and examined and soothed. A smiling stranger in an expensive suit, spoke to her of pre-meds, blood and saline.

She was silent, moody, sitting on the edge of an abyss, waiting to jump, hoping to be pushed.

They came at last to take her to the theatre. Act 1, Scene 1.

The cheerful porter who wheeled her along the corridor had a voice as thick and Scottish as porridge. He supported The Rangers he told her. He was missing the game.

Support the homeless, Support the needy. Support the Rangers.

She counted twenty-seven flat ceiling lights before the lift doors clanged shut. Somewhere, someone was moaning. She closed her eyes so that she would not see the face of the doctor who would take her son away. She wondered if they would throw him into a bucket or burn him in an incinerator.

She laid her hands on her stomach, a blessing and a betrayal.

She felt the prick in her arm.

It's been nice to know you. I would have loved you if I could, but there can be no place for you in this world.

Hours later it seemed, she crawled out of the blackness. The walls around her were opaque, thick, clouded. She clutched at them, her fingers splayed. Then she was slipping, sliding down again, plummeting into a bottomless well.

Her shame was anaesthetised, her mind empty, but the pain in her belly was real, an ugly twisting serpent of pain that carried her away on its back and made her moan and try to clutch at its source.

An angel bent over her later, a heavenly analgesic, and to her right, great ruby drops moved slowly along plastic tubes. Life blood taken to the taker of life.

She was too tired to cry and yet greedy for it. She wondered what he was doing. She hoped he was drinking, trying to forget what they had done. She moaned in her need to reach him, and they stuck a needle in her arm, to stop a pain that would never be stopped.

Days later her husband came, newly arrived from Spain and solicitous. The lies she told slipped off her tongue so easily. Outside in the wet empty Sunday streets she felt trapped. A spider was spinning around her. A gossamer web enclosed her mind and a tangle of threads cut into her heart.

A weak December sun was shining in the south. Wet washing hung sadly on tower block balconies. A gang of skinny boys circled a girl on a tricycle, like in some Glaswegian war dance. The green box lay on the seat beside her, a statement that things would be different now.

As soon as they reached the motorway she felt sick, and thin bile rose in her throat. She weakly leaned over the verge of grass and vomited beside the entrails of a seagull.

I need him, she thought, and yet I have nothing to say.

When her husband had gone, she carefully opened the box.

The dress was beautiful, more beautiful and delicate than she remembered. Black jet dewdrops sparked in the light of the Chinese lamp beside their bed.

It was too beautiful for her now.

Gently she spread open the wide skirt.

First , a gash from waist to hem and then a slash to open a seam. Her fingers crushed and tore at the lace. She was sobbing now. Great painful sobs tore from deep in her belly until the mutilated masterpiece lay at her feet.

She wrapped it, gently now, in the tissue paper and placed it in its green box.

Tomorrow when she was stronger.

She would throw it in the bucket.

Or then again, she might burn it.

The Glittering Prize

by

Lori Duffy

Gordon went to his wife and hugged her. 'He's a big boy now, and you did the best you could. Let the rest go,' he said. 'And come away from the window or he'll think you're watching him.'

Hannah nodded, and when Gordon released her, glanced back out the window over the sink one last time. 'I doubt he'd notice my watching him, Gordon, he's still waiting for the post van.'

Hannah Fairley let her gaze travel the snow-covered driveway to where her son, Scott, was leaning on the wrought-iron gate. He wore only an oversize t-shirt and worn-out jeans, his shoulders hunched against the wind.

'He's been out there for almost half an hour,' she said. 'And he's shivering. If he doesn't come in soon he'll catch a chill. Do you think I should call him in?'

'The mood he's in at the moment, he certainly wouldn't appreciate it.'

Gordon was opening the cupboard looking for a pen. 'Why is it absolutely impossible to find a pen whenever I want to do a crossword?' he muttered crossly. 'It's hopeless!' He slammed the drawer of the cupboard shut.

Hannah knew that his irritation stemmed from the anxiety of the past few days. She glanced back out. Scott hadn't moved but he watched the departing postman with a troubled expression on his face. She turned back to her husband. 'Did this young woman definitely say she'd write to him?'

'I've no idea,' said Gordon vaguely. 'But she did promise to contact him.'

'Yes, but when? Today? Tomorrow? Never? I can't bear to see him suffering like this.'

She poured a second cup of coffee and sat down at the kitchen table, considering the hold this woman, this Angela, had on Scott: the boyish grin and the sparkle in his eyes when he'd told her of their first meeting, the sudden interest in buying new clothes and having his hair freshly styled. He rarely smiled now, she thought miserably; he was so desperate, so dependent on the phone and the post.

Gordon broke her reverie. 'Try not to worry. He'll get over it, you know that. What about the article he wrote for the school magazine? He sat by the phone for almost a week before it got accepted. Then the time he had the holiday romance, the Italian girl. What was her name? Maria? Don't you remember how he waited for her to write?'

'How could I forget? But that was different, he was only sixteen.'

151

'I don't think the passing of a few years changes anything, Hannah. Besides, this seems more serious, somehow.' Gordon risked a quick glance. 'Oh, here he comes, maybe he'll put us out of our misery.'

But when the door slammed shut behind him a few seconds later, they knew that their waiting was not yet over. Hannah forced a brightness into her voice that she didn't feel. 'There's another post this afternoon, dear. Maybe-'

'Maybe the boy could do with some breakfast, Hannah,' Gordon interrupted.

'No thanks, Dad.' He looked at his mother. 'I'm not hungry.'

Hannah poured him a coffee and handed it to him. 'Well, at least drink this, Scott, you must be frozen to the marrow.'

'Scott nodded his thanks and sat down opposite his father. Hannah decided it was time to leave Gordon to have a chat with him. 'I'll make a start on the chores then,' she said finally.

Folding his newspaper, Gordon thought he'd better tackle his son. But where to begin?

'No word then?' he asked more abruptly than he meant to.

'No.'

'Chin up, there's always tomorrow,' replied Gordon. 'You've only been waiting a few days. Give the girl a chance.'

'A few days?' Scott gave an exasperated sigh.' You haven't been counting the seconds, Dad. And it's been one week and three days to be precise.' He fixed his father with a gloomy stare. 'I feel wretched. Did you ever want, no need something as much as I do now?' He raised the mug to his lips. 'I've been a fool,' he said dryly. 'I don't need anyone to tell me it, but she really seemed sincere. And when she said she'd be in touch, I believed her.'

'Of course you did,' Gordon said reassuringly. 'And I'm sure she'll do just that. In fact, maybe she'll just give you a ring instead. You did say she was a pretty busy lady.'

For a moment Gordon thought he'd seen a smile tug at the corners of his son's mouth. But he shrugged and stared into his coffee. 'To tell the truth, Dad, I think she's forgotten all about me.'

Gordon made one last effort. 'If you need to talk, you know where to find me.'

Scott nodded in reply.

Gordon went out of the kitchen, climbed the stairs to the attic which he'd converted into a studio, and put on his paint-covered smock.

He stood in front of the half-finished canvas he'd started to work on last week and began casting a critical eye over it. Scott's sad eyes stared back at him.

Why did he feel such a compelling urge to paint his son? Was it because somehow he wanted to keep alive the memory of how he used to be, sunny natured and outgoing, before he'd pinned all his hopes and dreams on this one woman?

Angela. The name echoed in his mind. He pushed the thought aside and picked up his palette. He started to work, painting away the pained expression in Scott's eyes. If only it were that easy in real life.

Again he heard his son ask him if he'd ever wanted anything in his life that badly. Had he? He should have answered him, told him that the only thing he'd ever wanted was sitting in front of him - a son.

But then he was a man of few words, unlike his son, Gordon thought grimly.

Now he could only wait, and perhaps ease the pain slightly by painting his son the way he knew him to be.

Two hours later he heard the attic door creak open.

'Dad?'

He turned slowly to see his son standing in the doorway. Scott grinned and his features were transformed into an irresistibly boyish expression.

'She phoned, Dad. Just like you said.'

'And?' Gordon prompted. But he already knew the reply. He felt pride swell in him until he thought he was going to burst. 'She read your short story?'

'Yes, she did!' Scott enthused throwing his arms up in the air. 'And guess what? She's going to include it in the book she's publishing later this year.'

Thursday's Forest

by

Marjorie S Brock

Jessie looked at her watch. She would go just a little farther. She had never explored this part of the forest before, and it interested her immensely. She pressed aside the lower branches of a large beech as she turned into a little clearing. Then she saw it.

It was unlike any tree she knew. It was at the far end of the glade, which was overshadowed by the trees on either side, but she could see that its leaves appeared to be very dark, almost black - far too dark to be any kind of a beech. And the outline was quite different. It intrigued her: she must find out what it was.

'Come on, Ben,' she called. 'We'll just have a look at that funny tree and then we'll go home.'

The dog appeared and followed her to the edge of the clearing. Then he stopped. 'Oh, come on, do,' she cried. 'What's the matter with you?'

But Ben refused to obey. He ran backwards and forwards at the edge of the little glade, barking frantically.

Jessie retraced her steps, and put on the dog's lead. His whole body quivered and he kept on whimpering. 'You silly little dog,' she scolded him. 'We're just going a little farther.'

She went forward again, but the dog just pulled at the lead and sat down. Then he howled - a long mournful howl as if all the troubles in the world were upon him. The girl tugged at the lead, but Ben resisted with all his strength, still whimpering. He was plainly unhappy.

'All right, then. We'll go - it's getting late. But I did want to see that tree properly, and you spoiled it all. Naughty!'

The dog looked up at her mournfully as she turned to take the familiar forest path. But he made no more protest, as she moved away he trotted after her quietly.

Jessie felt a peculiar sense of frustration. She had wanted to examine the strange tree - and Ben was usually quite happy to accompany her wherever she wandered. Maybe she'd try again another day. And without Ben. She wondered what had upset him. There were no foxes or anything like that in the forest - as far as she knew. But she realised she didn't know that part of the forest at all. And for some reason it seemed very different from the western area, but with a strange attraction. Well, she'd explore it again one day soon.

John laughed when she told him about Ben's behaviour. 'That dog's spoiled,' he told her; 'he does just what he likes with you. But I've no idea, either, what that tree could be - it sounds unfamilar.'

'Ben's usually obedient, even if he has his little tricks,' Jessie protested. 'What I couldn't understand was that he seemed so - so unhappy, so upset.'

'Probably wanted his supper!' her husband laughed. 'But if you go to see the tree again, take a few leaves and then we might be able to have it identified.'

During the following days the thought of the tree came back frequently to Jessie's mind. A week later - Thursday again - an opportunity occurred for her to take the exploratory walk she had promised herself. She studied the forest area on the local map. It didn't look much more extensive than she had thought, but perhaps it was just the scale of the map that confused her. She couldn't find the point where she had come upon the little clearing, but then, she hadn't been paying much attention that other afternoon. if she took her usual route no doubt she'd find it again.

It was a fine, sunny day, and she felt quite excited as she set off. John wouldn't be home till late, so she had plenty of time. And she had given little Ben a good walk in the park that morning and then left him in the garden, so she felt free to explore as she wished.

With no reason to hurry she wandered through the trees, picking some of the little wild violets. She was lucky to live so near such a lovely place - just on the edge of country. And she much preferred the wildness of the forest to the little lanes winding through the cultivated fields or the meadows with the cows which Ben would have liked to chase.

She was going in the right direction, she knew, but she wasn't quite sure where the entrance to the little glade was situated. She must be near it now. But the time was passing and the sky was clouding over. She stood irresolute, debating whether to turn right or left, when she saw a man coming towards her. A forester! She'd ask him about the tree.

'You saw it? You saw the jay-tree?' he queried, in a tone that suggested almost that he didn't believe her.

'Is that what it's called - the 'J' tree?' she asked. 'I wanted to see it closer, but the dog kicked up such a fuss that I had to turn back. And now I don't seem able to find it again. It seemed unusual - so dark, with a great spread of foliage on either side nearly down to the ground, almost like - like two wings. It's not a native tree, surely? Do you know its origin?'

The man shook his head. 'No - no, I've not seen it,' he said slowly. 'I've - just heard tell of it. And - this is Thursday, too! But I'd forget it, an' if I was you.'

What a silly thing to say, she thought impatiently. 'But I *want* to see it,' she exclaimed. 'can you tell me which is the best path to take? The dog pulled me away the other day.'

155

Again the man shook his head. 'More sense than we have, animals have sometimes. Best forget it, I tell you. Stay with the forest you know and don't go exploring the unknown.' He seemed reluctant to discuss the matter further. 'I must away now.' He walked off rapidly.

Stupid fellow, she thought. And what had Thursday to do with it? Was there some mystery here? But she'd get to the bottom of it. Maybe the forester was new to the area and just didn't want to show his ignorance. Well, she'd just have to find the tree herself.

She turned, and suddenly she saw the large beech tree which concealed the opening she was seeking. How had she missed it? The grassy sward beneath her feet changed to more stony ground. She had noticed the previous time how different this part of the forest appeared. It was darker, and there were no little wild flowers, no ferns, just rough barren ground. She was conscious of a feeling of unease, but suppressed it. The place seemed forbidding, but she was determined she would just look at the tree and then turn back. Suddenly, directly ahead of her, she saw it, just as she remembered. She quickened her pace, scarcely conscious in her excitement that the sky was darkening and there was a noise which suggested approaching thunder. The tree seemed farther off than she thought, and she hurried on; but again it seemed to recede, and she felt a mounting dismay. She stumbled over the rough ground, conscious of only one thing - her desire to reach the tree, to touch it, to feel it.

Suddenly she tripped. She tried to recover her balance, but with a cry of despair she fell forward. She felt a moment of triumph mingled with fear - she had reached her objective. Then all went dark.

Consciousness came back slowly. She was half lying, half sitting, with her back against the tree trunk. She felt exhausted, as if she had been through some untoward struggle. Fighting her weakness she made an attempt to sit up. Her hair was caught - evidently snared in a branch as she fell. Pushing her hands against the hard ground she tried to lever herself upwards, but she didn't seem to have any strength. She looked about her as she tried to get some sort of purchase to enable her to stand up. The forked root of the tree, beside her, was hard and horny - just like a bird's foot. The idea was unpleasant. Her ankle was caught under it in some way and she seemed unable to free it.

She stopped struggling for a moment, then put up her hands to disentangle her hair. There was a tug on it. But there was no wind! Now she began to feel afraid - afraid of something she didn't understand. A cold trickle of terror travelled slowly down her back as she remembered the forester's warning and Ben's distress. With an effort she lifted herself, wrenched her foot free, and got to her knees. Again she put her hands up to her head. What she felt was not the twigs of a tree - to her horror her hands touched something warm and clawed, which moved as her fingers sought to loosen her hair.

156

With a cry of anguish she dropped her hands and sank again to the ground. She dared not look up. What had she encountered? What danger had she walked into in her foolish persistence? The 'J' tree? The *jay-tree!* 'Don't go seeking the unknown' the forester had said. And as she realised that she was trapped she heard that sound again, high above her. Not the familiar crackle of anticipated thunder from the ever darkening sky, but the exultant cackle of a rapacious bird of prey.

The Hunter And The Hunted

by

Gary Fleming

The wind whipped the powdery snow into snarling flurries, shaking the ancient firs in the desolate valley. A single light shone forlornly through the obscuring snow, pinpointing the location of a tiny village perched on the steep side of the valley. The moon struggled to peer through giant, threatening clouds, and the night sky threw down blizzard after blizzard until almost dawn.

The winter sun blinked above the horizon, rheumy and pale. Snow covered everything. In the crisp, clear air, a dozen lines of black smoke drifted skywards from squat buildings of thick wood. A dog barked, shattering the cold, fragile peace. Doors creaked open, men emerged from their homes, blinking like miners hobbling from deep caves into sunlight. The snow was nearly two feet deep. Conversation drifted like the smoke above, talk of grain stores, firewood, fishing and fresh water. Fur-clad men walked from the little settlement into the surrounding forest, eyes scanning the ground for deer tracks. As the day went on, firewood was chopped, and the white snow was discoloured by busy feet. Deep in the forest, something stirred.

The man stood, dusted himself down. Snow trickled like sand grains onto his shoulders as he knelt in the shelter of pine branches he had constructed the previous night. He crawled out and surveyed the wilderness around him. His eyes, dark and malevolent, shone with an unnatural intensity, and his dark clothing clung to him in tatters. The wind ruffled his shock of raven-black hair threaded with silver, and his harsh, angular features tightened with the cold. In the far distance, a hunting horn sounded. They had found his tracks again. Unhurriedly he packed his meagre belongings and set off into a steep-sided valley.

A scream rose, long and loud, from the forest not a mile from the village. A second scream began but was cut off. In the village, heads turned in fear. Huge men trembled in their furs, knowing what that scream signified. It had begun again.

He watched from the crest of a hill. Below, steam rose from ripped bodies, snow stained deep red. Blood stained tracks were scattered all over the clearing, concentrated like hungry piranhas around the three corpses. Slowly, the man walked down the hill, coming to a halt beside the bodies. Behind him, he caught the sound of dogs baying hysterically. He sniffed the air like an animal, closing his mind to the persistent visions within. Figures surrounded him.

The villagers eyed the man nervously, seeing the long sword across his back and the livid scars twisting across his face. They had rushed to this spot, knowing what they would find, knowing that the bear was again awakened. They had not, however, expected to see this man. Their leader, a grey-haired giant in wolfskin, stepped forward.

'Stranger, what happened here?'

The man looked at him and cocked his head. 'Bear,' he said, his voice a deep whisper.

'Aye, and you are not safe in these woods,' replied the grey-haired villager.

'I am safe nowhere. I will kill it, but . . .' In the distance, now much nearer, a horn sounded, men shouted in harsh voices.

'. . . Help me.'

That evening, many horsemen rode into the village, huge black hounds baying at the horses' sides. A tall, sober man in black furs and a grey cloak went round the dark homesteads with two armoured bodyguards, searching each building. Presently, he joined the main body of horsemen, approaching a red-haired giant on a huge black horse.

'He has been here, I am sure of it!' said the grey-cloaked man, brushing his hair back with one gloved hand.

'Master, it's bin years! 'E could be dead as far 'n we know!' the red-haired man replied.

'No, Deacon, I feel him. He lives, as surely as my son is dead.'

'Me lord, it's bin so long, we go home, aye?'

The tall, grey-cloaked man didn't reply, instead he leapt onto his horse and called to his men. They swept out of the village, leaving it strangely silent.

He sat by the hearth, a pipe hanging loosely from his mouth. He smiled at the clustered faces, and patted an old dog which lay at his feet.

'The Baron has good reason to hunt me. I killed his son.'

Memories blasted their way into his mind, displaying themselves obscenely at his vision, filling every corner of his brain. He saw again the drunken night at the castle, the vindictive young noble and the hot-headed young warrior. The noble standing near him, trying to force a reaction in the smoke filled room. Finally the arrogant young man had slashed the warrior's face with a dagger. He had only to strike once. The youth was drunk, could not defend himself against the vicious blow. The noble had looked surprised, then dead. He had ran, straight out of the castle and into the wilderness. Years had passed. Names had been mentioned, and his face had been recognised in a lonely inn. Since then, the Baron had hunted him like an animal. Now, the Baron would himself be hunted. His consciousness surfaced and an idea slowly took shape.

The villagers then told their story, that of the Great Ice Bear, which appeared in the heart of winter and killed men when they hunted. Many in the village would rather starve than confront the Bear.

At the next dawn, he left the village, leaving not even his name and taking only what he arrived with. In the wild, his instincts again sharpened, he followed the tracks of his quarry with ease. Many hours passed. Far ahead, it chewed on a deer. He smelled the odour of death and knew that this was the Bear. He advanced sword in hand. It turned, a challenge growled, thunderous and menacing. In the distance, a horn sounded. The man smiled, and ran swiftly in the horn's direction. The Bear roared in fury, its white fur rippling in the moonlight. Man and Bear sped across the snow, racing among stately pines and snow-laden firs, and shouts floated like lifelines to the man.

Abruptly, he burst into a clearing. Faces stared at him in surprise, then cries of 'There he is!' and 'Get him!' rang through the night air. The man reversed direction, then climbed a huge, dark tree like a squirrel. The warriors and their Baron came face to face with the Bear. In the titanic battle that followed, the Baron and most of his men were killed, the few survivors running through the forest like frightened rabbits. The bear lay among heaps of carnage, its prone form jagged with thrown projectiles and weapons. The man climbed down the tree, surveyed the bodies. He looked up at the moon, then started walking. The trees enfolded him gently, and the night hid him swiftly.

Five Letters

by

Christopher Ellis

'Why have you let me kid myself for so long?' Hissed Karyer, his stare injecting a bitterness deep beyond the blue tinted eyes of Liberty. Karyer felt his mind seethe with anger, anger at her, for the destruction of something that had seemed perfect, almost the fairytale.

Liberty's eyes swung sharply away from Karyer's piercing gaze,

'I . . . I . . .'

, 'No . . . Just forget it,' Broke in Karyer, 'I don't want to know . . . Just get out . . . Get out!.' His shout made Liberty jump, her eyes darting wildly,

'Please . . . Let me . . .'

'Just shut up . . . I don't care . . . I've heard it all before. Just leave before I do something I might regret.'

Liberty started to weep, she had been trying to be strong, trying to do this right. She should've known that he would take it this way, but she had no option: Everything was too complex, it scared her. She had let Karyer get in too far, it was best for both of them to finish it. Best for both of them.

She stood and ran at the door, tears beyond control stinging at her cheeks as she ran down the stairs, grabbing her jacket from the coat rack at the front door and out into the crisp night air, gasping and whimpering, hurt and crying.

Karyer stood at his window, watching Liberty run down the artificially illuminated street and into the shadows beyond. He turned, angry, and took a swing at a wall with his fist, screaming as the pain burned in his hand. Cradling the injured arm on his lap, he sat on his bed and just let the tears come.

By the time Liberty got home and was safely locked in, her tears had dried and she had managed to compose herself slightly. The hardest part was over, now she just had to begin to forget. . . Get on with her life. Perhaps the future would hold someone who could give her the love she needed. Karyer could never give her that. She truly convinced herself that Karyer was out of her life forever.

It was two days later that she received the first letter. She knew exactly what it was long before she opened it, and even this she did wearily.

'Dear Liberty,

I'm sorry about the way I spoke to you last night, it's just that I got angry, I couldn't think straight. Please, I know you just want some space. If ever I was smothering you, you should have said. You know how much I love you and how much I need you right now. We can't just throw it all in the garbage like some piece of filth.

I guess what I'm trying to say is that I need you back, I'm begging you to come back. Please call me, I love you so much.

All my love,
Karyer.'

Liberty sighed as she carefully and deliberately ripped the letter into small pieces that would never be retrieved, and threw all of his words into the trash.

'Leave me alone. . .' She whispered as she watched the pieces float onto the garbage. She stared at them briefly, but snapped herself out of the dream. She had a life to be getting on with. Her other friends never saw enough of her while she had been dating Karyer. That would change now. It would be just like old times, she thought.

Liberty awoke one morning some days later, her mind still full of images from the night before. She smiled as she remembered the party. Oh yeah, that had been a good one. Who was that guy she'd met? Saul! yeah, that's right. She smiled again. Shaun Warrick really knew how to throw a party.

She wrapped her dressing gown tightly around herself and came down the stairs to make herself a coffee, picking up the post on the way. Junk mail and. . . Oh Christ, another letter from Karyer. She threw the letter onto the table and made her coffee, holding her mug tightly with both hands and blowing onto the surface causing steam to rise onto her face. She stood, gazing through the soft grey whisps of the letter. God, why couldn't he just leave her alone . . . ?

'Dear Liberty,

As I write I wonder what you're doing. I guess you're out there enjoying yourself, putting me out of your life forever, aren't you? How can you do that to me? How can all that we have done together mean nothing to you? You're not like that Liberty, that's not you. Please, please come back.

All my love,
Karyer.'

Liberty shook her head. No Karyer, it's over and I never want to hear from you again. Her guilt eased and she crumpled Karyer's second letter.

The third arrived three days later. Liberty removed it from her immediate memory by placing it in a drawer, where it remained, sometimes.

Picture Karyer standing at a window, looking onto the dark world. Picture him alone and lonely. See him turn and sit at his desk, pouring his heart into the third letter:

'Dear Liberty,

Why are you ignoring my letters? I'm begging you to come back so we can at least talk this through. I don't know what to say to bring you back, all I know for sure is that I love you more than anything else in the world. I want to spend the last days of my life with you, I want to share my life with you. I know you still love me because these things never die, not really.

You know what I'm going through . . . The thought of never being able to hold you again is driving me insane.

Don't you remember all the fun times? When we were at the zoo together and you said you loved me for the first time? I went back there yesterday, I sat at the same place and I remembered it all so vividly, I remember everything so vividly.

I know that I'm selfish, but all I want is to be happy, it's not too much to ask. I don't want to hate you. I never want to hate you.

I cant' say anymore. I don't know what else to say,

I love you so much,
Karyer.'

Liberty never read it. Sometimes she would want to and she would take it from the drawer and just look at it. Seeing Karyer's writing triggered memories that made her heart twinge, and she would be so tempted to return to him, but no, she had to be strong. She always knew it would be difficult for him, but God damn it! It was difficult for her. She wouldn't have broken up with him after four years if she was happy. Towards the end she had felt trapped and she was too young to deal with that, that and the other things. She had to leave, she just couldn't stay, she felt like he was killing her youth and she didn't want to hate him for that.

After some deep thought she decided to write to him, tell him it was over, that there was nothing he could say to save them, and to say goodbye, forever. This then was the fourth letter:

'Dear Karyer,

I know this is difficult for you, it's difficult for me too but I couldn't take it anymore. I was trapped with you and you knew that, you milked that for all it was worth and I just couldn't take anymore. I'm only twenty, I've got a life too. You always acted like I

163

belonged to you and I don't. I'm me, a free spirit, able to do what I damn well like, and for once I plucked up the courage to do just that. You've got to understand, it's over. I know I said I would always be there for you, but Karyer, I was never there for me, never, and I'm sorry but it was killing me.

Please, please, just let me go,
Goodbye Karyer,
Liberty.'

Time slips by, day by day. And soon it is almost a full month since Liberty has heard from Karyer. In that time she has seen Saul a few times. Liberty likes Saul, he makes her laugh and takes her mind of the trials of everyday life. To Liberty he is refreshing and so different from Karyer. Liberty thinks that soon, she and Saul might get together and that pleases her because all she really wants is to put the past behind her, that's not wrong? Is it?

But just this morning, Liberty received Karyer's last letter. She debated about opening it, or just hiding it away in the drawer with the previous one. She decided to read it. Why? She truly does not know, but the fifth letter read:

'Dear Liberty,
I understand. I will always love you, but I understand.

Goodbye,
Karyer.'

Now at last the shackles that held her to Karyer are broken, and a huge swell of relief rises inside Liberty and she sighs softly. When the cancer that eats away at Karyer eventually kills him, at least she can live, at least she has managed to save herself from that and all the pain it would encompass . . .

A Hell Of A Night's Work

by

Paul Forte

Jack pressed the screwdriver into the gap between window and frame. Globules of sweat, mixed with rain, ran from his forehead to his nose then leapt off. Silently he reached within his black pilot jacket and pulled out a small hammer. As he did this his watch chimed one am. Startled he let out a breath from his quivering lungs.

Moving position very slightly on the small wooden porch Jack proceeded to tap the screwdriver with the hammer. There was an audible click as the old window's lock gave way. He winced as the sound seemed agonisingly loud. After a few minutes of crouching, even lower, on the ancient mansion's porch he felt sure the sound had not been heard. With this relieving knowledge he felt it was okay to open the window and did so.

Once the window was open he then climbed through into hopefully, the master bedroom. When inside Jack allowed himself a sigh of relief, the strong shimmering moonlight had revealed that this was indeed the correct room. Feeling a little more relaxed he pulled the heavy black velvet curtains into place.

The room now deprived of any outside light was shrouded in darkness. Jack pulled a small penlight from the back pocket of his jeans and pressed it on. As he did so a thin beam of white light pierced the inky blackness of the room. This tiny amount of light allowed him to find a small table lamp and switch it on. The lamp, when Jack's eyes became accustomed to its light, allowed him to switch off the penlight.

The master bedroom was, he decided, rather plain. There was nothing that conveyed wealth in the room at all. He smiled though as his eyes fell upon the bedside table. 'The place where most people keep their treasured possessions,' thought Jack.

He sat on the large double bed facing the table and opened the drawer. Quickly and professionally he began sifting through the contents. He sighed as there appeared to be nothing of real value.

Before going to search elsewhere Jack pulled the small drawer right out of the table and looked into the gap. Switching the penlight on again he noticed a small back box. Within seconds he had the box in his hands and was opening it.

The small velvet covered box contained many very valuable items; gold chains, bracelets and rings, each encrusted with a myriad of jewels. He gasped as he saw one ring in particular. It was old, like the rest, but encrusted with a circle of diamonds and emeralds. In the centre of this circle of sizeable gems was an even larger ruby. The ring sparkled in the lamplight and Jack sighed at its beauty and the fact its gems would be cut up and the ring melted when he sold it. He couldn't help feeling sad about the fact that no one would ever wear the ring again.

Wanting to see what it looked like worn he pulled off his left glove with his teeth, still holding the ring in his right. He knew the ring was really a woman's ring so he placed it on the pinkie finger of his left hand. As soon as the ring slid onto his finger there was a blinding flash of white light and Jack was gone.

It was dark, very dark. Even with his eyes wide open Jack couldn't penetrate the light-less void. Before moving he decided to try and figure out where he was.

Well wherever he was he was lying down on what felt like a very comfortable bed? No couch. As he was still trying to figure out where he was he suddenly noticed a light which hadn't been there before. The light emanated through the cracks of what looked like a door. With this discovery Jack decided to sit up on the couch.

'Where am I,' he thought. 'In hospital? Yes that's it someone came into the room and hit me over the head with something. After that I fell unconscious, and here I am in hospital.' Even as Jack turned these thoughts over in his mind he didn't believe them. A few moments later though he had a thought which seemed more plausible and no matter how hard he tried to stop it the thought surfaced.

'Perhaps I'm. . . dead,' he whispered to himself, starting to feel a little worried. 'Then perhaps I wasn't hit over the head, perhaps I was. . . shot.' As he was beginning to get more and more frightened the door he had noticed earlier opened very quietly, allowing a vast streak of bright white light into the room. The light was so bright he had to put his hand over his eyes to shield them until they became accustomed to it. Once he could see properly Jack stood up and headed towards the door. Before he reached the door he paused as his overactive imagination started up again. 'Am I in heaven? or. . . hell?' he pondered.

'If I'm in hell then where are all the flames and screams of pain. Everyone knows hell is full of people being tortured and there are flames everywhere,' he thought trying to re-assure himself and failing. Closing the thoughts of flames and hell in his mind Jack stepped out of the door and into a corridor. 'A strange corridor,' he thought. 'There's plenty of light, but no lights.' Thankful for something else to think about he headed down the corridor which, a few minutes later, ended in another door.

This door was much the same as the other one, white and modern looking. There was a plaque on this door though, which read *The Boss*. Jack gulped and began to sweat profusely. As he was starting to wonder why the door had no handle a voice spoke. The voice was very loud and deep. It echoed in Jack's mind and oddly enough nowhere else. The voice said in a friendly tone,

166

'Welcome, Jack. Do come in.' With that the door opened.

Inside was an office. The office had a filing cabinet, a mahogany desk and a high backed leather chair.

In the chair sat a man. The man was wearing a black and white pinstripe suit with a white shirt and black tie. The man's face was young with deep set eyes. His neatly trimmed black beard and moustache did little to hide his sharp features. Black hair fell about his shoulders but still looked immaculate as did everything about this man.

'Come on,' he said. 'Don't be shy.' Jack stepped into the room very dubiously. The man motioned for him to sit in the chair behind Jack which, he could have sworn, wasn't there before. Despite this realisation Jack sat down. 'Now then Jack, em. . .' said the man.

'Morgan, Jack Morgan.'

'Ah, yes Morgan,' said the man turning to the filing cabinet behind him and pulling a file. Swivelling back round to face Jack the man opened the file. 'Let me see,' he said. 'Six counts of breaking and entry, four counts of theft and two counts for speeding. Not too bad Jack.'

'Yes,' agreed Jack feeling his past wasn't too lurid.

'I'm sure we don't need to send you to, the other place,' said the man. Jack sighed. 'Yes,' continued the man, 'You'll fit in nicely here I'm sure.' With that the man raised his hand palm facing Jack there was another flash of brilliant white light and Jack was once again gone.

The next thing Jack knew he was surrounded by a thick warm mist not unlike steam. As he began to get very frightened the mist started to clear. About thirty feet in front of him Jack could see the man. His appearance had changed slightly though, he now wore black leather trousers with nothing on top except a thin red cape. The man smiled and a long steaming red trident appeared in his right hand. Evil laughter filled Jack's head but the man's lips did not move.

'Guess where you are Jack,' said the man still his lips not moving.

'Em. . . Heaven?' proposed Jack.

'Guess again,' said the man.

'Hell?' said Jack shaking a little now.

'Rrrrright!' said the man, 'Or purgatory as some prefer, and I am, well let me see I have many names. For you though I think Satan would be best, yes you can call me Satan. Now to business,' said Satan. As he said this a large wooden crucifix appeared behind Jack. A few seconds later Jack found his hands bound to it by thick leather straps. Instinctively he struggled trying to free himself. Satan smiled at this obviously enjoying every moment of Jack's discomfort. Once Jack realised he couldn't get free Satan raised the trident like an athlete might raise the javelin, then spoke once more.

'In case you're thinking, now that you're dead you can't feel any pain Jack I'll let you into a little secret. You are not dead. The ring you put on transported you here,' said Satan trying to hold back the laughter. Jack looked at the ring on his left hand and started to sob. 'Another thing, if you think you'll be missed back on earth, don't. I was kind enough to send an agent to replace you, who will in time cause the premature death of your wife and daughter.' Jack stopped sobbing and began to shake with rage.

'No!' yelled Jack.

'Yes,' shouted Satan pulling back the trident then throwing it into the air. Jack watched helplessly as the trident headed toward him. The trident missed him though the shaft caught the side of his face and he screamed with pain as he smelled his own burning flesh. Satan laughed once more as though he could feel every ounce of Jack's pain and relished it. As Jack looked up at Satan another trident appeared in his right hand.

'Fire torpedo number two,' he yelled in a mad joyous frenzy and threw the second trident. This second trident whistled through the air missing Jack but striking the cross bar of the crucifix and hitting the strap holding his right leather clad hand freeing it. Instantly Jack reached over to his other hand and pulled the ring off his finger.

There was a flash of blinding white light. Once again Jack found himself transported. This time he was back in the master bedroom of the mansion he had been robbing. Things were exactly as he had left them apart from one exception. Another Jack.

The carbon copy of Jack was sifting professionally through the contents of a certain small box covered in black velvet. Jack watched on as his other self began taking off his left glove with his teeth. The glove fell to the floor and just as Jack's other self was about to put a beautiful sparkling ring on his finger a voice yelled.

'No!'

The voice was Jack's. The double reached into the gap between the back of his jeans and pulled out a small black Smith and Wesson. Jack noticed this and did the same. When he fired the gun he had already heard the other gun go off and felt the bullet tearing into the flesh of his chest and deep through his ribs. Jack fell to the floor watching his other self do the same. The last thing he saw was his other self disappear in a blinding flash of white light.

Two policeman walked down the flight of steps leading out of the ancient mansion.

'Sarge?' said the younger of the two.

'Yeah,' said the older one evidently a sergeant.

'I don't understand, why would a guy break into a place to kill himself?'

'If you ask me,' said the sergeant, 'there were two of 'em, one got greedy and killed the other. When he finished he wiped the gun clean and placed it in the other's hand.'

'How come we found two left gloves then, both with identical prints inside them?' persisted the younger one.

'Now there you got me,' said the sarge.

As Jack awoke he found himself lying on a familiar couch in a familiar dark room. Just then a familiar evil booming voice filled his head.

'Welcome . . . Back . . . Jack.'

The Rowan Tree

by

J Macdonald

Those who walk alone in the quiet solitary places are often aware of some undefinable presence that surrounds them. This is more evident in scenes where people once lived, and live no longer. There the lone traveller will pause a while, and tread gently, breathless, awaiting some challenge to his trespass; hearing in the rustle of the wind in the long grass the sad echoes of voices long dead.

In such solitudes all things are born, to grow together in harmony or hostility, each dependent on the other, until at last they go from the place where they grew, unknowing and unheeding. Yet there may remain, or appear again, some fragment of the past that will cause the wanderer to stop and look upon, and wonder.

So I remember Burnhead, a poor and lonely place standing high on the hillside where the pasture land yielded to the encroaching heather; just an old two-roomed cottage, a barn with an earthen floor, and a single rowan tree.

Here the old widow-woman lived out her solitary years. Her husband, long dead, had been shepherd to the farm in the valley. The new shepherd had a house in the village and the farmer, having no further use for the cottage readily agreed to her request to live on at Burnhead, although warning of the difficulties that would come with the passing of the years.

'But you'll mind now,' she said in her gentle voice, 'when I'm away, you'll see that the hill is made all trig and bonny. . .' The farmer said no word, but touched her hand lightly, and she knew it would be so.

Yet she was not alone, the wild creatures of the hill knew her and heard her voice and were not afraid. The broken barn gave safe refuge in season to blackbird and swallow and robin, and to this place she brought distressed birds and animals she had found on the hill; a tawny owl with damaged wing and near starvation was fed and sheltered until it was able to return to its natural haunts. A young fox cub lying beside a dead vixen caught in a trap, moorhens from the burn, even young lapwings - that most timid of birds - almost frozen to death in a late spring storm, were only a few of the wild creatures that survived in her care. And in the long summer days carefully tended the bright circle of wild flowers in the simple garden by the cottage door, campion, blue gentian, yellow iris and many others that she had taken from the hill when she had come to Burnhead so many years before.

One morning the travelling grocer, rattling up the track in his van on his weekly visit, saw no smoke rising from the chimney and found her lying dead by the side of the garden.

Soon after she was gone the farmer came with his men. They stripped and burned the roof timbers from barn and cottage, the tractor lunged repeatedly at the ancient walls until no stone remained upon another; they were taken down to the farm to fill in the weed-grown duck pond.

When all was cleared away, the tractorman put a chain round the rowan tree and fixed the end to his tractor, but the farmer held up his hand and went over and stood a while beneath the tree, shielding his eyes from the sunlight that filtered through the branches.

No, man,' he said gruffly, 'let it be; it's been a long time a growing. I'll not be destroying that. Just let it be!' He strode off down the hill without a backward glance.

Then the ploughshare cut deeply through the garden; the plants and flowers were uprooted and scattered on the hillside, the circle broken at last. The soil was levelled and raked and rolled and sown with new grass, till nothing remained to show that a dwelling had ever been in that place.

Winter came, the land was deserted, there was no life on the hill. But in time the storms were past, the plovers returned, swooping and crying above the heather.

One evening I was walking on the hill for no particular reason, and my footsteps took me, by chance it seemed, close by the rowan tree.

'Ah, old rowan tree,' I said as I walked in its shadow, 'the rowan tree that keeps witches and ill fortune from the door! But there's nothing now to protect . . . I stopped abruptly. Before me where the sheep lay content on the new grass were buttercup and gentian and all the others, in neat circle nodding in the soft evening air as if nothing had ever come to disturb their serene existence.

I was strangely compelled to linger in that benign place, and stayed there, quiet and thoughtful, hearing only the whisper of the burn and the curlews calling across the valley, until the sun went from the hill.

I never passed that way again.

The Old Man Of The Wild West

by

John Robertson

The arrival of Abe McCabe in Edinburgh was not the most important item in the Capital's history. His Wild West connection may have inspired a double-barrelled reason. Anyway, Abe was one hundred and twenty years old, give or take a day or two, and his visit was timed to coincide with a Clan gathering, of which he was to be the honoured guest, and a Television presentation concerning the Caledonian influence in the early days of the so-called Wild West.

Longevity had enabled him to be *The* Senior member of the Clan, and this was their way of showing it. For his age, his amazing good health had allowed the sponsors a little scope in bringing him to this country, though they were sensible enough to realise that much care and attention would have to be given to the old man, lest the hazards of travelling proved too much.

My encounter with Abe was brief, but I was no coward. He was reclining in a comfortable armchair, looking out of the Hotel window, enjoying that tremendous view of Princes Street, and the hustle and bustle of mid-afternoon. He had obviously managed to shake himself free of his captors, and seemed to be happy with the break.

I simply could not resist the opportunity to try and have a few words with him. A man as old as all that surely must have had some wonderful memories to recall. Tactfully, I approached him with,

'Please don't think me terribly forward, but may I join you for a little while?'

Old Abe looked stern for a moment, then he smiled, and said, 'Sure thing, buddy. Grab yourself a seat.'

As I did so, he apologised, 'Ma hearin' aint what it used to be, but heck, at ma age, I aint done too bad.'

'Quite true,' I said, then I began to study his face. It said everything. I was reading between the lines. 'Is it true,' I inquired, 'that Smokey Mountain Joe McCoy shot six men one afternoon in a gunfight at Dodge City?'

Abe sipped his coffee, puffed on his pipe, then recalled, 'Yep! McCoy was a mean ornery critter. Could shoot the wings off a bee at fifty yards. Him an' Billy the Kid just didn't get on. Didn't like each other very much.'

I put it to him, 'Whoever called it the Wild West wasn't joking?'

He slapped his thigh, and reminded me, 'Goldarnit, pardner, them days was mean days. Most men of ma age died when they was twenty. Lead-poisonin'.' The chronological logic of that remark escaped me, but I was able to capture Abe's retrospective journey, as he continued, 'That there Jesse James was a tough 'un. Him an' his brother, Frank, led that there Sheriff a merry old barn dance. When ya looked into Jesse's eyes, guess what was there?'

I hesitated, before suggesting, 'Death, perhaps?'

'Nope!' snorted Abe. 'One was blue, the other was brown. Meanest critter I remember was a gunslinger called Big Jake. He was nicknamed 'The Undertaker's Friend'. Hard-drinkin', hard-ridin', hard bitten son of a b. He was so prickly, they reckon he was weaned on cactus juice.'

Abe was clearly enjoying his sojourn into the past, as he regaled me with details about Abilene, Tombstone, the Younger Brothers, the Daltons, the Hole in the Wall Gang. Listening to Abe was like opening a window into the Wild West of long, long ago. They were all there . . . Wyatt Earp, 'Doc' Halliday, Kit Carson, General Custer. Very little escaped Abe's verbal analysis.

The odd occasion arose when he seemed to be forgetting, but gradually, the light in his eye would flicker, then gleam into a positive incandescent description of a time, or a place, or an event from those wild days in the old West. The reminiscent exercise was exciting, and I told him so.

'Fantastic!' I exclaimed. 'Absolutely fantastic!'

The old man looked at me, and he seemed a little puzzled when he inquired, 'Fantastic? What's fantastic?'

'I'm surprised,' I said, 'that you should even ask that, Mr McCabe. Everything's fantastic. The fact that you are the age you are, and the fact that you knew all those famous characters in the old Wild West.'

Old Abe stopped sipping his coffee. he stopped puffing his pipe. He stopped gazing out at Princes Street. He turned to me, and retorted angrily.

'What you blabbin' about, young 'un? I aint ever knowed any of them critters. I aint ever been to any of them places I've been tellin' you about. No sirree, not me!'

My confusion was complete, and, bewildered, I stammered, 'B-b-but how come you seem to know so much about the Wild West?'

Abe McCabe, the old man of the Wild West, shrugged, then informed me, 'Stands to reason. I saw it all on the Television.'

Well, goldarnit, pardner! . . . All my fanciful theories went that-a-way!

Siller For The Lochies

by

William F Hendrie

'Wha wants tae ken aboot Jamie the Saxth?' muttered Jimmy Johnston, the leader of the Linlithgow Lochies.

The Lochies were not famed for the attention which they paid to any of auld Tarry Beard's lessons and this was particularly true of last period on a Friday afternoon.

Suddenly, however, Jimmy was all ears, for Tarry Beard was describing how King James tried to solve his constant money problems with the English Parliament in London, by acquiring the silver mines in the Bathgate Hills.

'One of the mines near Torphichen, only about five miles from here, was so rich in silver that it was called God's Blessing,' he droned on just as the big bell rang for four o'clock, and freedom.

'Did ye hear whit he said aboot siller in the Bathgate Hills?' demanded Jimmy of the other Lochies as they barged down the school steps.

'Aw furgit it,' snorted Billy Sneddon. 'We dinnae want tae think aboot history in oor ain time!'

'Aye furgit it,' agreed wee Jockie Grant as he danced across the causies of the West Port and down into the High Street. 'Nair mair school 'til Monday.'

'Come on you lot. Am half starvin'. Let's get doon tae Cabs afore the rest,' chipped in Davie Dewar.

'Whits the use o' going tae Cabs?' shouted Billy. 'We hivnae ony money.'

'But dae ye no see?' demanded Jimmy again.

'See whit?'

'See that we could be rich, boys.'

Wee Jocky touched his head and shook it sadly. 'Aw Jimmy, a hale week at school's been too much fur ye.'

Davie and Billy nodded in sorrowful agreement.

'Listen ye glaikit bunch, it's a guid job yiv got me as leader o' the Lochies. Did nane o' ye listen tae whit auld Tarry wis sayin'?'

'Wha evir listens tae Tarry?' asked Davie as they reached the bright yellow painted door of Cabrelli's Ice Cream Parlour and Fried Fish and Chips Sitting Room, which was his idea of the next best place to paradise. 'Come on you lot, I got a shilling frae ma dad fur walkin' his dugs, so I'll treat ye.'

174

'Get yer waffers then maybe ye'll listen better aince ye'r fed,' sighed Jimmy patiently as they all settled round one of the round wrought iron tables, where the Lochies had held many a previous council of war.

'Auld Tarry Beard said that Jamie Saxth wha used tae bide up at the palace, wis short o' cash and found siller tae help him get by. And whaur did he find the siller?' He looked round at Davie, Billy and Jocky. 'He found it right here in the hills behind the palace. So whits tae stop us daein' the same?'

'The morrow ye'll aw ask yer mithers fur sandwiches, ginger beer an' aw, an' we'll awa up tae the siller mines.'

And so the great Saturday silver mines safari set out.

'Hey Jimmy! They hills is awfie steep,' panted wee Jockie as he struggled to keep up with the rest of the Lochies.

'Ye shid hae done yer exercises at drill,' Jimmy yelled back as he led the way out of the beech woods and on up the hill. But where exactly were the silver mines? Jimmy wished desperately that auld Tarry Beard had dealt with the mines in geography rather than history, then maybe he would have shown them on a map.

But it would never do to allow his men to know that he was not exactly certain where the mines were, so they plodded on.

'We're surely at the top, now,' declared wee Jocky. 'Remember ma legs is no as long as yours.'

'No quite, Jocky,' comforted Jimmy, 'but we'll stop for some rations.'

'Ma mither's pit potted heid on ma sannies,' grumbled Davie, 'An I'm half starvin'. '

'Here hae some o' ma ones,' offered Jimmy, anxious to keep up morale.

'Whits on them?' queried Davie.

'We'll at least it isnae potted heid,' Jimmy replied, flicking the top slice aside with his finger.

'Salmon,' announced Davie appreciatively before the offer could be withdrawn.

There was a moments silence while he devoured them, then his mouth still full of crumbs, he demanded, 'Hoo much further tae they siller mines?'

'Not aw that far,' countered Jimmy. 'Come on. Let's be haeing ye.'

Somewhat reluctantly the others finished their picnic, gulped down the last of their ginger and juice and struggled up the hill again.

'See! Thaur's some one comin', ' grunted Billy. The others looked up.

'Let's ask whaur's the siller mine,' suggested a breathless Davie, who was still licking the last of the crumbs. 'I'm still half starvin'. '

'As wis jis gaun tae,' declared Jimmy. 'Hey mister,' he hailed the passer-by. 'Whaur's they siller mines?'

'The siller mines? Are you looking for the old mine workings? Why laddie, they were drowned years ago,' announced the stranger.

'Drooned?' queried Jimmy, uncomprehendingly. 'Drooned, mister?'

'Yes, son, drowned. Look down there. That big pond is where the entrance to the shaft used to be, but its been flooded for years.'

'Trust auld Tarry Beard never tae gi' onything away,' groaned Jimmy to the utter confusion of the stranger, who went on his way with a cheery wave.

'Ye mean never trust him,' muttered wee Jocky as he wiped away a tear, which he hoped the other Lochies, would think was sweat.

'An' we should never have trusted you either, Jimmy Johnston,' muttered Billy as he massaged the big blister on the back of his heel. 'Ye said we'd git some siller, an' aw ave got is this muckle blister.'

In silence the Lochies trekked back down the hill. Even going down it seemed further than they had climbed up. A mood of black gloom totally enshrouded the four as they made their way back into the town.

Jimmy kept his eyes down. As a failed leader he just could not face his troops, when suddenly he discovered that every cloud does indeed have a silver lining.

For just as they passed the slaughter house, Jimmy's eye suddenly caught a glimpse of something in the gutter. It almost seemed to sparkle, just like silver. It did sparkle like silver. It was silver. In a flash, Jimmy was down on his hunkers and next moment his status as leader of the Lochies was fully restored.

'Look siller! Real siller,' he bawled as he showed Billy, Davie and wee Jocky the half crown he had spotted in the gundy.

And sitting in Cabs, it was the usual proud leader, who rapped his new found silver on the round iron table top and ordered, 'Slidders aw round, and make them big yins.'

Then there was a truly silver silence as the waffers slid down.

'Ye see, jist like Cabs' ice cream, I'm often licked, but never beaten,' concluded Jimmy. And Billy, Davie and wee Jockie nodded in agreement.

The Hunt

by

Craig Oxbrow

The Bush seemed dark to Andrew Gray that morning, although the sky was as clear and blue as ever. He ignored it, paying more attention to the herd of elephants running from his team's jeeps. There were only ten or twelve of them. Their ivory was rare now. The first shot echoed across the plain like thunder. Gray grinned as the lead elephant, an old bull, fell sideways. He reloaded his rifle as his men opened up on the rest of the small group.

They disembarked to view their prizes, blades ready to hack the tusks off, or put an end to any that were still alive.

As they moved around the massive corpses, Gray heard a scream of terror, from the other side of the dead bull. Scowling, he went to see what had happened.

One of his men kneeled on the ground, shuddering violently, hands covering his face, breathing loudly and quickly.

Lying beside him was another of his men, still, dead. His face was smeared with blood, but Gray could see that his teeth had been torn out.

Inspector Mabutu frowned as he piloted his helicopter over the barren Kenyan bush. Having spent most of his adult life fighting ivory poachers, he had gained an ability to almost feel if they were near, and the feeling was very strong that morning. It was probably that butcher Gray again. He would need his rifle today, no doubt.

Gray fired over the heads of his men as many of them turned and fled.

'Come back, ya cowards!' he shouted.

'No!' one of then screamed. 'You kill last of tribe! Spirits come! No!'

Alright, he thought, let the superstitious idiots lose their share.

Then he heard more screams.

Mabutu circled the site, looking for somewhere to land. There was a corpse on the ground below. As he approached it, he recognised who it was. It was one of Gray's native hired guns. Gray used them because they were cheap. This one had had his teeth pulled out.

'Ivory', Mabutu whispered to himself. A tooth for a tooth.

He followed the dead man's footprints to the bodies of the elephants, and the other hunters.

Gray found his men lying, each alone, dead, teeth removed. Then he heard the helicopter above, a police helicopter. He ran to hide until the police came.

Mabutu did not believe the legends that spirits would avenge the deaths of the last of a herd, or 'tribe' of elephants, although someone clearly did.

He realised that Gray was not among the corpses a moment before he leapt out of a nearby tree and attacked.

'You did this,' Gray snarled, pointing his dagger at Mabutu.

'Somehow, you did this, you evil nigger.'

Mabutu raised his hands, palms open.

'No, Gray. No. I did not.'

'Liar' Gray roared, raising his blade above his head and charging.

Mabutu took his gun from his back and aimed it at Gray. He did not slow down. Mabutu fired.

Gray fell to the ground, shot through the chest, dead.

A slight wind blew up as he went to radio in the massacre.

Although he never looked away from Gray, when he went back to check him again, he found that his teeth had been carefully taken out.

The Emotional Syndrome

by

James Soutar

The titanic object could easily be mistaken for either a meteor or a chunk of debris and no one would hardly pay much attention to it. Lieutenant Deasley adjusted the controls of the giant view screen which spanned the entire facing wall of Space Station Astra's command centre. The image blinked a moment until the close-up scan displayed a portion of Sirrune's blue-green surface beneath a majestic series of rings and the grey daylight arc of one of its six natural satellites. The obscure object was located in the central void, partly shimmering in the distant light of the twin suns.

This obscurity was one of Deasley's priority focal points for there were no lights, antennae nor even a sensor reading of vapour trails to indicate its wake. Perhaps he might have overlooked his initial point if he hadn't detected the dispersal of numerous egg-shaped pods. Following a close analysis, he concluded them to be of the organic phenomena. Such peculiar action could only lead to further scrutiny and the duty officer intended probing deeper before reverting to summon the colonel. His orders were to maintain communications with the expedition team currently on a surveillance of Sirrune's habitable surface while the remainder of the crew were on sleep period. Deasley initiated an interior sensor scan which was surprisingly a successful penetration and also indicated the lack of a defence shield. There were human-like lifeforms, but an accurate assessment as to how many present was inconclusive because their numbers were gradually depleting. They were in the process of abandoning their vessel which also remained inconclusive.

The matter at hand uplifted any thought of them being a physical threat to the station, but mentally it became the main problem. Even before he found it necessary to report his discovery, Deasley only now realised an error he made for allowing the scan to tap into the unknown. This became evident when he sensed something about himself was terribly wrong. One moment his consciousness was crystal clear and was able to control his own thoughts, then the next he found himself trying to shake off a strange sensation. It felt like invisible fingers of energy penetrating his subsconscience. He shook his head and blinked rapidly in a vain effort to dislodge the mind-bending phenomena, but it was taking control of him and was barely aware of himself reaching over and pressing the red alert switch.

This activated a high-pitched squealing noise which roused everyone from their slumber. For the first time Colonel Annest could recall, the alarm had been activated only as a drill to test the crew's reaction on emergency procedures and another practice wasn't due for sometime yet. He hastily dressed himself and stalked out of his quarters with the sole intent of disciplining the officer concerned if he had no adequate reason to cause this disturbance.

He barged past crewmen and women who were rushing about to their allocated positions within the station and stormed into the command centre.

'What the hell's going on?' he demanded. 'Explain the purpose of this alert!'

Deasley never answered, for he was sitting bolt upright and facing the viewscreen. He appeared oblivious to the commotion amidst the flashing lights and activated monitors. His ignorance only infuriated Annest even more to the point that tempted him to throttle this insubordinate individual. Then his dark eyes focused on the object which looked like a flower head with all its petals gone and dispersing its seeds by the aid of the wind. But there was no such weather pattern in space, other than a cold vacuum with fixed points of light and their solar systems dominating an otherwise blackened universe.

When the duty officer still ignored his superior, Annest reached out and swung the chair round. His anger remained within him as he watched streams of tears flowing down amidst an expression full of grief and pained suffering.

'What's wrong with you?' frowned Annest.

Deasley's glazed eyes met those of the colonel's. His erratic behaviour was totally diabolical from Annest's point of view.

'They're dying,' he croaked.

'Who's dying?' enquired Annest, irritably.

'Them,' sobbed Deasley. 'I - I can feel their pain. They're trying to escape, but its already too late for some of them.'

He swung back to face the screen which was an act that caught the colonel unawares. He never expected a junior officer to turn his back while he was addressing him and such a violation wasn't to be without its consequences.

'Don't you dare turn your back on me, mister!' bellowed Annest. He was totally unaware that the mental anguish from Deasley was now rubbing onto him, although his emotions were full of anger than of sorrow, 'I'm in command here and no one will do anything until I suggest otherwise! Is that clear?'

His last question was rhetorical because Deasley remained ignorant. His mind was totally disorientated that he hardly knew where he sat. All he could do was feel emotionally upset while Annest's enflamed expression bore into his back like twin brands.

He wasn't known to be this strict towards any of his crew, but the mental projections stemming from Deasley were far too powerful to control.

Annest spun round bewildered and noticed they were the only two officers present instead of the normal compliment of five. The absence of his 2i/c, who also acts as chief of security, a medical officer for monitoring lifesign readings of the expedition team and a computer engineer, added fuel to the furnace.

'Where is everyone?' he yelled at the walls of operating computers. The only response he received as a reply, were the internal humming and buzzing sounds stemming from the flickering jargon. Annest waved his arms as if trying to conjure up a trick to make the missing officers appear out of thin air. He slapped his sides just as the door slid open and in walked the officers concerned.

Their own erratic behaviour between themselves indicated these emotional outbursts had affected everyone on the station. Captain Rannell, who normally had an iron fist over the station's security, was now cowering under the threatening backlash from the medical officer.

'Don't yell at me,' pleaded Rannell.

'I'll yell at you if I want to!' countered Captain Tebre. 'You need some medical advice and if you resist, I'll break your damned neck!' Rannell shielded his face as he staggered towards Annest with Tebre displaying an expression and stance of intended aggression.

'What are you both doing?' scolded Annest. 'Can't you see I'm speaking to the duty officer?'

'Don't shout at us,' interrupted Tebre. 'I'm trying to give some advice to a potential patient.'

The engineer entered moments later and appeared oblivious to the other officers as he confronted the computers. He began muttering computer gibberish that had no meaning to the human ear. His actions, however, were enough to indicate his own aggressive emotions towards the machines. When he became dissatisfied at the lack of feedback, he fell to his knees and began to sob openly.

Before long, the atmosphere was a rabble of insignificant whimpering and arguing. It was as if an invisible plague had taken control and was spreading like wildfire, but like all diseases, there is always a cure somewhere and Deasley was the source.

The intelligence aboard the alien vessel was capable of projecting emotions using telepathy. From this link, Deasley was able to discover an actual plague currently effecting within the alien community. It also affected life support systems and major functions, forcing the survivors to use whatever emergency transportation was available to escape. Each moment a contingent of pods dispersed, lifted some of the strain from Deasley which in turn, affected everyone on the station. Only those who were presently with the infected officer were still contaminated and would remain so until the alien consciousness had lifted completely.

The sudden string of explosions with the brilliance of a supernova resulted in the remaining emotions being yanked from the crews' consciousness. Everyone was sent flying in all directions when the impact of the shockwaves shuddered the station.

It had taken several minutes for the crew to recover from their experience, but they were soon back on their feet.

'Where did it go?' Annest enquired after he was sure his mind and body were once again reunited.

Deasley didn't answer straight away because he had to wait a while longer to recover from his unusual experience.

'They're no longer within us,' he muttered. 'A few never managed to escape, but they were already beyond saving. The more entities there were, the stronger the emotions affected us. Now they're gone, their emotions are gone with them.'

'Were there survivors in those pods?'

'I'm not sure. I mean - I think so.'

'And where do you suppose they have gone to?'

'I can only guess they've scattered themselves in the hope that one day their species will be restored. When they were in those pods, they committed themselves to a destiny to which they had no control.'

'Then I assume its safe to continue the purpose of our presence so that one day, we too can find a safe haven for our people.'

'I expect so, sir,' ended Deasley.

The Path By The River

by

Emma Kay

The old railway track was now a charming grassy riverside footpath bordered by birches and rowans. It ended abruptly in a steep flight of rustic steps that led down to a side-road. Rob Armstrong disliked roads and hoped to find another footpath that would take him back to Leithen on the other bank of the Tweed, thus making a satisfying round trip. Looking around for someone to ask about it, he was pleased to see an elderly, benign-looking stranger leaning on a five-barred gate with a bright-eyed collie at his feet. Rob put his question to the stranger, who looked every inch a typical Border shepherd as depicted on many a Rural Scenes Calendar.

After studying him intently, but not rudely, for a few minutes the shepherd advised Rob, courteously enough, to return by the way he had come. Noticing that the other had not answered his question, Rob asked again, 'But is there a path?'

'Yes, there's a path. But nobody uses it now. Nobody has, for years.'

'But why? Is it overgrown?'

'Very much so. But there could be another reason.'

'What reason?' Rob felt a faint annoyance mingling with his curiosity.

The shepherd then proceeded to tell what was, to Rob, a totally ridiculous and fantastic tale. It appeared that in some unspecified century there had lived in a nearby hamlet a woman who was reputed to be a witch. Unlike the hideous hags of tradition she was young and startlingly beautiful. She was believed to be high in the favour of Satan, her master, and to possess extraordinary powers. She had been blamed for an outbreak of disease among the flocks. Vengeful local farmers had gone after her with dogs and had tracked her along the path in question. Cornered at last, she had in the midst of a violent thunderstorm cursed the place and all who approached it, calling down an unspecified dreadful doom. Her final fate was unknown, but locals had avoided the area ever since.

'This happened on a May Eve,' the shepherd concluded, 'and this just happens to be May Eve; that's to say, the day before the first of May. So, if I were you I'd go back the way I came, for sure.'

Despite the shepherd's very grave and earnest demeanour Rob had no doubt that he was being treated as a gullible tourist. He prided himself on being nobody's fool. No

183

doubt the locals took pleasure in spinning such yarns to any strangers who seemed fair game.

'I'll take a look at it anyway,' he declared finally. In a moment he glanced back, and saw that the shepherd's grave expression had not changed.

Crossing a swaying footbridge, he followed a rutted lane between crumbling lichen-encrusted dry-stone walls and soon found what he sought. On a wooden sign, much weathered, he made out with some difficulty the inscription, 'Leithen, 3 miles.' The lettering was Gothic in character. The signpost was at the start of a fairly broad path which looked inviting and, despite the shepherd's words, not at all overgrown.

Suddenly the light, which had been very bright, seemed to dim a little. Perhaps it presaged rain, he thought. He hoped not. Unbidden, a sentence flashed into his mind - 'Never start on an unfamiliar road in fading light.' He must have read it in one of his innumerable hiking magazines. Instantly he put it out of his mind. At his best pace, after all, he could very easily cover three miles in less than an hour.

The path, mossy and grass-bordered, wound between magnificent beeches whose broad limbs, meeting overhead, formed a rustling archway. Rob started along it at a fair pace. Gradually the path narrowed. The beeches gave way to sombre holly trees and dark yews. He became aware that the light was much dimmer. A storm must indeed be brewing. He quickened his pace, then, realising that he was almost running, slowed down again. There was no need for such haste, he told himself.

The path narrowed more and more, as the yews and holly trees gave way to a hedge of ash, briar, rowan and hawthorn. A wan light glimmered in the dimming sky. Was it not rather early for moonrise? It was indeed the moon, a pallid waning sickle moon that lay on its back as if ailing. The farther he went, the denser and higher the hedge became and the more closely it seemed to press on him. The light was fading fast - preternaturally fast, he felt, with a twinge of uneasiness. Surely, he thought, he ought to be very near his goal by now, and yet there was nothing to show that he was. He looked at his watch. The light was now so dim that he had to use the torch which he always carried in his rucksack. He had checked the time before starting on the path and he now saw, with a shock, that he had been walking for almost two hours. His unease increased. The distance given on the signpost, he assured himself, had been inaccurate. That must be the explanation. He had certainly not strayed from the path: at no point had there been any alternative way. Still, the sign could not be very far out.

The path went steadily downhill and the hedge became higher and denser, it seemed, with every step that he took, and the overhead branches made a more solid arch.

This detestable tunnel of gloom must end soon, he kept assuring himself. But it did not.

In time he checked his watch again. He found that he had been walking for over three hours. And still there was no end in sight. Should he turn back? Yes . . . no . . . that would take far too long, and he was dreadfully weary. Yet . . . could he go on? It might take longer still that way. But the path ahead was unknown. Yes, he would go back. He turned and retraced his steps for a few moments. Again he stood irresolute, then moved forward a few weary paces. He stood rooted to the spot in horror. The hedge now made a solid thorny wall that barred his way completely. Somehow, the trees had moved to cut off his retreat. He was forced to turn again and face the unknown under the mocking gaze of that eldritch moon.

Panic seized him. Hands held out in front of him as if he were blind, he blundered forward as fast as his labouring breath would permit. And still the path ran on and on, a tiny track with a ten-foot high thorn hedge hemming him in. On and on, changeless, with never an end in sight.

'This is not happening,' he sobbed to himself. It was only a nightmare, he thought. Yes, that was it . . . only a nightmare. He had only to wake up . . . But he could not wake up. On and on he stumbled, desperately weary, hour after endless hour, somehow unable to stop. And on and on went the path, stretching into infinity . . .

The Howlers

by

Graham Greig

It all began as a means to an end. A way out of the constant drudgery brought about by the work ethic that is somehow inextricably married to the democracy politics of old, where the seeing pipe the blind in a jolly little roundelay offering TV, hi-fi, Video - and almost anything else that inclines to make life that little easier - in reward according to style and cut of step. We knew that it had to be mass; everyone to a man. That way we'd weed out charlatans paving the way for only true adventurers of a kindred spirit whose sole aim would be to journey into death armed with what we believed to be the most - and certainly one that would afford freedom for everyone excepting they could hold the dance long enough to look at how it operated - comprehensively understood set of theories ever accumulated by five loyal friends and individuals in the last half century. Sure there were others that had acquired the knowledge in the past and had pulled through with spectacular results. You only have to look at the Beats: Burroughs, Kerouac, Ginsburg, Corso. The Parnassian. countless groups of singular minded souls in search of the truth kept from us by politics and the church alike.

We'd gather in the Raeburn apartment of Billy - January 25th - and get down to business as soon as everyone had arrived and made good their oblation, thus paving the way beyond the confines of all logical thought. This was highly illogical. . . Still. . . Billy had a copy of the Naked Lunch. Jack forwarded Howl. Matt, Confessions of an English Opium Eater. George, Nineteen Eighty Four and myself the complete works of Jean Arthur Rimbaud (1854-1891). A passage was read from each in ceremonial anointment whilst the means for procuring such a fascinating and mysterious journey were lain end to end on mirrored glass that reflected so convincingly on blackened ceiling that a doorway to the void could be perceived. And in this company anything would be possible: Coke, Smack, Sulph, Hashish and enough alcohol to drown a dozen of the best free-style drinkers of any town in the land, day or night. Still, the means was of little importance, only the end ranked in this theory.

All oracles, charts and numbers had been meticulously scrutinised over the seemingly short span of eighteen month and everything pointed to the 25th as *thee* day to go. Might never get the chance in a *hundred* years and by then . . . Well it would be too late. Everyone dead, only to return as a Joe in the roundelay ring being piped once again the tune of blind obedience. The I Ching had serviced us with No 56 'The Traveller' and this

186

was read and reread until all clarity and understanding had been drawn, not from the written itself but from the very essence of the thing. Everyone had to have in his mind a clear picture of what he was getting involved in and what would be detrimental to the securing of a successful outcome, otherwise the whole exercise would be best suited to the abortion table.

We were all aware - only too well, as this was perhaps the most prevailing feature in all suicides - that the resulting turmoil and confusion once the life expired would be our toughest test, but once overcome we were sure the rewards would be sweet. Because overcome them we could. We knew they were there, and once the paradox had been reached it was only a question of surmounting it and laying it bare for the others to see if only their vision could be sufficiently cleared in time for what would without doubt be the greatest single freeing of mankind since his humble beginnings here on this planet, Earth.

All number calculations had been methodically examined and gone over in great details, as these were perhaps the single most important feature in the whole theory and the only one on which all hope was pinned. Thus our obsession in specifics. All numbers for re-entry had to be calculated precisely along with star signs and parents. These would be selected from the other side in respect of what they had to offer by way of a helping hand or two, by thrusting our spirit forward at the very moment of conception and taking our chances from there. All conceptions to take place within a band of ten years, location irrelevant. The only things that mattered were date of birth, time of birth and sign. Calculations so fine that the merest fraction out would result in total and absolute failure and another journey of hope on the lookout for like-minds without guarantee of a find.

So say seven were aimed for as the come back birth number -20.11.2055. 20 + 11 + 2055. 2 + 0 + 8 +6 = 16. Rounded to primary number 1 + 6 = 7- with all its wisdom discernment and philosophy, along with Scorpio's strength and taste for the bizarre by one member, over his eighteen month accumulation of knowledge, and nine, with all its intelligence, artistry and genius, coupled with Gemini's love of the moral and ability for the word by another and so on until all five of us were suitably prepared with our hoped for date and time - to the second - of return. Nothing else could be done except for the execution of our theory and the journey it would entail, until eventually meeting back on Earth to carry our plan through to fruition, proving once and for all the idea of heaven and hell obsolete, and in one foul and mighty swoop render the God person redundant.

Thus prepared it was now only a matter of getting down to business and once again incantations from the various works of literature supplied were read aloud in the hope of furnishing the void with the credentials thought necessary for a favourable outcome. Needles and spoons were passed and the alcohol flowed freely whilst a passage was read aloud continually by one or other members of the group in the hope that an unbroken flow of offering would somehow effect success and ensure things went without a hitch. Hashish was inhaled from a bhung, its blue-grey smoke spiralling upward only to drop back and hang like a shroud of finest silk which oscillated inches above our heads, pre-eminent spectre of the void. All was going according to plan.

My companions and I have nominated ourselves 'The Howlers' who's duty will be the downfall of all convention through the art of the written. You will be hearing from us soon . . . Adieu.

Manhunt?

by

Jo-an Smith

Ten year old Alison Duncan hurried home from the supermarket with her mum's milk. She couldn't run too fast because of her asthma - sometimes if she got a fright or something, she couldn't get her breath and passed out. She always carried an inhaler with her, just in case. She looked at her watch, it was nearly five o'clock and her mum was waiting for the milk for tea. Alison started to run quicker. She could feel herself wheezing and decided to stop when she got to the tenements across the road. Stepping inside the close, she reached into her pocket to get her inhaler. She didn't hear the footsteps behind her until it was too late. The hands grabbed her shoulders before the inhaler could reach her mouth, and in her fright she dropped it. Alison could only watch helplessly as it rolled out of her reach, before the dizziness set in and darkness took over.

Detective Inspector Allen Davidson's moment of peace was shattered with the ringing of the telephone.

'Allen,' he said gruffly, into the receiver.

'Sir, that missing girl. She's been found strangled in the tenements out at Bridge Street in Paisley. Looks like sexual assault was the motive.'

'Jesus,' sighed Allen. 'What am I going to tell Kate? That was one of her friends. She's known her for years.'

'The case can go to someone else if you want, sir.'

'No, that's okay. I'll be right over.'

Allen replaced the receiver. He looked at the photograph on his desk. Kate, his 13 year old daughter had been frantic since Alison had been reported missing two days ago. He had no idea that the two of them had been so close.

When he arrived at Bridge Street, Allen took one of the uniformed policemen aside to find out more.

Rape had not taken place, but Alison's clothes had been torn off, and marks on her body suggested that some form of sexual assault had been inflicted upon the child. She had a cut on her forehead which looked as though she may have been hit with something, and finally, she had been strangled. Once dead, she had been bundled into a sack and dragged into a bin cupboard in the building.

Allen went inside to have a closer look at the body himself. He hated it when they found kids like this. It made him grateful that his beautiful, blonde baby was safe at home with her mother. He said a silent prayer of thanks.

The investigation began. The sack was found to be Australian made, and stocked at only one shop nearby. The shopkeeper could not help though. He said that, on the day of the murder, he had sold only one sack, and that was to a blonde girl, buying potatoes. The forensic scientists found no traces of sexual assault, making DNA testing imposs- ible. However, it was obvious that an assault of this kind had been attempted, but the at- tacker had been disturbed in some way. They also found blonde hair inside the sack - Alison Duncan had been a redhead. The fingerprints on the neck came from someone with a small build.

Police decided that they were looking for a white male, possibly in the region of 5ft 3 to 5ft 6 inches tall, with collar length blonde hair.

Allen was uneasy. Something wasn't right. As hard as he tried though, he couldn't quite put his finger on it. Now all he wanted to do was go home, put his feet up for a while, then get a good night's sleep. He felt mentally and physically drained.

'How's Kate?' he asked his wife when he got in.

'She's still very upset. It's funny though, I didn't think that her and Alison had been great friends. Alison really just used to tag along with her sometimes. Kate got quite annoyed with her.'

'Yes, I know. I was thinking the same thing. Anyway, let's change the subject. What's for tea? I'm starving.'

'You're always starving,' Sue laughed, 'first you can go and put out the rubbish.'

'Yessir, m'dear!' replied Allen with a grin. The smile froze on his face when he spotted a carton of milk lying at the top of the bag. They got bottled milk delivered. Why did they have a carton? He put the question to his wife.

'Kate came home with it the other day. I sent her for potatoes and she bought milk in- stead. It was the same day poor Alison went missing. I remember because she came in all upset, saying that someone had told her that Alison had disappeared coming back from the shops.'

Suddenly everything fell into place and the terrible truth dawned on Allen. Alison Dun- can had been buying milk for her mother. She bought the milk from the shops, but no milk was found at the scene of the crime. The teenage girl buying the sack of potatoes, the blonde hair in the sack - Kate knew Alison was missing before it had even been reported!

'I have to go out.'

His wife looked on, stunned, as Allen raced out of the door. He drove to the murder site as fast as he could, and with tears streaming down his cheeks, started searching the

190

rubbish. He went through bin after bin, bag after bag, knowing what he was looking for but at the same time dreading finding it, until finally, he found the missing link. There, lying at the bottom of a rubbish bag, were about a dozen new potatoes.

He keeled over and promptly vomited.

Allen drove home in shock. He went straight to Kate's room and confronted her. Kate broke down, and through heart-wrenching sobs, spilled out the truth.

'I didn't mean to hurt her, dad, I only wanted to give her a fright, to tell her to stop following me around. But I grabbed her, and she started breathing funny, then she fell and hit her head. I thought she was dead. I didn't know what to do at first. Then I thought that if I made it look like she'd been raped, then they'd look for a man. So I started to rip her clothes off, but she woke up while I was doing it, so I panicked, and I put my hands round her neck and just squeezed. You won't tell, will you dad? I don't want to go to jail.'

Allen couldn't say anything. He felt as if his life had just been destroyed. For two hours he sat in a shocked silence, until his wife's screams brought him out of his frayed mental state.

The funeral took place three days after Alison Duncan's.

'Why?' pleaded Sue Davidson, 'why did she have to kill herself? What could she have done that was so bad that she wanted to die?'

Allen could not, dared not, answer her.

Police never did find the blonde man wanted for the murder of ten year old Alison Duncan. The file was left open and the case unsolved.

Second Chance

by

Sarah Chapman

'Come on guys, lets get out of here,' complained the slender sixteen year old who was obviously scared. Pete, Ryan and Pam stared at Laurie as if she had grown another head.

'Jesus it was her idea,' Pam thought, but she had to admit, it was kind of scary to be walking in a cemetery in the middle of the night.

'Calm down Laurie there'll be no ghosts,' Pam said sarcastically, even though she was scared herself. Looking around, she experienced a shiver of fear.

'Hey guys lighten up, it's only an old graveyard,' Pete pointed out but still none of them moved. Ryan stepped forward, his dark hair flapping in the breeze. Looking about him he slipped the crowbar out from under his jacket. There was a crash as he broke through the rusted chains. Looking up into the night Pam saw the start of a storm. Pulling her hood over her long blonde hair she glanced nervously about. Reaching inside her jacket she pulled out the flashlight. Flickering it nervously about, she followed the rest of the gang. Laurie, who was hugging herself slowed down so that the two girls could talk.

'I wish I'd never suggested playing dare now,' she moaned.

'Never mind,' Pam said trying to comfort. She also wished they had never played dare.

'Hey guys, over here!' shouted Ryan excitedly. They ran over to where Ryan and Pete were standing. They were standing by a huge angel but it wasn't the statue, it was what was inscribed on it.

'Those who enter caring tomb, shall sleep forever until their doom.'

As Pete read those few words the wind started getting more than just a breeze and the rain more than a drizzle.

Putting her hands in her pockets, Pam realised that the torch which Laurie was now holding was starting to flicker, then it died.

'Oh no, this can't be happening,' she thought, they were all too shocked to move.

'Come on, let's find a shelter!' shouted Ryan over the thunder. They headed nowhere in particular but they found themselves at the stairs of a tomb. Pete started towards the door and tried to open it but there was no need to, for the door just swung open revealing a room lit by hundreds of candles and a coffin in the middle. Walking into the room Pam saw how the candles lit up Pete's face making his sharp features and blonde hair stand out. Then her attention was drawn by Laurie who was staring at something on the

192

coffin. Walking up she started to put her arms around Laurie to comfort her then she saw what she had been staring at.

'Oh God,' she whispered. This was definitely not their day.

'Caring Tomb,' Ryan whispered. Even he was pale under his tan. Just then a flash of lightening flashed outside the entrance. None of them had a chance to move before the doors slammed shut.

They all stood staring at the door in a terrified trance. 'This can't be happening to us,' Laurie thought as Ryan and Pete tried to budge it but it would not open.

'Man, there must be some way out,' Ryan said still walking around the room but they all knew that when tombs were built they were only built with one way in and out, the door. There was no way out of here until somebody heard their cries for help.

'On the gravestone it said that we would 'sleep forever until their doom', ' Laurie whispered. Sighing, she sat down against the coffin.

'Why don't we get some rest, it's been a very long night,' but Pam needed not to say it because they were already sleeping. None of them could really relax, they were thinking about their families. Slowly each of them fell into a deep sleep.

Slowly each of them awoke to darkness. Laurie slowly sat up feeling out of place then she remembered how she and the rest had got here. Her eyes wide with amazement she looked around at the burnt out candles with cobwebs hanging from them. Standing up she stretched her protesting joints. Then she realised that light was coming from somewhere, but before she had a chance to investigate, the others started waking up.

'How long do you think we've been sleeping?' she asked Pete who was glancing around suspiciously.

'God I don't know but it must have been a long time.'

'Hey guys before you all woke up I saw some light coming from out under the coffin,' Laurie said, trying to control her excitement.

They all crowded around the coffin, where she had seen it. When they had finally moved the coffin a dark staircase was revealed. Reaching across she grabbed a candle that still had some wax on it. Reaching inside her pocket she lifted out her matches and lit the candle. Walking down the stairs in the lead, the candle cast a eerie glow on the old worn walls. They stood in a strange room, all four of them looking around.

'Look, in that pile of rock, there's a light,' Pete said running over to it. He was right. There was a tunnel of some sort. As they all helped to remove the rocks Pam wondered if she would ever see her family again. Shrugging off the foreboding thought she returned to the work at hand, until there was a gap big enough for them, one at a time, to crawl through.

As they all crawled through they all had a feeling of déjà vu. As one after the other came out into the street, they were shocked to find and see a whole world alien to their own.

'No, it can't be.'

'Hello, anybody here?' Pam shouted but her echo was the only response.

A blue sky shone brightly, normally but a crimson sun shone hotly. The buildings were standing but dust and cobwebs hung everywhere. No birds sang and no bustle of the normal Saturday mornings.

'Come on let's see if we can find anybody.'

'We aren't sixteen anymore. We've grown up in the last few weeks or years,' Laurie thought as they walked past the drug store and Hypermarket. Usually on weekdays and every other day the streets would be jam packed.

'Jesus, how long were we in that tomb?'

They had all been wondering that but from the state of things gathered it had been more than a year.

'Looks like we did sleep 'til our doom,' Pam said staring at the sky.

'Alright, we can't sit here and cry all day. What's done is done,' she said wiping the last of the evidence off her cheeks.

'She's right, we have to know if anybody, apart from us survived whatever happened. Get food that's canned and anything else that looks fresh.'

As Pam and Ryan walked towards a different store Pete and I went to the drugstore.

'I thought we were to get food,' Laurie said , then it hit her that they would need a first aid kit.

While he was getting what they needed Laurie headed towards the newspaper rack but was stopped by something hard on the floor. Kneeling down she picked up the square package and glanced at the name and what was written on it, 'To whoever it may concern'.

'Pete, Pete!' she shouted. As he stood beside her unwrapping the package, she waited patiently while he read what was written on it. Passing it to her she skimmed over the page, letting them drop she now fully understood what had happened.

Someone had written the accounts leading up to someone pressing the button to a new weapon, designed to kill all humans at a programmed destination, but something had gone wrong in a laboratory as it had killed everything. The person who identified himself as only Robert had written how everyone died slowly and painfully. It had been a massacre. Pulling her into his arms, Pete hugged her until both of them were crying. Eventually when their crying had subsided she pulled away from him until their eyes were locked. Slowly, as in slow motion, he pulled her head until his lips were against hers. She had been kissed before but not like this; this kiss could coax the soul out of

194

the devil himself. They stayed in each other's arms for a while until Pam and Ryan came. When they got out into the street they told them what had been written in the letter along with newspaper clippings. She guessed that they all had one question that they needed answered. Why had they survived.

'We can't stay here, it holds too many memories,' she said quietly. As they stood up and gathered the food Pam and Ryan had collected, they headed west to old Baxters' stables. When they finally reached there they had decided that they would go away and find a new place to live and if they were lucky, find other survivors. Only three horses had survived so they used the third to carry the supplies. Pete and Laurie decided to share Christal a black stallion so Ryan and Pam had to share Cliff.

They all sat tall in the saddles and took one last regretful look around the town that they all had grown up in. Turning towards the horizon they felt as if they had left parts of their life behind.

When they finally rested, they were all mentally and physically exhausted. They all camped around a lone camp fire on a beach with a heavy burden on their shoulders. Standing up Laurie wiped the sand off her jeans. Walking down the beach she let the tears, she had been holding, free. She sat down on an old log and the tears rolled down her face. Thinking about her parents and brothers she hugged her knees, feeling more lonely than ever. Feeling a hand on her shoulder she looked up to find Pete looking down at her. Launching herself into his arms she let his warmth surround her, comforting her. Hand in hand they walked along the beach, none of them talking. When they spotted Pam and Ryan they all joined hands but still walked. None of them talked. Everything was said by the tears they shed for their families.

When the morning finally came they were all shaken by the emotions they had experienced. Mounting their horses they set off again on another lonely journey.

'What will become of us,' Laurie thought. Just then a dot in the horizon caught her attention. 'Hey guys do you see them,' she asked urging Christal into a gallop. Clinging to Pete she tried to twist around to see if it was humans. It was. Jumping off the horses they ran and hugged the strangers.

'Are you all real,' Pam asked still too amazed. They were. As they introduced each other they met John, Lisa and their daughter Shelley.

That night they exchanged stories over the camp fire. 'Their stories are the same as ours,' she thought. 'They were all underground and sleeping in some way! We are being given a second chance.'

After about a week they had met up with another group of people. As their group got bigger the love they had got bigger with it.

'We're going to have to stop travelling soon. We have altogether thirty eight including us,' Pete said, glancing around at the other five committee members they had picked.

'He's right, if there's more they'll find us. We have to start thinking about the future,' the small blond, Debra said. As they all were speaking she and Pam were staring into space thinking about a home.

Snapping out of her reverie she realised that she needed a home. Laurie stood up and cleared her throat. Immediately all eyes were on her.

'I agree. The children in the group need a bit of stability and to continue their lives.'

So it was agreed they stayed in the town that they were staying in and started over again. As they settled down Pam, Ryan Laurie and Pete all gathered around the flag on the dark night and pledged their love.

'We need a name for the town,' Laurie said looking at Pete. 'How about second chance?' she suggested. They agreed. They stood like that for sometime until they left for night.

'Grandma, do you miss your mama?'

Laurie looked at Pete with a sad look in her eyes.

'Yes child, I miss them and I hope you don't have to go through what your Grandpa and me had to go through.' Standing up, her old bones creaked angrily. Walking over to the bookshelf she reached up and grasped the old book and pulled it out. Walking over to her daughter she gave the book to her.

'This book contains everybody's stories, letters, paper clippings and how they came across this town. I got it from a very close friend - now I am giving it to you.' Smiling she hugged her daughter and looked lovingly at her husband, son-in-law and grand-children.

'Do you think it'll happen again?' Pete asked.

'I hope not for their sakes,' she replied. She silently prayed it wouldn't. Reaching for her husband's hand she took hold of it and squeezed reassuringly. They stood hugging each other. Two loving people on a now ordinary horizon. Secrets untold and terrors untold they shared. Forever.

Californian Poppy

by

Morag Hadley

Heels tapping, an hypnotic sound on parquet flooring drew his attention at first. Gradually, he learned to raise his eyes to retain impressions of the white tautness of the woman, relieved only by the lurid covered books cradled in her arms. Throughout the long summer evenings Stephen came to know that she would arrive about an hour before closing time and make a leisurely choice from the popular fiction section. From behind the Anthropology, Zoology and Ancient Civilisation section the librarian's coveting eyes followed her movements. Silently, he noted muscular calves, swept back shoulders, long thighs, cataloguing in his mind, not the maturity of the woman's beauty but her anatomical grace. All summer he watched. He waited. Time had no relevance.

Stephen was meticulous about all his research. At an early age he realised that his mother's tweezers facilitated the dissection of flies and other demented insects caught in sticky honey jars. Later, these same jars were used as formaldehyde containers for small lizards, mice and the like. He had just turned twelve when he skinned his first cat.

This incident was a vivid pivot in his pubescent state. It was the same week his mother, red haired, red lipped had teetered out of his life on high heeled, white, peep-toed shoes, a sleek, newly acquired fur jacket slung over her shoulders. Californian Poppy wavered in the stillness she left behind. She was never mentioned again. A few days later, the cat skin was stretched and drying nicely in the potting shed. Stephen had painted the claws vermilion.

During the long, solitary summer evenings Stephen applied himself to his hobby with an energy unknown to his colleagues. His scientific leanings, though amateur, had earned him some small recognition in the journals. None of his fellow librarians knew, or cared to think about, how he spent his time outside the reference library. It was generally agreed that being there rather suited his dry, dusty personality. They may have been interested, some surprised even, to know that Stephen's area of specialism was in the dating of bones, the odd Neolithic tooth, scraps of human hair. Their unassuming colleague longed passionately for that very particular identification which would thrust him into a blaze of glory and be recognised by the Royal Society. For years, he had hoped that the unusual, the rare find, would turn up.

Silently he worked behind shelves, rarely disturbed among the dull coloured spines and contents of the reference section. In his basement he came to life surrounded by

197

myriad shapes of objects and beings, some in glass cases, others floating in coloured liquids. All in a time warp, forever existing without decay, without change, just as they had been at the point of death. Catalogued like his books; impressed on memory, unchanging. Cared for, lovingly.

Autumn came. Now he looked for shades of red. She was easy to locate. Still her heels tapped, her red coat swinging, long thighs striding. His eyes followed, devouring her shape. Impressing it upon memory and senses. One evening, the first real night of winter, he followed her, stalking in his city shoes, shadowing her like an animal. She stopped only once half turning into the bitter wind that sped her along, shrugged and went on, her redness fading, dying.

Now the seeker of fame had to move fast. He had to be ready before Spring.

The kill had been easy. He knew his prey. Now he was ready.

He drained the fluids. Slowly, slowly he allowed the corpse to dry, turning it lovingly, treating the darkening skin, injecting the bones to age them. By spring, when the ground was softening and alive with growth he would be ready. Then he would place his newly made, Neolithic woman in her chosen grave. She was to be his discovery, his fame. His paper was already completed in anticipation of his presentation to the company of the Royal Society at the New Year lecture.

Winter was long that year. By spring, snow still lay, the ground frozen hard. The perfectly preserved corpse waited. Gaping holes of plucked out amalgam filled teeth formed part of her timeless grin. Time passed. Lingering odours of bark treated skin, and worse, filled the dry basement atmosphere. Stephen waited. Time passed. When winter came again he made a glass case like the others which lined his walls. He painted the nails vermilion. He waited.

The following year spring was as it should be, the earth opening to receive the sun's warmth, fronds of palest green struggling their way to the surface. The time was right. The shallow grave, as meticulously prepared as the corpse, received its occupant. Being the hunted, rather than the hunter, no flint weapons were laid alongside. No decoration adorned the body. The librarian returned to his basement to wait patiently for the time when he would make his discovery known. Time was of no importance; his lecture would have the same content and impact this year, next year.

One evening in summer, dozing at his desk in the stale library air, Stephen was roused by a tapping sound. Raising himself slightly he saw the blur of Mr Hewlitt-Thompson's ancient sports jacket disappearing round the corner of a cabinet and a flash of his polished walking stick. A few days later the same tapping intruded, this time, however, sharper and too fast for the old gentleman's pace. Stephen's eyes swept the library. It was empty as it often was just before closing time. He shrugged, locked up and went home to work on some undated bones.

Tap, tap-tap, tap. He looked up. A tree branch on the conservatory roof. Tap, tap-tap, tap. A gentle tapping then, louder, regular beating. Tap, tap-tap, tap. Concentration was hard. Tap tap-tap, tap.

Each evening, just before closing time, it started. Tap, tap-tap, tap. Consistent, rhythmic, hard, deliberate. Each evening, the library was empty. In the basement too. Tap, tap-tap, tap. The staccato of sound reverberated from the glass cabinets around the walls. It echoed from the stone floor. It followed him everywhere. Tap, tap-tap, tap. Day and night. He covered his ears with cupped hands; plugged them. Still he heard it.

His senses became acute. Denied normal hearing he became ultra sensitive to odours and his dull, daytime eyes greedily absorbed what his scientific mind normally rejected as trivia. He smelled the dust of unread books; floor polish; unwashed bodies dozing over crushed newspapers. At home, keen eyes saw cobwebs, peeling paint, points of razor sharp instruments. At work, rusty screws on angular cabinets, the patina of polished desk and floor imaged themselves on his brain. Sounds that were almost silent thudded into his ears; his eyes bulged with visual excesses; odours invaded his nostrils.

The constant drill of noise thudded behind his eyes. Dull red seeped in and around hard edges of objects, soft forms of people. His eyes, ears and head throbbed pulsating in time with tap, tap-tap, tap. The redness grew brighter, brighter. Midas like it touched everything he saw. It invaded his dreams, lapping the edges of nightmares, bursting into red lava, molten redness awful in its majestic slowness. His nostrils flared like a hunted animal scenting danger.

In the basement.

Sound.

Tap, tap-tap, tap.

Smell.

Dank earth. Rotting flesh. Dead animals. Musk. Dying, dying.

Sight.

Planets of fire. Meteoric crimson exploding. Blood.

Dripping, dripping.

They found his body some time later. His ears had been ripped from his skull leaving frills of flesh decorating the cavities; a black crater where his nose had been. His eyes, plucked, lay at the edge of the room where they had been thrown against the wall. A snail's stream of blood indicated their descent.

Somehow, his wasted, shrunken body had crawled into a large, glass case of the sort used to exhibit mummified, museum bodies. Had it not been for the painted toenails clutched in his locked, death fist the corpse, at first sight, could have been from any century. A strange, pervasive odour dominated the death cell. It could not be identified; it was heavy, musky, like stale perfume.

Later still, a sheep farmer came across a shallow grave on a lonely hill. An almost perfect specimen of a Neolithic body was gently unearthed. Seemingly, a combination of unusual conditions had preserved the body in a manner of almost perfection quite unknown in similar finds. The archaeologists and anthropologists concluded that the nails had been torn from the feet, either by a small animal or, in a ritual carried out shortly before burial. Many months were spent probing the surrounding hilltop for similar graves. None were found and, it was concluded that the woman had either been a person of high esteem or, guilty of some heinous tribal taboo to be buried in such isolation.

She was placed, finally, with great reverence, in a glass case at the British Museum. An excellent paper was read later that year at the New Year lecture.

Fare's Fair?

by

Colin Veitch

It had been a long day and I was knackered, I was also a little bit the worse for wear so I decided to get the bus home. I should also explain that I don't normally use public transport, however. . .

I got on the bus at the West End and asked for a 20p fare which the one-man operated driver/conductor gave me and duly settled in a seat near the front, (a) because I couldn't be bothered going upstairs and (b) to keep away from the smokers.

It was a mistake.

'Hey you,' shouted the driver, as we sat at the bus stop outside Haymarket Station, 'where are you going?'

'Roseburn,' I said.

'Roseburn? Roseburn - it's 25p to Roseburn.'

'It was only 20p on the way in,' I said, 'I know 'cause I asked the driver.'

'Well, it's 25p to go back,' stated the driver of Lothian Regional Transport's horse-less carriage.

I argued with the driver but to no avail, he insisted that it was 25p to Roseburn.

'OK,' I said, because by this time the other passengers were starting to mutter darkly, 'if it'll keep the peace, here's another 5p.'

'That's no good,' said the driver, 'I can't issue a ticket for 5p, you'll have to pay again.'

'What!' I asked incredulously, 'that's robbery - I'm not paying!'

'Well,' the driver went on, 'you either pay again, or get off the bus and walk.'

'I ain't payin' no more than 5p and I ain't getting off the bus,' I said defiantly.

'Well the bus ain't goin' nowhere until you do,' said the driver as he switched off the engine.

'Pay the man,' urged the other passengers, 'pay the man and let us get on our way.'

'I ain't payin' any more than 5p,' I said belligerently, '5p is the difference between what I've already paid and what he wants me to pay now, and anyway we've only come two stops and it's not worth 20p to travel two stops if you can travel six stops for 25p.'

By this time those passengers with bus passes were disembarking and getting on other buses, those who had paid cash were loath to do so.

'I ain't payin' no more!'

'I'll get the police,' said the driver.

'Get the police,' I said, ' 'cause I ain't payin' my fare again.'

After several minutes (I think it was about ten or so), and after several more passengers disembarked from the bus, the law arrived.

'All right,' said one of the two policemen, 'who's causing the trouble?'

I put my hand up.

'Why are you causing trouble? You don't look like a trouble maker to me,' said the keeper of the law.

'I'm not,' I answered. 'I'm just an Edinburgh citizen trying to get home and the driver's out to fleece me!'

The driver nearly had an epileptic fit.

'I'm not!' he shouted.

'Why, what's the argument?' enquired the second policeman.

'Well,' I said, 'I paid 20p to go from Roseburn to the West End on my way into town and I assumed that it would be 20p to get back again. The driver says it's 25p to get back and now I've agreed to pay 25p, or rather the difference to bring it up to 25p, he says I've got to pay my whole fare again. I don't think it fair, (fare? I joked) and anyway I've only come two stops for my 20p.'

The two policemen approached the driver to get his version of events as he had moved back to the front of the bus.

'As things are somewhat heated,' said the first policeman, 'it may be a good idea if we stepped outside to see if we can come to a compromise.'

'All right by me,' I said accompanying the police to the door of the bus where the driver already stood.

I got off the bus and waited to see what the bus driver was going to say.

The bus driver, however, had other ideas, he got back into the driver's seat and shut the bus door. He then started the engine and drove off.

I had been suckered!

'Night sir,' said the first policeman as he slightly doffed his cap to me.

'Safe journey home,' intoned the other.

They walked off . . .

A Drink With A Stranger

by

Tom Foggo

Sammy Sharp was one of those people who did not believe that a drink should sit untouched for longer than five minutes on any bar or table in a public house; moreover, he had made a resolution years before, proclaiming, if people were daft enough to supply him with drinks, free of charge, simply because he wangled his way into their company on the pretext of being hard up, then so be it. This practice earned him the name of 'Sharp Sammy' and forced bar managers to prohibit his entry into their establishments. Glasgow, however, is a large city, with public houses in abundance, so if a ban was imposed in one hostelry, Sammy moved easily to the next, with the hope that his character had not preceded him, then with his Social Security payment, he would buy himself a drink before weaselling his way into unsuspecting company.

It was almost 7.30 p.m. that Saturday night as Sammy weaved his way along the rain soaked streets of Glasgow, searching for The Ploughman's Dreel, a new public house recently opened, and when the neon sign, advertising the pub's location, came into view, he smiled craftily, rubbed his hands together, mounted the two steps and pushed open the glass swing door which led directly into the brightly lit lounge bar. He was disappointed to see the place so quiet. A couple at the far end of the bar glanced in his direction; the foursome in the middle of the room ignored him; the only other occupant, apart from the barman, was a well groomed middle-aged man sitting in the far corner, sipping a gin and tonic.

'What'll you have?' the barman asked abruptly, as Sammy strolled over to the bar, having divested himself of coat and cap.

'Ah'll jist have a hauf an' a pint. A wee bit quiet the night, are ye no?' Sammy questioned, again looking around the room.

'Sure now, we are,' replied the barman, placing the two glasses in front of Sammy, 'but it's early for a Saturday night, so it is.' He turned away and moved along the bar. Sammy downed his whisky in one gulp and settled down to sipping his beer. He appeared to be in a state of quiet meditation, but his mind was actively engrossed in assessing the free alcohol-customer potential, that surrounded him. With one more glance around the room, he disappointedly picked up the whisky glass and shook the dregs into his beer and was about to drain the mixture when a loud voice, close to his ear, startled him.

'I say, barman, might I have the same again, please?' It was the man from the corner seat.

Highly experienced as he was in cultivating handouts, Sammy turned quickly and stared hard at the intruder, who in turn, was quick to notice the look of consternation on the pale face.

'Oh! I do beg your pardon. I didn't mean to startle you,' he began, then without hesitation, he called to the barman, 'Oh, and a drink for my friend here.'

The bells in Sammy's head began to jingle his favourite tune and he almost sang aloud, 'Here we go - here we go - here we go,' but managed to restrain himself sufficiently, to answer in a dignified tone.

'Och, no need - no need at all,' he simpered, but quickly added, 'Ah'll jist have a double whisky an' a pint. Yer over there in the corner - aye?'

The man nodded his reply and Sammy ambled over to the corner table, pulled out a chair and with a tremendous sigh of satisfaction, settled down into the seat.

The man returned from the bar to join his guest and as he walked across the floor, only a close observer would have noticed the faint smile of evil that touched upon his lips.

Sammy was delighted to have found such a wonderful provider and as the evening wore on, his tongue was up and running. He became master of exposition. The man was a good listener, only nodding in agreement, or asking Sammy to repeat something in his non-stop commentary, but then, quite suddenly, he changed the conversation with a direct question.

'What do you know about good and evil?' he asked quietly.

Sammy tried to focus his eyes on his partner's face.

'Aw, c'mone,' he slurred, 'when yer good - yer good, an' when yer bad - yer bad, an' so say all o' us.'

The man's eyes narrowed at the childish answer.

'Let me put it another way,' he said quietly. 'Do you believe in heaven and hell?'

'Aw, whit is this? Question Time?' Sammy retorted, lifting his glass to his lips.

'Please answer the question,' the other said coldly, his face reddening with impatience, but Sammy was in a jocular mood.

'Here pal,' he commented, ignoring the man's demand, 'the last time ah saw a face like yours wiz on a haggis, at a Burns supper.'

The man repeated the question a second time.

'Do you believe in heaven and hell?'

Sammy was drunk, but not stupid. He was not about to kill the goose that laid the golden egg.

'Right then,' he said, 'ye mean if ah die, an' I've led a good life, ah go to heaven - an' if I've no led a good life - ah go to hell?'

The man nodded, 'That is what I mean,' he replied.

'Naw, naw,' said Sammy, 'ma policy is this. When yer deid - yer deid, an' that's that! Here, are wi no havin' another dram?' he hiccuped, changing the subject quickly. The lounge was empty now and the man signalled to the barman to fetch another round of drinks.

'You're quite wrong, my friend,' he said softly, continuing the original conversation, 'there is a heaven and a hell. Do you believe in God?' he added quickly.

Sammy changed his position, leaning now on his left elbow, his chin cupped in his left hand, 'Aye,' he said innocently.

'Then,' murmured his interrogator, 'you must believe in the Devil.' He paused for a moment and smiled. 'You see, my insignificant, little friend, I am the Devil.' The small scar above his right eye, unnoticed till now, became iridescent. The whisky was now coursing through Sammy's brain in such quantities that he didn't even notice the change in the scar.

'Is that right,' he retorted, 'in that case, ye better come home wi me the night, fer am married to yer sister.' He then burst into a fit of laughter. But his laughter was short lived, for even as he peered into the face across the table, the features began to change. The eye sockets in the face curved upwards, rapidly, into angled slits; the eyes changed from small burning points of light to ghoulish lumps of white hot cinder; bluish trails of smoke curled forwards from the terrible eyes and wreathed themselves across the grinning face. Suddenly, as Sammy watched fearfully, the skull bones enlarged, expanding to bursting point and gnarled pointed horns pierced the scalp on either side, protruding through the misshapen head. The face pushed down and forward into a snubbed protrusion and the body size increased, enveloped in a reddish mist, the whole manifestation rising upwards in the shape of a goat, the cloven hoofs striking down at him. Sammy screamed and buried his face deep in his hands for what seemed an eternity, until, breathing heavily and sweating profusely, he dared to look again. The table was empty, but for his own glass.

Rising unsteadily, still watching the table, he moved backwards slowly towards the bar.

'Right then, Squire,' the barman declared, 'closing time, it is.'

Sammy, almost a nervous wreck, turned on him quickly. 'See you - what kind o' place is this? What kind o' folk do ye get in here?' he shouted. 'Ah've been sittin' drinkin' wi a man dressed as a bloody goat. Who was that la-de-da nyaff that wiz sittin' in the corner ower there?'

205

The barman looked at him in dismay. 'The only man sittin' in yonder corner has been yersel an' you argued harmlessly with yersel all night. Besides, ye spent the best part of fifteen quid. Yer a grand customer.'

Sammy delved into his pocket and pulled out a crumpled five pound note instead of the twenty he was carrying. In a daze, he staggered into the street.

Two nights of sobriety led Sammy back to The Ploughman's Dreel. The building was in darkness. He stepped back looking for some sign of life and caught sight of a name above the door - 'Miranda's Boutique'. He staggered in total disbelief and collided with a passer-by.

'Sorry,' Sammy muttered. 'Lookin' fer a pub - the Ploughman's Dreel.'

'No,' the man said slowly, 'there has not been a pub here for fifty years.' Unconsciously, he touched the scar above his right eye and walked away from the lamplight.

Sammy thought the man's voice sounded familiar.